OUTCOME,

A NOVEL

Barbara Ebel

Outcome, A Novel

Barbara Ebel, M.D.

Barbara Ebel

Second edition:
(New 2017 Edition)
Paperback ISBN: 978-0-9977225-3-6
eBook ISNB: 978-0-9977225-4-3

This book is a work of fiction. Names, characters, places and events are the product of the author's imagination or are used fictitiously. Any resemblance to actual events, persons, or locations is coincidental.

*For organ donors and recipients,
and in celebration of the unconditional
love of our pets.*

Barbara Ebel

Chapter 1

Diana Devlin scanned the September night from the window of her Cessna 402 as the twin-engines purred. She enjoyed listening to the smooth and familiar motors. The mechanical music was like a fine symphony to her ears and part of her fastidious nature wanted to make sure nothing sounded amiss before she commanded her plane to cruise at 200 knots.

Her passengers seated themselves in four of the six seats and placed their equipment, paperwork, and white jackets on the available floor space. She smoothed a soft wisp of butterscotch hair away from her forehead and peered outside to the FAA control tower and fixed-base operator office at Standiford Field. She would be back home in Louisville by morning depending on how fast things moved once the transplant team disembarked in Birmingham. Not that she was in a hurry. She had made trips for organ retrieval before and liked the adrenaline rush, the pressure of the medical necessity, and the involvement in saving a recipient's life.

Retrieving organs wasn't even Diana's main job. During weeks off from flying UPS cargo, she leased trips on her private plane. She planned on giving up flying UPS Boeing 757s by the time she turned fifty, in twelve more years, when her retirement assets would be dependable and flying would be at her discretion. She piloted her Cessna for sheer joy and exhilaration and charged handsomely for some excursions, but tonight's trip, except to cover the cost of gas and landing fees, was charity. Her husband, Peter, was an anesthesiologist; they only partially depended on her full-time salary and didn't need her extra-curricular income.

A passenger's voice broke into Diana's thoughts. "It would be allowed for me to sit there? Up front?"

Diana motioned to the right seat. "Go ahead. I'm pilot, co-pilot and crew. Seat's empty."

Sukhdev Bhagat planted his buttocks into the seat and sighed after arranging himself. He was a large man with pudgy cheeks, dull black hair, and sloping eyebrows. He unfastened his top shirt button and folded his white coat on his lap. He was one of the two main surgeons for the impending liver transplant, but his partner stayed at Samaritan Hospital while he headed to procure the donor liver. A senior surgical resident accompanied him as well as a United Network organ representative and a registered nurse.

Diana tuned the cockpit radio frequency to Louisville clearance. "Organ Life Zero One requesting clearance to Birmingham."

A voice on the other end crisply responded, "Organ Life Zero One cleared to Birmingham as filed, climb and maintain ten thousand feet. Contact ground on 121.7 for taxi."

"Roger," Diana said. "Organ Life Zero One cleared to Birmingham as filed, climb and maintain ten thousand feet." She looked at Dr. Bhagat and then craned her neck to see the passengers behind her. "Are all items secured and are you all buckled? And, are there any last minute questions regarding the emergency drill I gave you?"

"We are ready," the thirty-five year old surgeon said. "Your briefing did not involve us learning brain surgery." He faced the right window and lowered his voice. "Please, let us get this plane moving."

Diana frowned but continued her eye contact with the other passengers. They nodded and she proceeded to switch frequencies as instructed.

"Ground, Organ Life Zero One is ready to taxi with information Alpha."

"Organ Life Zero One cleared to taxi and hold short of Runway 17 Left via taxiway Echo," said a voice from ground control.

Diana read back the taxi clearance, released the brakes, and headed for the runway. Her 20/20 vision gauged the small truck to the side of the plane to be far enough away from her right wing.

"Organ Life Zero One monitor tower on 124.2 for takeoff."

"Roger that." Diana set the brakes and completed the before-takeoff checklist.

"Organ Life Zero One ready?" queried a voice from the tower.

Diana viewed the panorama to her left - the 150 foot wide runway and the white runway lights stretching forward 200 feet apart like white-spotted dominoes in the dark.

"Tower, this is Organ Life Zero One ready for takeoff."

"Organ Life Zero One. Maintain runway heading. You are cleared for takeoff on Runway 17 Left."

Diana echoed the tower's instructions, taxied onto the runway, and pushed the throttles forward. She quickly and methodically checked the engine instruments and the air speed indicator as the plane accelerated to takeoff speed.

Inside the unpressurized aircraft, her passengers remained quiet. The spotless white plane rolled forward. Diana's pulse quickened along with her accelerating toy. Her ears keyed to the roar of the engines, her sharp eyes to what lay before her as well as the incandescence passing to the right and left.

But something wasn't right. She sensed it and felt it - as well as she knew her own capabilities. Was her keen vision betraying her? Ahead, she could swear, a flickering - right, then left. Again, a set of runway lights ahead blinked as speed drew them closer. "Shit," she mumbled.

"Tower," she said loudly. "Organ Life Zero One is aborting."

Diana maintained control of the aircraft, kept it centered, and noted the air speed as she started slowing down in a few quick seconds.

Sukhdev turned sharply towards her. "You do not decide to stop taking us."

"Roger, Organ Life Zero One do you need assistance?"

"Negative."

"Did you hear what I said?" the doctor yelled, pushing physically towards her.

Diana shot a piercing glare at the surgeon. "You may be god in your OR, but shut the hell up in my cockpit."

"Organ Life Zero One what is the nature of your problem?"

"Tower, I think nature is my problem."

Chapter 2

After successfully generating enough steam off the African coast, a tropical storm churned across the lower North Atlantic. The National Hurricane Center named it Ivan, but it didn't capture much press. After all, if it didn't have the "H" word in front of it, it didn't give visual images of property damage, palm trees swaying horizontally, or weather reporters blowing in the wind. All eyes focused on Hurricane Frances, storming itself in the Atlantic Ocean. As Frances slammed into the Palm Beach area with 105 mph winds, Ivan boldly grew from a Category 1 to a Category 4 hurricane within sixteen hours.

Karen Puno and her husband Rick bought their dream home on Pensacola Beach in the spring of 2004. With a three-mile view from their second and third floor windows, the white sand and the clear Gulf of Mexico substituted as their back yard, and since Karen lived in paradise, she had little reason to watch weather reports.

Karen sat outside on the second level deck and answered her husband's call from Lima, Peru on her cell phone as the western sky danced with blues and pinks from a setting sun and a group of pelicans soared above.

"Hey, baby," Rick said.

Karen smiled. Whenever Rick crooned out the word 'baby,' his accent reminded her that his father was from South America, making Rick's upbringing in the U.S. multilingual. Rick worked for Southern Telecommunications and his transfer from Indianapolis to Pensacola had landed him heavy consulting in the southern continent, reacquainting him with his family's heritage and solidifying his speedy Peruvian dialect.

"Hey, yourself," she said. "How was your day?"

"Fine. I'm going to grab dinner in the hotel, but not before talking with you."

"You're missing another stellar evening," she said, patting their dog's head. They had found the mixed Labrador retriever after their move and couldn't resist giving him a home.

"Soak it up while you can. I'm catching television coverage of this Ivan. Wind of 135 miles per hour is no joke."

"I saw that. I'm going to read up on hurricane preparations since I haven't given the storm much thought."

"Karen, no telling where it's going but it could track west through the Gulf. The beach could lose power, so be ready."

Their dog, Putt-Putt, arched his head back to Karen and whimpered. The adolescent pup made no attempt to bark. His sweet little face with a jet-black nose and his big, dark eyes made him resemble a seal and his slight build was shrouded with snow-white fur except for two tan spots off to the side of his shoulders. Karen scratched around his ears while finishing the call and then went inside to watch the tropical update.

———

Karen and Rick lived in a small subdivision nestled between the gulf and the bay and homeowners around them with storm experience knew exactly what to do. They didn't watch and wait; one of them even told her "this could be the big one," as if islanders anticipated the danger.

At first, she watched the increased activity. Down the street, a neighbor moved his antique car out of his garage into a moving truck. Two men unfastened the security gate to the subdivision entrance to store off the island. The couple next door loaded their RV.

The turmoil heightened on September 8th when Ivan intensified to a Category five hurricane after raping Grenada and roaring into the southeastern Caribbean. Off the island, Karen waited in line at the pump as people filled red portable gas cans as well as topped off their car tanks. At the big box store, shelves normally stocked with water jugs were almost empty and tear-open tuna fish packages were sold out. Plywood destined for windows flew off shelves at Lowe's and stuck out from pickup truck beds on U.S. Route 98. Residents pulled into mainland storage facilities. They'd been through Erin and Opal in 1995 and swore not to lose possessions to surging floodwaters again.

Over the next few days, Ivan oscillated between a Cat 4 and Cat 5, violently powering 145 mile per hour winds. As the storm's projected path became more ominous for Pensacola, Karen sprang into action. She needed to move items up from the furnished room in the corner of the garage in case gulf waters plowed through. She hurried upstairs with Rick's phonograph records, her childhood art collection, and school degrees. She filled the bathtub and the two second-floor bedrooms with treasures, but she barely made a dent in the piles. The last big item she hoisted upstairs was her daughter Tonya's road bike, which had not accompanied her to college the previous month.

"I'm sorry I can't be there with you," Rick said, raising his voice because of the fuzzy cell phone connection. "I have at least ten more days of work in the Lima area. Please, find someone to put those shutters up."

Karen couldn't handle the large aluminum shutters which came with the house. Several were needed to cover the windows and full length glass doors. She asked a young gardener securing the subdivision's sprinkling system to assist her and offered to pay him handsomely. She helped steady the ladder and handed him bolts until dusk as they went from the two gulf decks to the deck facing the bay. The sky began to darken and the Gulf began to approach, much angrier and taller than Karen had ever witnessed.

The shutters blocked off the outside world, pitching their home into an eerie darkness. Lights strangely illuminated the inside cave as the weather channel blared Hurricane Ivan's northward progression in the gulf. Karen rarely slept in two days and gathered precious belongings to take with her. She stacked family pictures into boxes and collected her coin collection and her husband's woodwork. She took art off of the walls and covered as much furniture as she could with tarps. Neighbors told her that if water trickled in, mold could grow, especially if residents weren't allowed to return for some time due to major damage.

By now, there was not a question that residents should leave. A storm surge could wash over the island to engulf buildings and easily snap them like spaghetti. While Karen listened to the television at 2 a.m., she heard local officials announce that the beach bridge would close in the morning; by then, evacuation of all islanders should have occurred and police would be blocking the entrance back onto the bridge. She more hastily continued her plan to leave while Ivan plotted his coastal landfall.

Karen stopped the frantic packing of her car for a mere ten minutes, downed a cola and a handful of pretzels, and then petted Putt-Putt. His normal sweet expression was absent and replaced by a crinkled forehead and drooping head. She opened the cabinet and scooped out the dog's travel necessities: dry dog food, vet records, brush, and a bowl. She placed them along with water bottles in the front of the car while thinking of the long drive north in the morning. Hotels were booked as far as Birmingham.

At 5 a.m., she took the last food from the freezer and put it into a plastic garbage bag. She dumped all the ice cubes into the sink, switched off the air conditioning, and shut off the lights. She patted her thigh for Putt-Putt to follow her and they descended the steps. Downstairs, Karen opened the back of her Honda CRV.

"Okay boy, we're going for a ride," Karen gestured. Putt-Putt readily jumped in the back behind piled-high back seats. She threw in his leash and closed the hatchback. Upon opening the garage door, she sulked at Rick's Corvette because she was unable to drive it away from potential harm. She backed out and speed dialed Rick, who answered immediately with a groggy voice.

"I'm leaving the island," Karen said loudly, pulling onto the main western road of the overbuilt sand bar. Crashing waves to her right sounded like muffled thunder and the sand blew hard, pelting her vehicle.

"Be careful," Rick said, but she barely heard him. "Call me later, anytime."

"I love you," she yelled.

She pieced together his response of, "I love you, too," as the connection severed and she saw a vehicle's tail lights further ahead. Putt-Putt whined in the back and she checked the rear-view mirror to see his wide-open eyes glued on her.

Karen felt terrorized by all the sights and sounds. She trembled and her heart rate sped. As she began ascending the steep bridge incline to cross the bay, waves chased in her direction, towering south in the Gulf to what would eventually be fifty-two foot monstrosities.

The wind and turbulence helped push Karen's car as she descended the summit of the beach bridge going to the larger barrier island of Gulf Breeze. There, police Officer Kent Milton was parked perpendicular to Karen's northbound lane and monitored the evacuation.

———

Meanwhile, an island dweller has forgotten his insurance papers. In the poor visibility the brazen driver sped southbound towards the bridge and through the police barricade. Officer Milton dropped his coffee as he bolted across Karen's lane to chase down the car on the other side.

———

Karen descended past the final concrete pillar of the bridge as her CRV pitched out of control. The patrol car rammed into her and sent her spiraling into a light post with a resounding thud and the gnarling of twisted metal.

Jarred and injured beyond pain, Karen's last thoughts and vision ebbed away into unconsciousness.

Chapter 3

Jennifer became aware of her symptoms more than a year ago, thanks to her seventeen-year-old son, Johnny. An early summer heat had sapped her usual energy and the sun had been unforgiving to her skin, so she began wearing a wide-brimmed hat.

"Mom, why the straw hat every time you go out?" Johnny had asked her. "You've never done that before."

"I'm getting too tan," she had said, noticing her forearm. "I look weathered like a dried prune."

"Why? The Ohio River valley isn't exactly Florida." He studied the bronze color across her face and arms and which had descended down her thin legs protruding from baggy shorts. "Your skin has never turned this yellow." He peeked under her hat. "Maybe you should see a doctor."

Johnny had a point. Once a year she went to the gynecologist; otherwise, she didn't have a family doctor. After a month's wait as a new patient, she sat before a freckled family practitioner and rattled off symptoms affecting her quality of life. After the physical, blood work, chest x-ray, and CT scan, he sent her across the river to see someone more specialized.

Like Jennifer's other appointment, the internal medicine doctor, Dr. Liu, auscultated her chest and heart and she flinched when he palpated on her right upper abdomen. He scribbled in his chart and then asked her to change and step into his office.

As Jennifer watched pedestrians on the ground below J-walk from one medical office building to the next, and traffic turn in and out of parking garages, she was thankful to get the bothersome appointments out of the way. She was a teacher and wanted to concentrate on decorating her classroom bulletin boards before fall classes resumed.

While she waited, she considered bringing Johnny in from the reception area, but instead slouched into a chair. Dr. Liu finally hurried in, all the while talking. "Hot day today." He patted her shoulder as he passed. "All your test results were expeditious. That's a good doctor you went to in Indiana." He sat swiftly, his short stature meek in a big chair behind his desk.

"Mrs. Barns, I do not like what I tell you now."

Jennifer's sighed and clenched her fingers into her hand. She hadn't considered that she could have cancer. That possibility sent a drum roll of nausea from her gut to her throat.

"You have hepatitis C," Dr. Liu said softly.

"Oh," she mumbled. She eased off on pushing her fingertips into the palm of her hand. "I thought you were going to tell me that I have cancer."

Doctor Liu grimaced. "Mrs. Barns, your liver is in a bad condition. That is why you are jaundiced."

"I suppose I don't remember much about livers and what they do."

"You are sure you never receive a blood transfusion?"

"I'm sure."

"And you never do drugs? Share a needle with someone?"

"Never. Not interested."

"No tattoo or body piercing?"

"No, except for pierced ears as a teenager." She toyed with a costume pearl earring and smoothed her hair alongside her ear.

"Hepatitis C is caused by infected blood. But sometimes patient have no risk factor."

"Bad luck, huh?"

"Not good," he said. "Your liver do many things. It make protein, clear waste, metabolize drugs, regulate your glucose, and produce factors that make your blood clot. Many, many things." Doctor Liu's tone became more serious. "We evaluate the liver by liver function tests. Yours way too elevated." His arm shot up in agreement.

"What's the treatment, Dr. Liu? Antibiotics?"

"We will attempt to clear virus from your bloodstream with weekly injections, but your liver extensively damaged."

Jennifer thanked him as he handed her follow-up instructions and liver disease literature at the front desk. She pulled her wallet from her shoulder bag. The medical insurance policy she retained as a grammar school history and geography teacher had hefty copayments, but it was better than nothing. She handed the card to the woman at the desk to copy.

Johnny scanned his mother's face while he held the door open for her. "Hey, Mom. What did he say?"

"He diagnosed me with hepatitis C. Which means squat to me," she said, smiling up to him, "except that I feel terrible and wear a funny color."

Johnny wrapped his arm around her shoulder and squeezed. "Don't worry about your color. I bet it will go away after they treat you."

———

Johnny attended high school and had not studied enough human physiology or anatomy to ask many questions so he planned on searching the internet to understand his mother's condition. His sister, Amelia, had lived with his mother all along but, when Johnny was twelve, he had moved back in where he belonged with his mother and sister. He had lived with his father after his parents break-up when he was eight but finally realized his blowhard father and his business endeavors held no substance.

Jennifer and her son drove back home through their sleepy town and turned right towards the cliff which paralleled the water. It was a matter of time before the low income properties along the Ohio would be scoffed up by builders recognizing the potential for voluminous homes or condominiums facing the river … which had occurred on the Louisville side. Their little clapboard ranch needed a pressure washing, but Jennifer's purple pansies spruced up the front, thriving from routine afternoon thunderstorms.

Jennifer hugged the right side of the driveway going into the one-car garage while Amelia stopped roller skating and waved her fifteen-year-old lanky arm. She had scraggly black hair and a pretty smile and wore a pink T-shirt exposing midriff. Her loose capris sat on skinny hips.

When Johnny stepped out from their two-door Ford, he grabbed a basketball from the corner of the garage. "Mel, Mom's got hepatitis."

"Nothing to be worried about," Jennifer said as Amelia eyed her with concern. Jennifer went in the front door and Johnny sprang around the driveway tossing the ball at the portable basketball stand while Mel watched.

"What do you think about Mom?" Mel asked when Johnny slowed.

"I don't know. I've got to look up hepatitis. She seems awfully tired, like she's really changed."

"Yeah, that's what I was thinking. Especially compared to a summer or two ago."

"Come on," Johnny said, setting the basketball back. "Why don't you boil corn and I'll light the charcoal and grill some burgers for dinner."

"Okay. My feet are getting sweaty anyway." Mel sat on the asphalt to untie her laces while Johnny waited. After slipping off socks, she carried the skates with pink wheels into the garage and placed them in a box. She'd spent practically six months of babysitting money on them in the spring. Mel stuck her feet into flip-flops and they went inside.

Jennifer sat on the couch, her legs stretched forward on the cocktail table, a glass of ice water nearby. She ripped envelopes with credit card applications and opened bills, pausing to smile at her children. But her eyes were heavy.

———

By February 2004, Jennifer toiled with standing at the blackboard, preparing tests, and grading papers at the nearby public school where she'd been teaching for twenty-one years. Previous enthusiasm to explain the likes of Thomas Jefferson, the Liberty Bell, and the acquisition of each state dwindled. Perhaps it was Jennifer's imagination, but her students seemed less interested anymore in what she said.

Her homeroom class emptied out for the day. Outside the windows, gray clouds mirrored her mood. She rolled back her chair as if making space for her decision, which had become inevitable. She tucked another tad of skirt material into a safety pin hidden under a belt, acknowledging to herself that she had picked at her sandwich at lunchtime and had left the fruit uneaten. She rose and progressed slowly to the principal's office.

Jennifer knocked and entered. "Mrs. Waverly, may I discuss something with you?"

"Sure, Jennifer, come in." The gregarious woman motioned to sit. "I'd actually like to talk to you." She moved paperwork to the side and leaned forward. "I'm concerned about your health."

"That's why I'm here. Mrs. Waverly, I'm trying my best to sustain enough energy to get through normal days. Frankly, I find this term too difficult. I'd like to only sub next year. I don't think I'm going to feel any better by then."

"Jennifer, all of us will try to accommodate you in any way." The phone rang but she ignored it. "That would affect your pay check, so, if things change in the next few months, let me know and we'll give you a regular homeroom schedule." She cracked a smile. "Besides, if you don't work full time, the kids will miss you."

"Thanks, Mrs. Waverly. I'll be sure to update you." Jennifer gathered her parka and purse, locked her fifth grade classroom and drove to her monthly doctor's appointment. The thought of partially undressing and slithering into a paper gown on a bitter cold day made her quiver.

———

"Hello, Dr. Liu," Jennifer said, when he entered the examining room. "There's no change in my liver enzymes, is there?" She looked at the floor, avoiding his response.

Dr. Liu cleared his throat and nodded. He flipped pages on the chart, listened to her lungs and heart, and hung the stethoscope around his neck. "Mrs. Barns," he said, "irreversible damage to your liver is now 'end-stage.' We must consider a liver transplant."

Jennifer's heart quickened. "I could die if I don't have it, couldn't I? Or die anyway?"

"Yes. You now know much about this big important organ and we discussed your illness at length. Surgery very dangerous. You have huge clotting abnormality because your diseased liver cells cannot synthesize clotting factors. For transplant surgery, many blood transfusions will be necessary. It is much specialized surgery." He wore a serious expression, not camouflaging the gravity of her situation.

Thoughts of Johnny and Amelia surfaced as Dr. Liu spoke. She would do anything to preserve every single future day she could spend with them.

"Can you still be my doctor?"

"Yes. And I do extra hematology, so I will be a useful consultant to the surgeons. And anesthesiologists who do liver transplants very, very knowledgeable in this. But, I send you to liver transplant center. They evaluate you for eligibility."

Jennifer sighed. "I don't see how I can pay for it, even with some insurance."

"Your life more important than that problem."

———

Johnny and Amelia insisted on attending Jennifer's first visit to the Kentucky chapter of the United Network for Organ Transplants, so Jennifer picked them both up after school. They sat in a private cubicle off the waiting room as Jennifer amassed a stack of forms, answering questions regarding her medical and family history, social life, and present circumstances including health benefits. Dr. Liu had forwarded them a copy of her chart.

"Hey, Mom," Johnny said, "I'll take it all to the desk for you." He walked over while sniffing in through his nostrils, which never seemed to relieve his sinus congestion. Although plagued by allergies, he complained little in front of his mother and avoided her remarks about seeing a specialist because he didn't want to burden her with more medical bills.

He passed a mirror and grinned at his overdue need for a haircut while hastening back to Jennifer and Mel. His dark hair spooled with humidity, his shoulders had masculine breadth, and his eyes sparkled like his mother's when she'd seen better times. After sitting again next to Jennifer, he opened his backpack and handed her a graded English essay.

"Nice," Jennifer said. "Your grades are going to get you into a decent school."

"I've applied to our community college for next year, Mom."

Jennifer rested her arm of the side of the chair. "That's not where I think you should go."

"It's where I'm going." They sat in silence, Jennifer realizing her son spoke the last word.

"Mrs. Jennifer Barns, please come in," said a woman in the doorway, giving them all an invitation with her eye contact.

Inside, the woman introduced herself as Mary. "This is the beginning of a long process. One in which you are the most important member of our team, if indeed, you're selected as a recipient for a liver transplant. We have tons to discuss."

Jennifer smiled meekly across the table at her. "If you're agreeable to all of today's conditions, we'll send you for further testing; upper and lower GI series, pulmonary function tests, and much more. The process will eventually include evaluation by everyone involved; social worker, coordinator, dietician, professionals involved with the actual surgery, and soon, a psychologist or psychiatrist."

Jennifer arched her eyebrows. "A psychologist?"

"There are concrete reasons for all members of a transplant team to be involved with the patient. A psychologist may recognize that a patient may never be able to stop an unwanted behavior, making his transplant more apt to fail. After reviewing your case so far, you would make a sound recipient. You are not an alcoholic or drug abuser. For that matter, you don't even smoke, and you have no other chronic medical problems."

Johnny glanced sideways at Mel, who appeared as overwhelmed as her mother. His eyes squinted and he nodded to her. His mother's addition to a transplant list would be a lucky privilege - he couldn't think of anyone more deserving.

———

Jennifer watched a young girl amble by in front of the house. The girl waved emphatically when she noted her teacher sitting on the step. "Hi, Mrs. Barns. I hope you feel better tomorrow."

"Me too, Mellissa," Jennifer responded.

"We didn't like our sub today," the girl added.

Although the temperature hung around sixty, Jennifer pulled a sweater around her arms, waiting to break a huge development to Johnny and Amelia as they approached after school. Johnny had stayed over to play basketball and Amelia had gone to cheerleading practice.

With a renewed vigor to their step upon seeing their mother outside, Johnny and Amelia came up the walkway, dropped their things and nestled next to her. "Hey, Mom," Johnny said, scrunching his nose. "Nice day?"

"For March."

"What's going on?" Amelia asked.

"Did you see the polite driver stop to let that stray slowly trot across the street? Or have you looked at the sky? It's beautiful." She pointed, her face reflective, yet holding back a surprise.

A light wind circulated, flowing from the west, carrying a scent like fresh rain, as Johnny and Amelia followed their mother's gaze.

"You made it," Johnny said. "Didn't you? You're on the transplant list."

Jennifer's eyes moistened and her lips quivered. She rested a hand on Johnny's knee. "Yes, they called me before I left for work today. I went to the center and received my instructions. Look...." She produced a black pager. "I'm to carry this at all times. I could be called whenever." She sighed. "It means...it means...maybe, just maybe, I'll get a new liver and live to read to my future grandchildren."

"This is just great," Johnny said. He sprung up with joy, took her hands and pulled her up. Although he frequently hugged her, he laced his arms around her and held her like a picture of a guardian angel clutching a child.

"We love you, Mom," Mel said as she rose and waited her turn.

In a few moments, Jennifer breathed without a teenager engulfing her and said, "You're making me feel like popping open a bottle of champagne."

Chapter 4

As Diana taxied toward the FBO building, two emergency vehicles shot past her. She cursed under her breath. The aborted takeoff would generate a cascade of paperwork. She rolled her Cessna to a complete stop for brake cooling time and as she entered the facility, her passengers single-filed in behind her.

"An entire entourage awaits me in Birmingham," Dr. Bhagat said.

Diana quickened her pace. He pressed her like a supermarket cart too close to her ankles.

"When I arrive in Alabama," he continued, "all the wheels get set into motion. The patient will be readied only for me. You delay me; I'll see that you never fly us again."

A man with a face like dark polished river rock stepped from behind a counter, uniformed smartly in gray and carrying a belted weapon. Mr. Temple had been hired post 9/11 by the Department of Homeland Security after retiring from thirty-five years of police work. "Diana, is there some trouble here?"

"Not yet," she said and then glared at Sukhdev. "I haven't heard a word from you about the lives of the recipient or donor." She relaxed her stare and smiled at the officer. "You see, Mr. Temple, Dr. Bhagat here thinks everything is about him."

"I know where the doctor can wait while you expedite this trip." Mr. Temple led the way as Sukhdev trailed and the transplant representative, resident, and nurse followed without a word.

Diana walked into a small office with big windows where a man sat with his feet on the desk and another stood, shoulders slumped, watching Mr. Temple escort the visitors.

"Guys," Diana said, "something obscured the runway lights. Deer! I think there were deer crossing the runway."

"Damn it, Diana," said the man, bringing his feet down. "Good call. The truck just called in. You were right." The young man acted as the direct liaison between the airport and the FAA and Diana's smart maneuvering made his night run a lot smoother.

"Diana," said his coworker, "you deserve a fresh cup. Grab some while your engines cool."

"Really. And that doesn't only go for my plane."

"Be careful with your next departure," the first man said. "Just because the tail of that hurricane has blown through, it doesn't mean clear skies."

———

For Diana's next attempted flight, ground crew swept the perimeter fencing for any wildlife that evaded the screening process. The flight took off without incident. This time she appreciated the empty seat next to her. She contemplated taking a catnap in the Birmingham FBO. It usually took hours for organ procurement; sometimes she even went to the particular hospital to hang around the OR waiting room. But she no more wanted to follow this doctor than to trail a troubled skunk. If she changed her mind, she could go later, when he'd surely be in surgery. That way, she could overhear surgery updates and grab a bite to eat in the lounge or cafeteria.

———

After their smooth landing and the medical team's trip to the hospital, Sukhdev Bhagat selected the largest Styrofoam cup in the doctor's lounge and poured coffee nearly to the rim. He stared out the window at the slice of moon high in the sky looking like a page in a children's story book and then went to check on the formalities of the paperwork.

The donor's papers, except for the medical chart, sprawled on a round table. The United Network woman, Sally Ryan, looked at the consent which had been gathered by the local chapter's representative while Sukhdev's resident scurried to the OR.

"Dr. Bhagat," Ann, the accompanying nurse, said, "if you'd like, I'll verify out loud." She fought to open a wrapper of crackers.

Sukhdev flailed his hand for her to continue.

"First, a copy of Karen Puno's license."

"Karen Puno?"

"The donor. And I obtained confirmation by her spouse, Rick Puno."

Sukhdev reached into the basket and also tore into a packet of saltines. "We happen to have a good match on both the women's weight, correct?"

"Yes," Mrs. Ryan answered. "Your patient on the table is one-hundred thirty. Recipient one-ten."

Ann also nodded. "Donor AB positive. Recipient AB positive." She slid the blood type sheets toward him.

"Both AB positives," Sukhdev said. "Do you have brain death documentation? A copy of the electroencephalogram?"

"Right here," Mrs. Ryan said.

Sukhdev pushed away a wayward thick eyebrow hair pointing at his eye. He drank the last remnant of coffee as the front desk informed him his patient was ready in the OR. He changed into scrubs, scrubbed, and entered the swinging door to a room bustling with activity. Two poles with wires cascading across the floor held old and newer infusion pumps.

On the table, drugs slid into Karen Puno's right neck central intravenous line. The ventilator bellows pumped up and down, raising and lowering Karen's chest. She was paper white and an endotracheal tube jutted from her mouth.

"Are you the transplant surgeon?" the anesthesiologist asked while adjusting the rate of a drug.

"From Louisville. What's your assessment of renal function?"

"Adequate urine output since she's been here, but I'm fighting to keep decent pressures. I'm basically maxed out on vasopressors."

Sukhdev turned for OR staff to tie the back of his gown. The scrub nurse gloved his hands. His resident stood ready. "Brain-dead organ donors aren't that simple," he said to his accompanying resident while selecting the available instruments on a sterile draped table.

The female anesthesiologist adjusted a monitor while the young resident took a step towards the head of the table to see the patient more closely. "For the anesthesiologist," she said, "keeping a brain-dead patient alive for organ donation is acute critical care. Most of these patients are hypovolemic so we resuscitate them with fluids and transfusions. Maintain their blood pressure with inotropes. We fight to keep their bodies alive so that the organs to be taken and transplanted are well perfused. If the kidneys aren't managed well prior to harvesting, there could be a graft malfunction." She took an empty bag of red blood cells off a pole and chucked it into a half-filled garbage container.

"Over here," Sukhdev said to the resident. "Let's get going." He made a long, thorough abdominal incision and neglected the chest. "We're not taking lungs or heart. Only the liver and kidneys, but the kidneys are staying here for transplantation."

"They'll probably be on the morning's schedule," the scrub nurse said.

After adequate exposure, both Sukhdev and the resident examined the renal arteries and kidneys. Sukhdev palpated and examined the liver, dark and slippery like a manatee's skin. "They seem to be good organs," he said.

"I heard it was a car crash," the resident said.

"She lived in Florida," the anesthesiologist said, working hastily. "She was evacuating due to Hurricane Ivan but was hit by a patrol car, just a mile or two from her home on a beach." She glanced at the patient's identifying label. "She was only forty-one years old."

"The paramedics brought her straight here," said the circulating nurse. "Local hospital ICU's had little space. Plus, they were worried about accumulating too many patients there if Ivan hit as a Cat 4 or 5."

"I guess they were right," said the scrub tech. "Yesterday and today the outside world had no contact with Pensacola, Florida."

As everyone thought about the multiple disasters, the room chatter abated. "It's time for some music," Sukhdev asked after the soulful silence irritated him. "Can someone pull out a CD from my small black bag on the floor?"

———

Upon the removal of Karen Puno's liver and two kidneys, her remaining abdominal contents sank into the newly formed available space. Dr. Bhagat folded her skin back over and ran a heavy stitch across both sides. All persons involved left the room except for the scrub nurse, circulator and anesthesiologist. The female physician turned the ventilator knob to off, and as she removed intravenous catheters and various monitoring devices, Karen Puno's normal sinus rhythm EKG converted to a flat line.

The anesthesiologist sighed heavily. Thank God, she thought, that someone else's miracle would occur because of what they just did.

Chapter 5

A feeling of uncertainty and alarm mounted up in the medium-sized dog as grains of sand blew across the dune and pelted the aluminum shutters on the face of the house. Putt-Putt had been scared before, but never like this. Not only did his instincts tell him that over the last few days the atmospheric pressure, the winds, the surf, and the growing darkness had grown unnatural and that now something was vastly wrong with the weather, but also Karen, his master, scurried everywhere and with such haste and busyness that she barely glanced at him.

Normally, he liked to lie on a rug or the carpet inside his open crate. But well into this night and the early morning hours, he preferred to stay on the cold tile floor before the hallway entrance to the basement steps. That was the best spot to stay out of Karen's way as she ran up and down the steps, carrying things down, but not back up, and to keep his paw on the pulse of what she was doing, wondering what her increased activity meant.

The furious shaking and blowing against the house intensified as the hours ticked by. The unstable situation made his blood speed and his heart race, and also increased his need to urinate. He got up once and circled by the main side door to give Karen his usual signal. After a half hour, to no avail, he went back to his previous perch. She had never ignored his cues before and he almost whimpered.

After 4 a.m., Karen disappeared downstairs with her arms full and when she returned she slid onto a stool. Putt-Putt trotted over to her and sat while she sipped a soda and crunched on brown snacks. She had let him taste those once, but now she didn't share and sighed heavily toward the refrigerator as if something about it, too, was a burden. Putt-Putt imploringly asked her with his eyes to tell him what she knew. What was turning the predictability of their life into chaos? Were they in danger because of this strange weather? And why didn't she go to bed the entire night?

———

Before, life had simply become a joyous endeavor for Putt-Putt. Each day he tackled with renewed vigor, as if the previous day had only been a test, a practice run for the present day. Every morning after waking up and planting his front paws deeply into the rug, arching his back, and sticking his hindquarters and tail in the air, his full-body stretch announced his glory to have food and shelter and to be loved. Then he'd sit straight, his back facing Tonya or Karen's bed, and arch his head backwards for a hand to stroke between his ears. Although Karen and Tonya sometimes got lost in their busy days, he demanded their attention that time every day when the sun bloomed above the horizon and sneaked its rays straight into their eastern windows. It was then he'd try and express the warmth he felt in his heart to be a member of the Puno family and let them know his appreciation of yet another day.

When he thought he would burst with uncertainty at this night's unfamiliarity, Karen looked down at him. Their eyes met. Her gaze confirmed to him that she loved him, and would take care of him, and finally she stroked the top of his head. Her fingers ran behind his ears and massaged. He nuzzled her hand as she stopped. She got up and gathered all his things he knew so well from the closet – his food, his brush, and his bowls. But she didn't put the bowl down to put kibbles in it, nor did she groom him. She tossed the objects in a box and they too disappeared with her down the cellar stairs.

For a short time, the long lack of sleep caused the frightened young dog to relax and he closed his eyes. When he woke again, Karen took ice from the freezer, pitched it in the sink, and the garbage disposal ground it into chips. In a few minutes, she shut the light and beckoned for him to follow her. Perhaps she would let him pee after all. But downstairs, she coaxed him into the back of her vehicle. Maybe she would drive him somewhere and walk him there, hopefully far away from the monstrous wind which made their house shake and the shutters shimmy.

As the car crept from the subdivision, Putt-Putt couldn't sit. The sounds and the vibrations worsened, more than being in the house, and the darkness was creepier than a normal 5 a.m. pre-dawn. He wanted to bolt, he wanted to hide, and he wanted to feel safe. He heard Karen talking very loudly on and off, like she did when one of her hands held that contraption to her ear. He heard her shout "I love you."

In five minutes the car turned left, the familiar route to go over the bridge where he normally wagged his tail excitedly at the pelicans dive-bombing into the water below. But this morning there was no sign of life.

Instead, the car rattled around like when he shook water off after a bath. Conditions grew worse at the top of the bridge and he couldn't hold back whimpering. He tried desperately not to pee in his small space which would cause him to stand in it but, also, he didn't want Karen to scold him. She had reprimanded him once for urinating in the house. She had called him a "bad dog," which made him feel very sad.

His body leaned forward against the back seats as the car descended to Gulf Breeze and then he huddled in the left corner as the car drove at the base of the bridge. At that moment it wasn't the weather that created a thunderous explosion and pitched their vehicle leftward off the road and into a pole, but another car, whose front end made ripped canned dog food out of the right side of Karen's car. The experience overwhelmed him and he peed and he cried and he scampered over piles of boxes and bags inside the car. His back leg didn't work correctly and when he got close to Karen, her head was jammed between the car door and head rest.

He sniffed; she didn't move. She didn't acknowledge him, nor could he arouse her. If she awoke, she might be angry he wet the car. No, that would be okay, because what had happened, he sensed, was frightfully wrong - worse than not minding his manners in the car.

Voices and sirens now howled in the wind from around the vehicle. The metal crunched on the door Karen laid against and from the back window came a blast of air as someone accessed the hatchback window and door. A uniformed man crawled in, shouting. "Ma'am, talk to me!"

But Karen didn't answer.

Putt-Putt inched along the pile of packed items and passed the man who headed for his master. He jumped out, but a shattering pain shot through him when his back leg hit the ground. He slithered between the confusion and limped off across the southbound lanes and to a subdivision street. On the left were shrubbery and trees flanking the bay and he trotted along disoriented. The gusts practically picked him up, and now and again, sticks, tree limbs and garbage blew past him.

The stabbing pain in his right thigh intensified as Putt-Putt ambled down the street, seeking shelter from the elements. Along the left side of the road, the bushes and trees continued along above the shoreline, but they shook and snapped so he set his sights to the other side. Homes came into view so he detoured along front lawns looking for anywhere he could bed down. He spotted a smaller ranch house than the others, with two front steps and a wooden porch. The space underneath might suffice. It would have to do, because his limp and pain had grown worse.

The determined dog reached the crawl space, discouraged to find it already entangled with loose debris. A soft pile of leaves and shrub material looked as good as a haphazard bird's nest so he circled several times and lay down. Part of him was flush with the end of the porch so he gained only some safety with the spot. He curled around to the fresh gash which had turned his stark white coat to crimson and began to lick. His tongue pushed further and with more pressure into the material already matted, and more gingerly on the open raw meat oozing a strange tasting liquid.

After grooming for some time, Putt-Putt glanced the way he had come. Was Karen still back there? Why hadn't she followed to come get him? Would she wake up from that nap? Over all the noise around him, Putt-Putt could now make out voices from the back of the house.

"One more look, and I have to bring in the hoses," a male voice shouted. A man stepped on the side of the porch. He ran his hand along the bottom of a window frame which was covered with plasterboard, checking the security of the nails he'd banged in the day before. Satisfied with his handy work, the man stepped towards the edge and gathered a half-coiled hose.

Putt-Putt trembled. If the man saw him, he might decide to shoo him away. Before Karen, Rick and Tonya gave him a home that had happened too many times. One day at the beach, a stranger threw a can at him which hurt his head and yelled "I don't do no strays."

But this time, Putt-Putt whimpered with fright knowing he couldn't go anywhere because of the weather's fury and because of his injured leg. He whined and cried longer than ever before.

"Well, I'll be. What are you doing there, pooch?" Putt-Putt looked up, his dark black eyes like pools of pain. A man stood above him with a long water pipe draped over his elbow. "Don't you know it's no time to be gallivanting away from home?"

The man with little hair on his head and caterpillars for eyebrows came down the steps. "Why, you're hurt."

What Putt-Putt heard was a gentle voice. He waited anxiously, holding himself still while the man extended his hand and held it near his muzzle to let him sniff. The man stood straight and quickly left the way he had come.

So many minutes ticked by that Putt-Putt closed his eyes with exhaustion. Shut them tight to make the fury go away. Again, he heard voices, this time a woman trailed the man and they stood together in front of him. He couldn't smell her and she didn't offer her hand to him.

"But, Jim," she said, "I really don't want you going anywhere now."

"Janet, I won't take long. She's only five minutes away. Storm or no storm, this little guy needs fixing up."

Putt-Putt didn't expect it, but the man eased his forearms underneath him, pulled him out a little further, and scooped him into his arms. It hurt to be moved, but not as bad as walking himself. When the man stepped away, Putt-Putt felt more secure with the wind buffered from his face. The man headed to the yard with the woman following, and without a word, she opened a maroon sedan's door and the man put him on the front passenger seat. The dark leather had a vertical gash and the fuzz inside warmed Putt-Putt's right leg.

"Good luck, little fella," Janet said. "And you be careful Jim."

Jim planted a kiss on his wife's cheek; he climbed in, and backed out. Although her extra weight was a force to slow her down,

Janet walked as quickly as she could with the help of the wind to the back door of their house.

————

Holding the dog in his arms, Jim pressed the buzzer at the veterinarian's front desk. A woman in a puppy-pictured scrub top poked her head around the corner. "We're closed, sir. We'll be leaving as soon as Doc Ricker puts her last minor surgery in a back kennel. We shouldn't still be here."

"But look," Jim said, nodding towards the bundle in his arms. "This stray took shelter at my house. I couldn't just leave him; he's hurt pretty bad and needs stitches."

The young lady glanced for a second at Putt-Putt's wound and longer into his eyes. "I'll go mention it to her." She came back in a few minutes with the veterinarian, who was drying her hands on a paper towel.

"Hi," Jim said. "I'm Mr. Kent. My wife and I live back here on Bay Watch Road. This dog showed up and I don't know where he lives. I'll pay you to fix him. Then maybe someone'll come claim him or you can send him to the Humane Society."

The woman surveyed the dog's leg while Jim still cuddled him. "We're not in the animal placement business, Mr. Kent. And I don't really have room to board him. We just secured the dogs we have right now. I'm not sure this little place is going to keep its roof on, so the security of the dogs already here is questionable." She frowned. Putt-Putt blinked his eyes tightly.

"Oh, hell," she said, "the look of despair on your face is almost as bad as the dog's. Just place him on the scale inside, and then give Andrea your address. We'll bill you when we're finished with him."

"Forty-eight pounds," she said to herself as Jim gave the dog one last glance. The building creaked and moaned, reminding Jim to hasten home.

————

Gradually, Putt-Putt eased awake from the spell of a deep sleep. He felt so groggy, like the time he had dumped over the aluminum can on the deck and licked up its contents while Rick had gone inside. When Rick had come back out, Putt-Putt had tried to greet him, but his legs wobbled. His master had laughed and said, "No more Bud Lights for you."

The earlier leg discomfort had subsided and a big white bandage replaced the slit skin he'd been compelled to lick. He was lying on a blanket against a wall and there were cabinets on either side of him. Across the aisle were steel cages, similar to his crate at home, and each one was latched with a dog or two inside. In these unfamiliar surroundings the man who picked him up and gave him a ride was nowhere to be seen. Events were becoming more complicated. How would he follow his scent back to Karen? He missed Tonya and Rick, too.

The reverberations from outside had gotten stronger. His eyes locked onto the Weimaraner opposite him and they spoke with their eyes, both sensing unavoidable imminent danger. Putt-Putt burrowed his chin into the blanket while the long-legged dog stepped forward in the kennel and pawed at the door. A heavy-set neighbor in the next crate barked several times and several others followed suit as a tremendous thud sounded on the roof. A ripping noise ensued as well as the sound of hurling objects in the front room.

Chapter 6

Satellite dishes mounted on adobe houses in the hills outside Lima had confirmed Rick Puno's suspicions that Peru wasn't as unsophisticated as many Americans might think. New market acquaintances in South America had expanded Southern Telecommunication's influence in the region by bringing better equipment and know-how. But there was still room for improvement since his transfer and, due to Rick's likeable charm, he had the quality of making people feel special; that almost always put them on his growing consultant list.

Although certain areas still had spotty cell phone coverage like where Karen and Rick lived in Florida, his ultimate test of their network would be placing calls outside of Cusco, even up at Machu Picchu and Wayna Picchu. Besides, doing that field work would give him an excuse for a journey to Machu Picchu, the Inca forgotten city that he so craved to see.

Rick unbuttoned the collar of his Panama shirt as the traffic crawled in Lima while his driver told him they must take a detour to Miraflores. Certain streets were barricaded due to a strike, something to do with water, a touchy subject. Streets were congested and Rick shook his head wondering why people lived in the densely packed city, but, like most urban areas, it meant having a job and making a living. Rick finally arrived at the Casa Andina, paid the young cabbie, and entered the automatic doors, nodding at the doorman.

"Senor Puno," said one of the receptionists. She walked from one end of the mahogany front desk to the other as Rick veered towards her after setting his things on the lobby piano bench. The clerk had scrutinized his full lips, curly dark hair, and big brown eyes that morning when he had reached for a complimentary newspaper.

"Buenos noches," he said. He smiled and gave her a crisp look as if his day had just begun. She wore a black-skirted uniform with short sleeves and he noted her gold name tag.

"Your company is trying to reach you," she said. "They left voicemails in your room but called us to make sure we also relay the message."

"Muchas gracias, Senorita Canesa. I'll call my office in Florida." He turned and hurried. After pressing number four in the elevator, he checked his cell phone which didn't indicate any messages.

Inside Rick's room, the telephone red light blinked. He put his brief case on the bed and washed his hands. Calling Karen would have to wait until he found out what the office wanted, if anyone was still there after hours. He dialed the number and looked out the window at the flat rooftop below.

"Sumners," a gruff voice said.

"Mick, it's Rick."

"Rick, we've been waiting anxiously for your call. There's been an accident."

"It's not Karen, is it?" Rick asked with worry. His wife or daughter were the only ones that would warrant his company's sense of urgency.

"I'm sorry to tell you this. Karen was pulled from her vehicle at the base of the island bridge after a car crash. They've stat-flighted her north."

Rick's thoughts grinded to a stop. Afraid to ask Mick any further questions, he imagined an accident scene; his wife motionless and smashed into a steering wheel. Perhaps a car had rear-ended her. Maybe she was suffering from a broken bone or two. Perhaps there was no bleeding.

———

Karen and Rick's daughter, Tonya, eased open the door to her dorm room. Inside, the bed on the right looked tidy but spillage from her roommate's bed on the left cluttered half the floor. She went to her desk, put down her books, and sat down on the graffiti etched into the wooden chair.

College choices had haunted her. Because she loved the gulf coast and living with her parents, the decision to go away had been difficult. Nevertheless, pursuing her favorite subjects of history and archeology at Butler University in Indiana was proving to be the correct decision and she liked residing in the familiar territory of her original home town of Indianapolis.

After eating a pizza slice and salad in the cafeteria, Tonya ate a sugar cookie she carried from the cafeteria and turned on the small Zenith. She eyed her cell phone, making certain she had turned it on. Her mother was supposed to call at lunchtime and should be on the road, heading north with Putt-Putt, getting out of harm's way. By the looks of the satellite images behind the gesturing weatherman on television, Ivan could jeopardize their piece of paradise at home.

At one o'clock, Tonya headed for music class, then nestled into a back library cubicle to study. She tugged a wad of hair behind her right ear while reading about Chopin and Bach. At four o'clock, she temporarily abandoned her books, went outside the building, and left a voicemail on her mother's phone. "Mom, where are you? Call me after you listen to this. Love you."

————

Rick called Birmingham's University Hospital to speak to the social worker who had contacted Southern Telecommunications.

"Mr. Puno," she said, "the hospital and doctors have tried to contact a family member. I'm glad your company tracked you down."

"My wife, please …"

"She's in the ICU. I'm going to transfer you directly to the physician hospitalist. Her name is Dr. Gregory." Rick waited a minute, thankful for the time to absorb the meaning of "the ICU." That admission meant something quite different than Karen being on a regular admission floor.

"This is Dr. Gregory," said a new voice.

"Hello, I'm Rick Puno. I was told my wife, Karen, is there."

"She is, Mr. Puno. She suffered multiple injuries from the accident and is unconscious. Her mental status is what we're most concerned about. She's in a coma."

Rick hadn't braced himself for that. "Are you saying that she may not wake up?" Stupid question, he thought. How could the doctor predict that? And if anyone knew his wife, it was him. Karen would make sure she woke up.

"That's a possibility," the soft voice said, "but I'll thoroughly evaluate her again in the morning and run some other tests."

"Right now I'm in South America. I'll make travel arrangements right away."

"We're doing our best for her. A ventilator is breathing for her and we're giving medicines to maintain her blood pressure. In other words, she's on total life support."

Rick gritted his teeth and squeezed his eyes.

"Mr. Puno, please keep in touch."

"I'll try to be there as soon as possible."

Rick took twenty minutes to compose himself. He paced the room, his thoughts cloudy, as if he were in someone else's dream; someone else's tragic circumstance, not his. Karen always said he carried tons of luck. Why couldn't he be the one? He should have been there helping her with evacuation preparations. He shouldn't have been away on work.

How could he call his daughter? Their only child? Karen's only girl after they'd tried to conceive for three years. When they'd given up and relaxed, Karen said the love between them took root and sprung life. He frowned and dialed Tonya's cell phone. The first time, he lost the hotel connection. Then he heard his daughter's rushing voice.

"Hi, Dad," she said, after seeing the foreign number. "Do you see this Ivan the Terrible on television? And I haven't heard from Mom all day. How are you?" She stopped. "Are you there?"

"I'm here, Tonya. Sweetheart, I've received bad news this evening. Your mom was in a car accident this morning. She's in an intensive care unit in Alabama."

Tonya dropped her head and fixed her eyes on the tile floor. Several students in the lounge sprawled over the two oversized couches as they watched an old movie.

"Dad, is Mom all right?" She wanted to ask detailed questions but figured she might cringe at the answers.

"It doesn't sound good. They said she's in a coma." He lingered a long minute "I'll call you tomorrow morning. I have to figure out arrangements with the office. If you go, you may get to Birmingham before me."

"Where were they, Dad? When it happened?"

"They?"

"Mom and Putt-Putt?"

"Going off the island. But, sweetheart, no one said anything about Putt-Putt."

————

Rick peeled his socks off, undressed, and showered. He opened an internet connection and discovered that all flights going north or northeast, to North America, were cancelled. Mick was probably going to tell him the same thing in the morning. He shut off the TV after a pregnant weatherperson gave the update. Hurricane Ivan was gradually turning north as it moved through the Gulf of Mexico, a Category 4. It was 1 a.m., September 15th. In a few hours, it would be twenty-four hours since his only true love had lapsed violently into a coma. He longed to take her hand and whisper into her ear that he sat alongside her. With nothing more that he could do, Rick slipped under a light blanket and tried to sleep.

————

Tonya passed the cafeteria, mounted the brick steps, and purchased a bottle of orange juice. She didn't want breakfast, nor did she want to see her friends. She continued along the path to the Administration office.

Like her father, Tonya had big brown eyes and, this morning, they were moist. She waited for Tom Roberts, her student counselor, to complete his phone call.

Mr. Roberts gestured for her to enter. "What can I do today, Tonya?" he asked smiling.

She summoned up a small smile and pulled her short hair between her fingers. "I'm … probably going to miss some classes. Maybe a lot of schoolwork." Her composure started to break down and her words broke into sobbing. "It's my mom; she's in a coma in Birmingham."

Mr. Roberts quickly came around his desk, closed the door, and handed her a tissue. "When you leave town, let me know. I'll advise your teachers where you are and we'll figure out the rest later. If you need someone to talk to, I'm here. But right now, I'm sure you have a list of things to do."

She sniffled, and put her hands on her cotton pants.

"Tonya," he said, "classes, even a college semester, are replaceable. But your mom isn't.

———

Rick pulled on trousers, deck shoes without socks, and left his casual cotton shirt untucked. Downstairs, the receptionist said "Buenos dias" and waved a newspaper as he passed. He reluctantly took it and poured a cup of complimentary coffee from outside the dining room. When he brought it back to his room, he called Mick.

"Rick, Ivan's predicted landfall is tomorrow. Scheduled flights are available when the storm passes. We can book you to Miami in the morning, then to Birmingham. It's anybody's guess if your second flight gets disrupted. Ivan's wind and rain is going to track into the southern states."

Rick sipped his coffee. "Thanks, Mick, give me the details later."

"Have you talked to Karen's doctor today?"

"I'm calling right now."

———

Rick's call reached Dr. Gregory as she sat in the central desk area of the ICU, her eyes glancing through the glass window of Karen's cubicle. Except for Karen's chest rising and falling due to the ventilator, she appeared lifeless and small in the middle of the thick white mattress. A taped breathing tube jutted from her mouth. Intravenous tubes exited from her forearm and neck and pumps cycling life-sustaining drugs carried liquids into her bloodstream. Monitors on shelves displayed her heart's normal sinus rhythm, blood pressure, and oxygen saturation.

"Mr. Puno," she said, "there's been no improvement in your wife's condition."

"I sensed that," Rick said softly.

"We ran a battery of tests this morning. Your wife has no spontaneous movements. She doesn't respond to stimuli and has no reflexes."

"Could that change?"

"I don't think so. The electroencephalogram also confirms the diagnosis of brain death."

The words cut through Rick like he'd been stabbed. How could this happen in so short a time?

"I'll repeat these tests later."

I have to get there, Rick thought. "I'll be leaving South America tomorrow morning."

"We'll do our best. We need twenty-four hours, in any case, to legally establish brain death."

Rick thanked her, but not for the grim news.

"You're welcome. If you're a praying man, your wife is going to need that."

"It's awful to think God allowed this to happen. But, yes, I am a religious person."

"Mr. Puno, are you aware that your wife signed the back of her driver's license? To be an organ donor?"

Chapter 7

Rick fidgeted in his first-class seat to Miami. The stocky man sitting next to him drank a Bloody Mary after he stopped snoring and ordered one for Rick. But the drink sat untouched as Rick stared out the window, plagued by the uncertainty of his wife's condition. As he waited for his connecting flight in Miami, he called Tonya, and they agreed to make a plan after he talked with Karen's hospitalist.

In Birmingham International Airport, Rick made his way to the baggage carousel where his squatty suitcase rode towards him. He stacked his duffel bag and briefcase on top of it, went outside and caught a taxi to the downtown Courtyard hotel. He checked in to leave his luggage and walked the short distance to the University Hospital. By the time he arrived at the ICU waiting room and asked to see his wife and Dr. Gregory, a sleep-like state fogged his mind.

Rick sat and rubbed his eyes. He regretted not changing his wrinkled shirt but seeing Karen as soon as possible was more important. A short, bristly growth covered his lower face, tweaking his features into a more rugged look.

In an adjoining area, television newsmen discussed Ivan's landfall the day before and weather professionals marked Pensacola down in history as the storm's ground zero site. The northeast quadrant of Ivan, the area mounting the greatest surge of gulf water, swept the barrier islands and bay fronts, but much of the area was out of contact because of downed power and cable lines. A Civil Air Patrol crew reported that whatever hadn't been devastated by flooding, the wind had taken care of. National Guard troops were en route also by air to land and assess the city, look for possible survivors on the beach, and begin making roads passable.

As Rick continued listening, the reporter's coverage shifted to the possibility of a major mobilization of out-of-state utility companies to help out and the Red Cross and FEMA's impending decision to implement disaster plans. Rick buried his face in his palms and closed his lids. Because of Karen, their home was his last priority, but sooner or later, he'd have to deal with that, too.

A thin wristed, petite woman in a white coat walked towards his chair as he unburied his face. "Rick Puno?" she asked. "I'm Doctor Gregory." Rick extended his hand. "Getting here this quickly must not have been easy. Would you like to see your wife before we talk?"

Rick nodded. He felt grateful for the woman's silence as they went through the automatic doors and passed windowed cubicles. They turned into the third door as several nurses buzzed back and forth from the central desk.

With disappointment, Rick realized that the visions he had played out in his mind beforehand were quite accurate. His pretty wife, so full of life, was not the woman before him. His fingers slipped under the sheet to gather her limp forearm. Although a taped hep-lock jutted from a vein, he put her fingers to his mouth. He wanted to kiss Karen's lips but tape plastered on her upper lip held a breathing tube in place. The cold plastic pipelined oxygen into her lungs ... a vital life support, like an umbilical cord to a fetus. His spirit sank so deep that he had to prompt himself to breathe along with his wife's ventilator.

Rick moved a chair close to Karen as Dr. Gregory left. He sat for a half-hour, the stark ICU lights contrasting with the blackness outside. When he finally let go of her hand, he was ready to face the doctor, who closed a bulky chart at the desk with apparent relief.

They walked into a dimly lit room, the sign outside noting *family conference room,* and sat at a table where Karen's paperwork lay stacked. Dr. Gregory poured two coffees from the orange decaf pot and handed one to Rick. "Thank you," he said as she pointed to the tray of creamers and sugar. Rick declined the extras.

"I have all the results from the repeat testing we did, Mr. Puno."

Rick looked into the young woman's worn eyes for the first time. "My wife's mind... her brain. She'll never speak to me again, will she?"

"I don't think so."

Staring into the rich beverage, Rick spoke slowly. "What's left of Karen's beautiful existence?"

———

Back in the waiting area, Rick contemplated his wife's organ donor decision. He imagined his wife procuring her Florida driver's license and scribbling her signature in agreement before she left their office. That's the way she was; when it came to helping others, she didn't pause. Whenever he looked at the back of his license, he contemplated – but never made a commitment.

After waiting another fifteen minutes, a local representative for organ transplantation arrived. "Mr. Puno," she said, "thank you for extending your stay. We're sorry for your loss. We commend your wife for her charitable decision, one which is going to benefit several people." She spoke deliberately, her dangling earrings totally still. "I would like to explain the details and we'd like you to sign accompanying paperwork. After that, the process moves expeditiously."

"Anything I can do to comply with my wife's wishes," he said.

———

A light rain sprinkled the streets late the next morning as Rick crossed the traffic-laden street from the hotel. After settling into a Waffle House booth, he ordered pancakes and scrambled eggs and a waitress attentively refilled his coffee cup. He then made the definitive phone call to a well-known funeral home in Indianapolis and explained the situation. His wife's body would be forthcoming but he wasn't sure when; then he gave them the details of the family's cemetery plot for her burial.

Rick finished, paid the bill, and called Tonya while standing under an awning outside.

———

Tonya decided to attend her 9 a.m. elective music class, but her heart wasn't in it. She kept pulling at her hair and checking her cell phone. She went to the upper deck of the cafeteria with a hot chocolate and finally felt the vibration of her phone.

44

"Dad, what's going on?" I've been waiting for your call. How is Mom?"

"I'm sorry, Tonya." Rick turned sideways as a fine, misty rain blew his way. "It was too late last night to call." He fell silent and took a deep breath.

"Dad?" Tonya whispered in the phone.

"Sweetheart, your mom isn't going to make it. Her body is being kept alive, but her brain is ... well ... not the same."

"Oh, Dad. This is so hard. What do we do?"

"Tonya, your mom wished to donate her organs if something like this ever happened."

"Doing that is a charitable gesture, but my own mother? This is too difficult to contemplate."

"But what if it were your mom who needed a transplant? And no one volunteered their organs?"

"I don't know. I suppose if Mom wanted to donate, we don't have a say in it. She was wonderful like that. I mean, she is wonderful like that." Tonya cupped her left hand over her eyes. A sob escaped and tears gathered. "How did this happen?"

"There is a network around the country which oversees organ donation. They've talked with me. Karen meets their criteria." A woman opened the exit door and stood eyeing Rick as she opened a collapsible umbrella. "Tonya, I'll be having your mom brought back to Indianapolis to be buried there."

"When, Dad? And when will I see you?"

"I'll stay here until the end, then catch a flight there, even if it's standby. And I'll start making phone calls to family."

Tonya wiped her cheek while more students filtered in downstairs for a late breakfast.

"Tonya, you don't need to attend classes if you're not up to it."

"I know."

"I'll call when I know more. I love you."

"I love you, too."

———

During Rick's morning visit with Karen, Dr. Gregory stepped in and touched Rick's shoulder. "They've found potential recipients for your wife's liver and kidneys. Information is being cross-checked and potential arrangements are being made."

Rick stayed seated and glanced at her with acknowledgement as he kept his hand wrapped around his wife's, knowing her wedding ring finger was tucked into his palm.

"If all goes as planned," Dr. Gregory continued, "a transplant team will be here tonight to take her organs. You can visit with her as long as possible."

Rick nodded as she placed her stethoscope over Karen's lungs. Then time stretched throughout the afternoon as Rick stayed and decided to pray. At 3 p.m. he thanked Karen's nurse who left for the day and assumed a first name basis with the next shift. Health care providers maintained a revolving door, writing in her bedside chart, fixing monitors, injecting medication every few hours and adjusting infusion rates.

In the evening, an anesthesiologist stepped in. "Mr. Puno," she said, "I don't mean to disturb you. I'll be quiet." She had a clipboard and intermittently wrote on an anesthesia preop form.

"Anesthesia? My wife will get anesthesia?"

"Perhaps, but not necessarily. I will be maintaining her circulation. Her vital functions, Mr. Puno. I will be with her to the end." She waited as Rick thought about that, but he couldn't talk. "It's very charitable. What you and her are doing."

———

A harder rain pounded outside when the daylight disappeared and Karen's nurse came to usher Rick away from his vigil. A sudden realization gripped him. As long as he had stayed at Karen's bedside, he had held on to fortitude for a one percent chance that his wife's eyes would open and she would acknowledge him. But now, as a respiratory therapist and others readied Karen for the trip to the OR, he choked back emotion and prayed for the courage to say good-bye. A drop slid from Rick's eye onto Karen's lid as he leaned in and kissed her cheek.

Outside the ICU door, Rick waited for his wife, the staff, and all the machinery to pass. The therapist inflated Karen's lungs with an Ambu bag, the thick green oxygen tank sat at the bottom of the bed;

orderlies pushed poles, and a nurse tried to assemble the loose papers from the chart. Rick stared but turned away before they disappeared through another hallway. He wanted to retain previous memories rather than have this last vision persist.

————

Rick moved downstairs and sat in the OR waiting area. He hadn't checked out of the hotel, and needed to do that in the morning, as well as to catch a flight. He delayed the initiation of his grieving process. Karen was simply in the OR and he'd wait until they did the surgery; wait until activity with her case ceased. Then, he must face the fact that his wife would never come home.

He focused on a little girl across the room quizzing her parents about her brother's surgery. After some time, a surgeon came to tell the adults he removed their son's appendix, he was stable and groggy in the recovery room. The family left for the cafeteria and Rick allowed himself to slouch deep into the upholstered chair.

————

A woman with creamy butterscotch hair turned into the waiting area. The humidity outside had corkscrewed her short hair, almost as much as Rick's black curls. She waved toward the open neck of her long-sleeve shirt and headed for the assortment of beverages. She settled on a coke and peanut butter crackers and turned around.

"Excuse me," she said. "Have you heard anything about a transplant team working in the OR?"

"Yes," Rick said. "They went back."

'Thank you." She sat on a chair in a row perpendicular to Rick and turned off the cell phone on her belt. The woman munched on a sandwich cracker before going to the doctor's lounge to quiz people there for more specifics. When she came back, she glimpsed at the man who had a curious accent and exotic handsome features.

"Do you work for the United Network?" Rick asked.

"No, but I flew the team here. I'll fly them back with the liver they're harvesting."

Rick straightened his posture. "Where to?"

"Louisville."

"Hmm. I need to get to Indianapolis. That's where my wife is going to be buried."

The woman took a seat closer to Rick. "Your wife?" she queried softly.

"My wife was in a car accident and was declared brain dead." He leaned over to speak low and point-blankly to the woman. "She's giving them her liver and kidneys."

The woman took a deep breath and exhaled poignantly. "Sir, I'm sorry about your wife. My name is Diana Devlin and if there is anything I can do for you ..."

Rick nodded but a sob crept forward, the one he'd been holding back all along.

———

Rick picked up his pace to the hotel then stopped at the lobby desk. "I'm checking out," he said. "But first I'm going upstairs to get my things."

The printer churned and the receptionist handed him a bill. "Just drop off your room key on your way out," she said.

In his room, Rick lightly towel dried his hair and face, and called Tonya.

"I hope you weren't sleeping," Rick said.

"Dad, it's early for college students. Plus, I'm monitoring my phone like crazy."

"In a way, I have good news."

"It's probably not what I'd love to hear though."

"No. A miracle hasn't occurred to your mother. But, would you like to pack a few things and drive down to Louisville? You could meet me at Samaritan Hospital."

"Why? What's happened?"

"A pilot of a small plane offered me a ride tonight. She's taking your mom's liver and the harvest team there, where a recipient will undergo surgery. We can stay in a hotel and head north after we've rested."

"But what about Mom?"

"They'll send her on to the funeral home in Indianapolis whenever they can. And then the director requires time to, well, make her presentable before we can have a family service."

Tonya closed the binder on her desk and pulled up MapQuest on her computer.

"I'll leave as soon as I can."

"You must promise me that you won't drive over the speed limit."

"I promise. And I'm getting directions for that hospital right now."

"I'll call when I get there. I love you."

"I love you too, Dad."

Chapter 8

For three months, Jennifer considered the black pager an extra appendage. She slept, ate, and went everywhere with it and changed the batteries once a month for peace of mind. She didn't have the energy but, if she did, she wouldn't take a trip away from the Kentuckiana area. If that little box beeped, she had a bag ready for the hospital with fresh pajamas, a lightweight robe, slippers, and new toiletries.

The gorgeous July day had given Jennifer, Johnny, and Amelia an excuse for an excursion and yet still be in southern Indiana. They drove along East Market like bears escaping from a winter den.

"I'm sorry I didn't take you here when you were little," Jennifer said when they reached their destination and squatted in exposed fossil beds. "I brought kids on a school trip here last year. I want to show you this before …"

"Hey, Mom," Johnny said, "nothing's going to happen to you." He tried clearing his sinuses with a good sniffle. "You're going to get your transplant and the results are going to be like magic."

"Johnny's right," Amelia said. The sun warmed her face while she held a clam-like brachiopod.

Jennifer gingerly sat down on the bumpy ground at the Falls of the Ohio. "It's amazing," she said, pointing a bony index finger at Mel. "In your hand is a fossil probably hundreds of millions of years old."

"No way."

"Really. This area lay beneath an ocean at that time." Jennifer leaned on her hands extended behind her. "These Devonian age fossil beds are testament to a coral reef. This is the oldest, largest exposed fossil reef in the world."

Johnny whistled and took off his baseball cap. "Do you want to sit on this, Mom?"

Jennifer gently shook her head. "This place. It reminds us that our presence in the history of the earth is nothing. These geologic rocks persist, but our bodies will turn into dust. And our lives don't even provide a comma in the stream of time."

Johnny and Mel frowned at each other. A peregrine falcon swooped, headed for the rushing water as his eyes scanned for fish descendants from the age of dinosaurs. Mel sat next to her mother and straightened her legs for the sunshine. She felt cool water slightly moisten her denim shorts as Johnny bent over and picked up a sand dollar.

"Mom, do you want to explore the water's edge?" Johnny asked.

"No. I'm too nauseous. I'll make my way back up to the interpretive center. You two can stay and meet me there later."

Johnny extended his arm. "We're coming with you." Jennifer clasped her son's hand and allowed him to pull her up. They waited as she zipped her nylon jacket. She gazed again at the Ohio and the distant bridge before turning, and then locked her arm into Johnny's for the ascent.

"I need to sit," Jennifer said inside the building. She yielded to a wooden bench while Johnny filled a paper cup from the water fountain and handed it to her.

"Mom, what is that?" Amelia asked. She nodded at the lobby's circular display where long, curved tusks extended from a massive skeleton and a couple stood reading a plaque mounted on the railing.

"It's a cast of a skeleton which came from Utah; a woolly mammoth from the Ice Age, descended from an extinct genus of elephants. Some of these gigantic beasts' bones have even been unearthed in Indiana. In Fort Wayne." Jennifer took a sip as Johnny's face lit up with a smile.

"It must also be why Indiana-Purdue picked the *Mastodons* as their athletic mascot."

The burly man in front heard Johnny and nodded emphatically. Jennifer managed a smile. When she felt less queasy, Johnny and Amelia escorted her to their Ford and they left Clarksville to go home, her pager as quiet as a casket.

———

Saturday, September 19th, Jennifer sat at the kitchen table in the early afternoon slicing parboiled potatoes into a bowl. She mixed in a hardboiled egg, onion slivers, and mayonnaise. The radio piped soft rock and intermittent talk continued about Hurricane Ivan's wrath on the gulf coast.

Johnny walked in without his shoes and grabbed a pill bottle. He peeked into the bowl. "Even being congested, that smells good."

"It's only potato salad to accompany sandwiches for tonight."

Johnny popped out a decongestant, opened the refrigerator, and pulled out a gallon of milk.

"Do you have much homework for the weekend?"

"Not much. And I'm almost finished. I know you're concerned about the college I chose but, so far, I like Indiana University." Johnny didn't travel far to the southeast campus and his flexible schedule allowed him and Jennifer to still share the car.

"You won't have a problem wherever you go." Jennifer grinned. "You can drop me off to school on Monday. I'm subbing." Johnny looked at her skeptically. "Don't worry. Mrs. Waverly said I'll be in a homeroom class and it will be an easy day."

"All right." Johnny commented. He tasted her salad with a teaspoon, handed her the salt and pepper, and headed for the hallway. "I'm going to go get a haircut," he said over his shoulder. "Just a little trim. I don't want to cut my hair real short all at once." He passed Amelia's room on the left where she lay on the bed and her friend, Bonnie, sat below her on the floor. School books, magazines, and clothes surrounded them.

"Johnny, if you're not driving," Mel said, "we'll follow you on our skates."

"Sure," he said. He went into his room and put on sneakers.

Amelia and Bonnie checked themselves in the mirror and weaved around the clutter. "Meet you in the driveway," Mel said. "We're going out to lace up."

———

Jennifer put the plastic bowl into the refrigerator and sat down on the couch with a laundry basket. She folded slowly but longed to rest her head on the pillow. After she topped the pile with two boxer shorts, she succumbed to the plaid cushions. A top of the hour weather news brief interrupted the stream of music. Jennifer couldn't imagine why people lived in harm's way on coastal properties but she supposed they loved the sun and the sand and the water as much as she loved the familiarity of her small town and brackish Ohio River. But the federal government would probably help bail the coastal people out with federal dollars after the storm and she didn't know about taxpayers doing all that. No one helped her with her medical bills and she hadn't done anything stupid to warrant hepatitis C. Her weighty eyelids and legs got heavier until a strong sleep took hold.

———

After some time, dark brown eyes gazed knowingly into Jennifer's. The eyes of a wooly mammoth were almost as huge as Jennifer's hands. She smoothed her hand from the base to the point of the curved, elongated tusk, so smooth and perfect to the touch. The animal nudged her and Jennifer accepted her invitation and sat. Carefully and tenderly, the beast raised her in her tusks. In the safety of ivory, Jennifer saw an entire valley as the day broke, anew with strange and beautiful animals. Two younger mammoths joined alongside them, guiding the older beast's care of Jennifer.

Abundant food and shelter awaited them across a large perilous river. The older mammoth stepped into the water and a scaly crocodile arose and smiled at them. Once the thick leg of the mastodon went forward, the crocodile grabbed it. The animal shook it free and stepped back on land as Jennifer watched the smaller beasts attend to her caregiver's bloodied leg. After some time, they set out again through a smaller river, the young ones close by to thwart danger. Underwater, a smart, otter-like creature thwarted another crocodile, nipping at its leathery shell to let the group pass to the other side.

———

Johnny exited the side door of the barber shop where Mel and Bonnie rolled along the driveway from the back parking lot.

"You had it trimmed shorter than normal," Mel said. "You going military?"

"No. Not yet, but I'm working up my nerve," he said. "It does look kind of cool."

"Johnny," Bonnie said, "since you're my best friend's brother, I'll tell you. The girls that like you don't care if it's short or long."

"Bonnie," Mel whined.

"I'm not talking about me," Bonnie said. "I'm just reporting what I know." She dug her hands into her hoodie for her ringing cell phone. "That's my mom. I gotta go. Later," she said, and skated away.

Johnny and Amelia made their way towards home. They talked about annoying fall term teachers as Johnny's spindly legs kept pace with Mel's wheels. Mel ditched her skates in the garage and they both entered the front door where they heard a *beep-beep, beep-beep.*

"Hey, Mom," Johnny shouted. Amelia shook her mother, yanking her mind from a convoluted dream while Johnny dove to grasp the shrill pager sitting on the coffee table. Jennifer hazily righted herself. As Johnny held the square box, they stared at each other in disbelief.

"Maybe someone made a wrong number," Jennifer said.

Johnny looked at the incoming number on the screen and shook his head. Amelia picked up the touch tone phone on the end table and handed it to her mother. Jennifer's hand trembled as she pressed the buttons.

"Mrs. Barns," the voice on the other end said, "would you like to use that packed bag? The one we know you have waiting beside your bed?"

————

Jennifer's heart thumped as she put down the phone and nodded at her children. Johnny and Amelia hugged her until her bones practically cracked. "Ease up," she said, "or they'll be gorilla gluing me before they transplant me!" She giggled and her children's eyes widened. They hadn't heard her laugh in months.

"I'm taking a quick shower, putting on fresh clothes, and picking up my bag." Jennifer stepped towards the hallway.

"Otherwise, I'm clueless; I don't know what needs to be done to leave the house. You two are in charge."

"We'll take care of what needs to be done," Johnny said. He put the laundry away then shut the window over the kitchen sink. He brushed hair off his shirt and popped a 24-hour decongestant.

Amelia put an English class novel, her wallet, and two apples into her tote bag. She put on a headband and tucked her T-shirt into her Capri's.

Jennifer dried and combed her hair and steered clear of deodorant and moisturizers. She slipped into a wrinkle-free dress and denim shoes.

"I'm the driver," Johnny said, when Jennifer appeared with the overnight bag. Johnny closed the blinds and curtains, motioned them out, and locked the door.

———

While crossing the bridge, Jennifer, Johnny and Amelia's jubilant emotions waned as their thoughts centered on the uncertainty of Jennifer's plight. Jennifer gulped as the skyline of downtown Louisville approached. It wasn't too late to back out except that the terminal nature of her disease only plodded forward. Her future lay in the hands of a surgeon who would remove her sick liver and sew in a new one.

Johnny found a handy parking space in the garage. When they got out of the car, Amelia carried Jennifer's bag. "Thanks," Jennifer said. "Now, I'm tired of being tired and sick of being sick. I don't want to be a worn-out mother to you both any more. Let's get this behind us."

Chapter 9

Mumblings of an impending liver transplant filtered into the anesthesia department of Samaritan Hospital throughout the day. The busy elective surgeries started to unwind and emergency cases remained slow but anesthesia staffing for the next day remained uncertain. If the transplant was booked, which doctor and nurses would be available to handle the increased manpower needed for a liver transplant after the department assigned anesthesia providers for the next day's regular cases?

Joan, the schedule coordinator for the group, shook her head. If Dr. Sukhdev Bhagat or Dr. Arnold Morris added on a liver transplant, it would take three people out of the normal schedule and rearrange others. The three anesthesia providers chosen may be sight unseen for six to twelve hours, depending on who did the surgery, and totally taken away from all the other cases, which would come and go in the interim. Other cases required one doctor to do them, or one nurse anesthetist staffed by a doctor who was also responsible for other cases. Joan put down her pencil. She believed her job would end up easier if Arnold Morris' role was primary surgeon. She questioned Sukhdev's skills and the longer length of his surgeries.

By late afternoon, the transplant team informed the operating room head nurse that they had a donor and a recipient match and they would go south for harvesting the donor's organ. The head nurse rushed into the anesthesia office with a thicker clipboard than Joan's and announced, "Looks like a liver transplant is in the pipeline for the early hours of the morning. Sukhdev Bhagat's the surgeon and Dr. Morris will help him get started." She spun around and left in a flash leaving Joan readdressing her department's needs.

Walking past the office, Dr. Peter Devlin heard the news, and stopped at the door. He grinned sheepishly at Joan.

"And what do you want?" Joan asked. "I swear, Dr. Devlin, you're a glutton for punishment."

"No. I'm a magnet for a challenging case." His sandy brown mustache stretched while he managed a dimpled smile. "Plus, I know you'll give me the day off after I staff it."

"That's never your motive," she said. "Okay, best to put your skilled hands to good use. Your mind, too."

Peter usually ignored remarks like that; he shrugged his shoulders and held out his hands, giving Joan the benefit of the doubt. He had grown up in the Carolinas, gone to college and medical school in the northeast, and sailed through his residency on the west coast. With knowledge and know-how from all over, he ended up in Louisville, Kentucky for no particular geographic reason. He had liked the description of the practice during his job interview; complex cases, medium-sized group to spread call nights, state-of-the-art medical center, and some teaching of residents.

"Thanks," he said, pushing his lean body off the door.

"I'm putting Kevin and Cindy in there with you. The three of you better start setting up the OR room."

"Yes Ma'am." He walked away with a glint in his eyes.

———

Peter stepped into OR 3 and the anesthesia technician wheeled in the extra equipment needed over and above a routine case. The anesthesia machine was stacked high with Hewlett Packard equipment for pressure waveforms for the femoral arterial line, pulmonary artery line, and central venous line. The oximetric Swan Gantz catheter equipment also stood there for direct readouts of the patient's ongoing cardiac output. And to his satisfaction, he checked the other equipment - EKG machine, capnometer, vaporizers, oxygen flow meter, the circuit, and suction.

A red anesthesia cart also stood adjacent to the head of the table. The certified registered nurse anesthetist, Kevin, walked in and began assembling things on top, preparing labeled syringes, endotracheal tubes, laryngoscope blades, drugs and other tools. "We're going to have a long wait and a long case," he said. Like most of the group, Kevin stood shorter and carried more pounds than Peter. He'd been doing anesthesia for years and had developed gray hair along his temples.

The anesthesia technician pushed in another bulky cart with the other CRNA, Cindy, following behind. On the top shelf were more invasive monitors for another arterial line in the patient's wrist and the noninvasive Dinamap machine for blood pressure. Cindy smiled under her mask at both men. "Nice group," she said.

"Now that you're here," Kevin said.

"Thanks. How do you want to split up our breaks, Kevin?" She evaluated the pulse oximeter on her own finger and put temperature probes out for the patient; one to be used rectally and one for his or her esophagus.

"Together for induction and then switch off every hour until we're all together coming off bypass. After that, we can switch off again every hour until we get together again for wrap-up and transport." This came out in one quick stream and Cindy chuckled.

An IV pole stood at the top right and left of the OR table. Peter set up bottles or bags of nipride, mannitol, D50W, and regular insulin. He checked for ketamine while listening to Kevin and Cindy arrange their own breaks. At anytime, he could call them both in together if needed. He would be present almost the whole time except when things were manageable by one of them, he needed a quick break, or when he ran a special laboratory device for an important piece of bleeding information in a nearby room - a TEG or thromboelastogram. Their end-stage liver patient could profoundly bleed; it wasn't just the clotting or red blood cell function he had to worry about, it was platelets and fresh frozen plasma transfusions that he needed to be equally diligent about.

With only enough space at the top of the room, a young man busily prepared his area of equipment. Robert would work with a complicated machine - a rapid infusor system or RIS - and would correlate closely with Peter. Robert had an unsightly scar on his cheek and appreciated covering it with a mask. He handed Peter a one-quarter-inch tubing to be hooked to one of anesthesia's stop cock ports.

Robert patted his resuscitative machine which could deliver warmed, filtered premixed fluid at an incredible rate. 1,500 to 2,000 cc/min or 1.5 to 2 liters/min could be infused into the patient at a constant rate or a bolus of 400cc/min. And the ratio of red blood cells, fresh frozen plasma and platelets would be a specific cocktail.

Peter, Cindy and Kevin would be transfusing their own blood bank products, tweaking the patient's blood based on lab values for whatever the patient lacked. They knew the total blood volume of a normal-sized adult to be approximately five liters; their patient could lose and gain back his or her entire blood volume.

Peter handed Kevin a bottle to pour some liquid isoflurane into the vaporizer because the window gauge showed it to be half full. Kevin carefully put the bottle lip on the filling device and poured, the scent of the liquid permeating their nostrils. When turned on, the liquid would vaporize and travel along the plastic circuit to the patient's lungs.

"It always amazes me," Kevin said, "that in liver transplants, the anesthetic part is the least of our worries."

"It's because we're careful," Peter said, "and delivering amnesia and pain control is second nature. But you're right." Peter nodded. "This is acute, resuscitative care like no other. They didn't say anything about this in medical school or even in residency."

"Do we have a patient's name yet, Dr. Devlin?" Cindy asked.

"Not yet. But I'll go see the patient as soon as I get word he or she has arrived, and I'll fill you both in." Peter walked over to the thermostat while OR nurses and techs continued assembling their own equipment. He nodded to one of them his approval of the room temperature. He always checked a separate list in his mind, to scrutinize the materials needed to keep a patient warm, important in preventing hypothermia. Besides the RIS and thermostat setting, they had fluid warmers, a concha humidifier, and would wrap the patient's arms and head. They would place a silver blanket and a warming blanket on the table. Practically the only non-warmed area of the patient would be the surgical site, a major area of body temperature loss.

Peter was in OR 3 for an hour before they called him on the walkie talkie. Looking around the room, he was satisfied and relied on Kevin and Cindy to finish. Cindy assembled the separate clipboard dangling from the liver cart where they would write all the TEG results as well as all the product bags they would hang and infuse. Kevin sorted the regular anesthetic paperwork and neatly arranged it on the top of their machine.

"I'll see your frazzled body tomorrow morning," Joan said to Peter while grabbing her purse from the bottom drawer in her office. "Here's the patient's name. She's on the fifth floor. Give Cindy and Kevin a dinner break before dust hits the fan." She turned around once more as she headed for the automatic doors. "There's pizza in the nurse's lounge from an orthopedic rep salesman, besides yesterday's pot luck leftovers in our refrigerator. Anything's fair game."

"Good night," Peter said, pushing his hand forward to make her go.

Peter scoured a fifth floor nurses' station for the patient's chart. Jennifer Barns' prior record, diagnostic tests, and paperwork were loose in her unassembled chart and orders were pending from Dr. Morris. Peter looked over the grim data and copied some of it onto his preanesthetic evaluation form. He went to the forty-seven year old patient's temporary room. A frail, jaundiced woman in a hospital gown sat on the edge of the bed while a young teenager slouched in a chair with her feet nestled against the mattress and an older male teenager sat in the corner. The girl's novel perched face down on her pants.

"Hi," Peter said. "Are you Jennifer Barns?"

"Yes," she said.

"I'm Dr. Devlin, the anesthesiologist. Do you mind if I sit?" he asked glancing at the teens.

Jennifer introduced Johnny and Amelia.

"Nice to meet you both. If either of you have any questions, chime in. What are you reading, Amelia?"

"*To Kill a Mockingbird* for English class."

"Still a classic."

Peter looked at Jennifer. "I have questions to ask you and then I'll explain what to expect. We'll talk about your anesthetic and overall risks and benefits. I bet things are moving fast for you, so if you'd like me to repeat anything, I'd be happy to."

Jennifer answered Peter's questions about her illness. He listened to her heart and lungs and asked to see inside her mouth. Jennifer frowned.

"They aren't operating in my mouth, are they?"

"No," Peter explained. "Looking at your neck, your mouth, and the back of your throat lets me know if I may have a problem putting a breathing tube into your windpipe."

"So besides doing that," Amelia asked, "you're going to give my mom anesthesia? She won't know anything, will she?"

"We'll be sure to give your mother the anesthesia she needs. And no, she shouldn't have any recall. This is, however, a serious operation and the risks are many." Peter spoke in a soothing tone and Johnny leaned forward and listened intently.

"Doctor, it's been a long road for me to get here. Telling me risks won't deter me now."

"I understand, Mrs. Barns. Nevertheless ..."

———

When Peter arrived back in the anesthesia lounge, Cindy and Kevin huddled over the circular table.

"Did you two eat?" Peter asked.

"We did," Kevin replied. "Pizza from the lounge. But it's gone. What about you, Dr. Devlin?"

"I guess now's the time."

Cindy pointed to the left-over Subway sandwiches.

Peter cut an end slice off a foot-long with deli meats. He slid his preanesthetic note to them. Cindy's bright eyes dulled as she read.

"Her two kids are upstairs with her," Peter said softly. "She's forty-seven and was a full-time teacher. She's thin as a dime on its side and I suspect some ascites." He took a bite and poured lemonade from a container. "We'll do our best to get her to the blackboard again," he said.

Peter strode to the doctor's lounge. He called his wife, whom he hadn't spoken to since leaving the house in the morning. She had put herself on the hook for the weekend; whether to volunteer or get reimbursed for flying, he didn't know which. Being in the air was her thing, especially if it meant flying her cherished Cessna.

"Hello," Diana said.

"How's your day?"

"Great. Just did a walk around of my plane. I'm flying a transplant team to Birmingham for a liver. It must be for you guys."

"Spot on. And I'm doing the case."

"Hmm," she crooned. "We make strange bedfellows."

"That's because we never sleep together."

"We'll have to do something about that."

"We'll have to make a date."

Diana watched the security officer in the Standiford Field FBO office nearby. Mr. Temple fished for a Winston in a cigarette pack and stepped through the automatic doors for fresh air.

"We'll have to get our calendars," Peter added.

"Looks like you've got a long wait. For the transplant, I mean."

"The team isn't there yet?'

"No. But they should be any minute. I'm heading to the plane when we get off the phone."

"You're welcome to see me if you come into the hospital when you get back. When I duck out for a break."

"Any call rooms available if I'm half awake?"

"Sure. You can use mine. I surely won't be using it."

With a brisk step, Diana again headed to her plane. Mr. Temple gave Sukhdev Bhagat and his team directions to the plane when they arrived several minutes later.

The overnight anesthesiologist on call supervised the other cases being booked. Peter excused himself, entered the call room, and sat in a comfortable chair with a magazine. Within minutes, his eyelids dropped like acorns. When his forearm jerked, he slinked his way to the bed. Hours later, he fumbled for the wall phone blaring above the bed.

Peter jumped up. "Doctor Devlin."

"Dr. Devlin, we're sending for the patient. The donor liver and our people are on their way back from Birmingham."

"Thanks to a lovely pilot," he said rubbing his eyes and glancing toward the digital clock. "Please bring our recipient patient, Jennifer Barns, to the holding area. I'll do preliminary lines in there and let me know when the plane touches down. Then we'll take our patient to the OR."

———————

Peter added Jennifer's recent lab work to his forms as he scrolled through her record on the preop holding area computer. An orderly wheeled her in on a stretcher and the OR room 3 nurse visited to do an identity check and preliminary assessment. Jennifer groggily rested. She had signed and agreed to all consents, and now lay under the spell of Peter's preop anesthetic orders. His intramuscular benzodiazepam had gone a long way. Although she could haphazardly answer his questions and stir when aroused, she already couldn't remember the elevator ride.

Kevin came in and introduced himself to Jennifer. He put an inclining arm board under her right wrist and Peter inserted a catheter into her pulsating radial artery for continuous blood pressure monitoring. They hooked it to a heparin syringe and flushed. Peter sutured it in and Kevin taped it securely.

Jennifer turned her head to the two men. "Where … are my children?" she asked trying to command her eyelids to stay open.

"I believe they're in the waiting area," the nurse said. "They'll be comfortable there. While you're in surgery, someone will routinely let them know about your progress."

Kevin inserted a small IV into the crook of Jennifer's arm.

"Mrs. Barns, are we hurting you?" Peter asked.

Jennifer's chest rose with a deeper breath. "My hair is a mess," she mumbled.

Peter and Kevin nodded to each other, acknowledging her satisfactory preop medication. Both men worked on documenting what they had done so far while Cindy went to get fentanyl from the drug dispensing machine, the potent narcotic they'd give Jennifer during her case.

A voice sounded over the call box in the holding area. "Dr. Devlin, we just received word. The plane landed at Standiford Field."

Chapter 10

Tonya pulled a T-shirt over her head with 'Butler University' on the front. She tucked it into faded jeans and then packed: athletic shorts, pajamas, a toiletry bag and another change of clothes in her backpack. A paperback from her archeology class followed, as well as her CD player, paper and pens. She wrote her roommate a note, grabbed her cell phone and directions, and left the building with the smell of marijuana in the staircase behind her. Instead of causing a delay by eating dinner on campus, she wanted to get on the road. Plus, any excuse to avoid dorm food.

The monotonous drive south on I-65 would have normally caused Tonya to insert her favorite music into the CD player. Not this time. Over and over, memories of her mother sprang up, causing a crowded feeling in her chest.

Tonya recalled their visit to Butler. They had pulled off the interstate and as they walked through the parking lot after lunch, Karen popped a wad of paper into her mouth, moistened it, and then stuck the spitball inside the coke straw. Tonya watched as her mother blew out the paper bullet above their car. "What? You never did that before?" Karen had asked.

Tonya had rolled her eyes and said, "Mom, that's so five minutes ago." She had always wondered what other teens meant when they said their parents were so old. Hers didn't act that way.

In two hours, she crossed the dark river into downtown Louisville, followed the directions, and parked on the third floor of the hospital parking garage. When she called her father, the voice prompt steered her to his voicemail. "Dad, I'm at the hospital. Call me when you land so we can link up."

Tonya ambled to the elevator and rode to the ground floor. She passed a Burger King in the causeway and stepped inside. An employee hastily stacked chairs to wash the floor. "Can I still buy something before you close?" Tonya asked at the counter.

"Yah man," the employee said. "But the machine isn't working," he said nodding at the soda dispenser.

"Cheeseburger and fries," she said and wondered when her dad had last eaten. "And another cheeseburger, bigger, and with everything on it." When all the closing chores from the worker behind her subsided, the clerk handed her the order.

Inside the hospital entrance was an unstaffed desk and a closed gift shop but no sitting area. A directory listed the operating room on the second floor, so she went there to find some place to sit. When she exited the elevator, she followed the arrow sign pointing to the OR. Around the corner, waxy plants lined a hallway partition and she looked over them to see an ample waiting room. A woman wearing a nylon jacket came forward, away from her son and daughter behind her, to flip through the magazine selection on the corner front table.

The woman's little girl lay face up on a two-seater couch against the wall, her long hair draped over the edge, while her brother ran around in full ecstasy. The mature toddler abruptly stopped in front of his four-year-old sister, grabbed two fistfuls of her hair, and yanked her to the floor.

Tonya's jaw fell. In a chair to the left, a girl wearing a light blue T-shirt gasped. The male teen with her straightened his developed shoulders and winced with empathy for the girl on the carpet. He spotted Tonya and their eyes held.

"Go away," yelled the little girl on the floor. She seemed barely perturbed by the startling disturbance as her brother bolted off.

The mother settled on a woman's magazine, spun around, and hastened across the room. "Nancy! Get up off that floor." The mother pulled her up and directed her back on the couch. The little girl rubbed the back of her head.

Tonya walked towards the rear left wall. She put her things on a table between chairs and sat. The little boy stopped bubbling spit in the middle of the room and ran a circle with outstretched airplane arms. He hit Tonya's backpack and kept going.

The woman slapped the magazine on a chair. "Let's go you two. For a walk or something while your dad's in surgery." The youngsters trailed her reluctantly and disappeared down the hallway.

"Like adios," Amelia said. She glanced at Tonya and then at her brother, shaking her head.

Tonya and Johnny cracked smiles. Tonya pulled her wrapped burger and fries from the bag and placed them on the seat next to her. She munched on a French fry as Johnny cleared his throat.

"Is a Burger King nearby?" he asked her.

"Very. But they closed after me."

"We missed it Johnny," Mel said, nudging his arm.

"I bought one for someone else," Tonya said. "But he's probably going to be too late." She dug the plump burger out and stepped over to Johnny.

"No way," he said. It smelled so good and he wondered if she had bought it for a boyfriend.

"It's yours, really."

"Ours," Mel piped in.

"To share then." Tonya shrugged. "But the drink dispenser was empty."

Johnny stood and noticed 'Butler University' on her shirt. "Thanks. Then I'll find us something to drink. Any preference?"

"A cola or a root beer."

"Mel, you can split it," Johnny said. "I'll be back."

———————

On his return, Johnny handed Tonya a chilled can. "What year of college are you in?" he asked.

"First. But every time you finally gain seniority in a school, you're starting at the bottom in the next one."

"I know what you mean."

"You in college?"

"First year at Southeast IU."

"I'm at Butler," she said and took a sip.

"I figured," he said, taking his half of the burger from Mel.

Tonya tilted her head. "How did you know that?"

"By your shirt." He nodded and admired the shapely contents under her shirt.

She looked down and rolled her eyes. "I forgot I put that on. I just drove down here from campus, not under the best of circumstances."

———————

"Mrs. Barns, we're going to do all the work," Peter said when they lined up Jennifer's stretcher beside the OR table."

"I didn't plan on helping. You've made me loopy but I don't remember if that is a real word."

"Mrs. Barns, right now, you can write your own dictionary if you'd like." Everyone grasped the sheet underneath her. "One, two, three," Peter said, and they slid her over to the operating table. Cindy slipped more versed into her IV and loosely fastened the plastic mask blowing one-hundred percent oxygen over her face.

Jennifer breathed shallow until she took a good gasp. She stared at the ghost-white lights above while Dr. Devlin painted a cold solution along the top crease of her right leg. Everything happening to her seemed so strange.

Why was the anesthesiologist sticking something into her groin area? Why was the anesthesia nurse hooking tubing to that syringe they had attached to her wrist area and why had someone tilted the table head down and why was someone smearing a solution on her left neck? What did the things they were doing to her have to do with surgery in her abdomen? She couldn't sort it out, although she'd been told her transplant was a big deal and many procedures and risks were involved. Finally, she settled on thoughts of Johnny and Amelia, and closed her eyes.

Kevin converted the temporary right antecubital fossa IV to a monster IV using a guide wire and sutured it in while Peter stood between the right arm board and the OR table. With a sterile technique, he prepped Jennifer's groin area and palpated to find her femoral artery. Once he located it, he injected a bee sting amount of local anesthetic and used a number 18 arrow kit to insert a femoral arterial line for pressure monitoring. He sutured the second arterial line into place. Although rare to have two arterial lines during the same case, Peter felt it mandatory for a liver transplant in case something happened to one of them. In any case, they would monitor both and note discrepancies between the femoral and radial pressures along the way. The two lines would guide resuscitation and allow trending of blood pressures going up or down.

When Peter and Kevin finished, Peter began a sterile procedure at Jennifer's left neck. He inserted a seeker needle into the area, avoiding the carotid artery. On his first attempt, dark venous blood returned into his syringe. He inserted a different needle with a catheter into the same spot and removed the last seeker needle, inserted a long guide wire, then nicked the skin to make a bigger hole and removed the catheter. Over the wire, he gently pushed the big central line IV with side ports for medications and drips, removed the wire and checked for venous blood return again.

Cindy helped Peter with the insertion of the Oximetric Swan Ganz catheter into the 8.5 French line which would allow them to follow Jennifer's cardiac output and other important pressure data to guide therapy. Meanwhile, Kevin constantly scanned Jennifer's vital signs and began the tedious job of charting everything they had done so far.

Dr. Morris came in for the second time, assuring himself that the surgical equipment was in order and the anesthesia team had no difficult delays. "Mrs. Barns," he said to Jennifer as Peter removed the blue drapes off her face and mask, "it's Dr. Morris. Dr. Bhagat just arrived at the airport. As soon as he gets here with your new liver, we'll be getting underway."

Peter and Arnold Morris nodded, both understanding they still had much to prepare. Jennifer dozed off again. This time the darkness behind her lids deepened and the noises in the room echoed like talking in a tight canyon.

––––––––––

Since Tonya had offered to share her French fries, the three teens intermittently stabbed them into ketchup. After Johnny ate the last one, he crumpled the paper and Tonya helped him gather the assorted garbage. The two older teens walked to the hallway where Johnny mimicked a basketball shot into the can, reeling forward on his sneakers, grinning with the sport of it. "You play?" she asked.

"Just for fun, with some neighborhood guys. How about you? Like any particular sport?"

"I like basketball and I like to ride, but my bike's still not at school."

The automatic door opened nearby and a woman in scrubs came out. "Johnny," she said when she spotted him, "your mother went back and they've been getting her ready for some time. They'll be putting her to sleep within a half hour." She spun back around. "We'll keep you informed," she added over her shoulder.

"My mom's here for surgery," he said, noting Tonya's questioning look.

Tonya wished her mother was having surgery, but Karen must now be officially dead. Tonya rolled that word around inside her head. Maybe somebody was lowering her into a big wooden box for transfer to an airplane. As cargo to Indianapolis. Moisture swelled in her eyes and she hastened to the sitting area.

Johnny sat in his previous chair and pulled a tissue from the box on the table. He sniffled and blew his nose lightly. "Mel," he said. Amelia tilted her head sideways to see her brother. "I guess the transplant doctor is here or something. A nurse just told me mom will be going to sleep soon."

Tonya dabbed her eyes with her fingertips and gazed at Johnny. She wore a questioning awareness like a city pedestrian scanning an intersection before stepping off the curb. "Is your mother getting a liver transplant?"

Johnny stared back and nodded.

Tonya paled. This was all too much to absorb at once.

Chapter 11

Rick left the hotel and met Diana in the hospital's front lobby as planned. "I'm not an imposition, am I?" he asked.

"I invited you," Diana answered. "My plane can accommodate one more, and I am happy to help. Your wife just passed away and you just shot up here from South America. Under the circumstances, you can't impose on anybody."

He raked his hand through his wavy hair as they walked out and she waved down a cab driver.

"You can make yourself comfortable in the FBO office where we're going," Diana said in the vehicle. "I have preflight details to take care of. We should be ready to go by the time Dr. Bhagat, his resident, and the network coordinators arrive."

"He's the surgeon who worked on my wife? And he'll put her liver in the patient in Louisville?"

"As far as I know."

"I can't even imagine that," Rick said with admiration and became silent. He made errors working on mundane matters, he thought. How do surgeons fix moist, beating parts of bodies as routinely as people drive cars?

————

Diana left Rick in the airstrip's office after giving the airfield information on her flight. She sprang across the flat cement to her plane, completed her tasks, and then went back for iced tea and graham crackers. When they walked back outside together, she thought the night was clear and perfect for flying. She left Rick to his tortured thoughts, a man so fresh with grief that she wanted to tuck him into her airplane like helping a blind man cross the street.

In the cabin, a few belongings from her previous passengers lined the seats so Diana asked Rick to sit in the back left seat. He closed his eyes with fatigue, but twenty minutes later a hand jostled his shoulder, rousing him from his nap.

"Rick," Diana said, "this is Dr. Bhagat."

"And, Dr. Bhagat, I asked Rick to join us because he's going to Indianapolis after we drop him off in Louisville. He's the husband of Karen Puno who, as you know, was the donor patient you just did surgery on."

The group gathered on board, settling into position. Diana weaved between them, evaluating their items, particularly the safety of the doctor's organ cooler he had placed behind the last right seat. She scanned the group for secured seat belts.

Sukhdev buckled up and had stretched his legs comfortably in the front cockpit seat. He turned around to Rick. "Glad she could help you out."

Rick peered at him between the seats and nodded. Sukhdev turned to the front and checked his Seiko aviation watch with multiple time zones. No matter how long he'd been in the States, during the day he still thought about his family and what they may be doing in Pakistan. He was more clever than his watch, though, because it didn't show him that Pakistan's Greenwich Mean Time was GMT+5. In his experience, many adult Americans stared at him blankly if he mentioned Greenwich Mean Time, let alone the world's variety of time zones.

Sukhdev stared out the window while Diana rambled on with her safety spiel. He looked forward to dosing off, which he figured the hitchhiker in the back of the airplane would do. He needed it more than that guy.

Diana paused for emphasis. "And," she said, "a US federal aviation regulation prohibits the use of any personal electronic devices or PED's on board an aircraft. If you don't believe the reasoning behind this, next time you're staying at a hotel, pocket your electronic hotel key card with your cell phone. Electronic interference from you cellular phone will erase your card of all data and you'll be locked out."

Diana continued her data and instrument checks, and gave and received Organ Life Zero One's information with the Ground and Tower. She began her departure as Rick's downcast eyes finally succumbed to sleep.

That's strange, she thought in a little while. She zeroed in again on the flight management computer, or FMC, map. She quickly studied the raw data VOR position. A clear disagreement existed between her FMC map display and the VOR position. Diana sensed a déjàvu, two years ago in a flight simulator for requalification. Due to solid training, she had assumed correctly at that time that the FMC had erred. She had immediately switched over to raw data, impressing her instructor. But now? Diana looked out the window to a beautifully clear, unchanged night and the FMC seemed accurate.

"Hello." Sukhdev's cell phone was on vibrate and he answered a call from the OR front desk at Good Samaritan. "I am on my way," he barked. "Tell Doctor Morris the liver looks good."

"I said," Diana vehemently voiced, "*no* person may operate a PED in an aircraft. Nor may I, as the operator in command of this aircraft, allow cellular phones to be on in my US registered civil aircraft."

Diana's cheeks heated like lava while Sukhdev turned off his cell. She glanced at her VOR and FMC map which now correlated. This time, she raised her voice. "I am directly responsible for the safety of everyone on board this aircraft as well as any and all safety degradations."

"You're interfering with our medical mission," Sudadev said, ramping up his glare. "Communication is required between transplant surgeons and the two hospitals."

"You're going to make us all organ donors, Doctor! Even Air Force One follows protocols." She desperately tried to swallow the insults she wanted to hurl.

"I've never heard of an aircraft crashing because of a cell ph…, I mean a PED," he said smartly.

Diana inhaled a long, deep breath and counted to three. "Late in the 1980's five Blackhawk helicopters went down. All indications pointed to electromagnetic interference with electronic flight controls." She gritted her teeth. "Which is what you just did to my Cessna."

Several seeds of sweat trickled down inside Sukhdev's shirt. It was getting too hot in the bitch's plane.

———

An hour and a half later, Diana smoothly landed at the Standiford runway and taxied to a stop. Rick awoke from a deep, rich sleep and glanced around. Sukhdev had catnapped and practically opened the hatch door himself.

The transplant team went ahead lugging the paramount liver cooler, fled the FBO, and left in Ann's CRV. Diana lagged, tidying up work-related issues while Rick waited.

"I have my car," Diana said as they entered the office. "You're welcome to come downtown to Good Samaritan Hospital with me." She motioned to the chairs in case Rick wanted to sit. "My husband, Peter, works there. He's the anesthesiologist in charge of the transplant."

"You mean he's taking care of the person receiving Karen's liver?" Rick asked, surprised. "Dr. Bhagat's case?"

"Yes."

He slipped down into the first chair. "It must be interesting for him, working with surgeons."

"Mmm, I'm sure it is."

"Thanks, I'll take the lift. I was going to call a cab." Rick managed a smile. "I asked my daughter, Tonya, to drive down to the hospital from Indianapolis. She should be there by now."

Diana entered the office to leave flight data. "Looks like you've got the place to yourself," she said to the man at the desk, who needed to screw his eyelids open.

"We're down to only me at eleven. Even Mr. Temple goes home to his wife."

She frowned at the pot with the muddy coffee. "You don't want to drink that," the man agreed.

————

Rick called Tonya while he waited for Diana. "Hi, honey. I'm in Louisville. I have a ride to the hospital. Where should I meet you?"

"I'm in the second floor waiting room outside the OR." She watched Johnny while his fingers beat to a rhythm; she'd lent him her ear buds and portable CD player. She moved to the hallway and spoke in a hushed tone. "The lady that's receiving Mom's liver is in the operating room right now. I'm sitting with her kids. One of them is in college like me."

"What a coincidence. I'm glad you have someone to pass the time with."

"I think their mother has been really sick."

Rick tried to imagine the woman with liver disease. His wife had spent her last days with sensors, machines and computers keeping her alive. How close was this other woman to death?

"The surgeon left ahead of me and the pilot," Rick said. "We should be leaving in a few minutes."

"Dad, this is mind-boggling and I'm so tired."

"I know, sweetheart. I feel the same way." Rick watched Diana approach, her steps not as bouncy as before.

"And we don't even know if our house is standing," Tonya said.

He wished Tonya hadn't reminded him. He couldn't deal with thinking about that.

———

"Mr. Puno," Diana said while driving along the Watterson Expressway.

"Please, call me Rick."

"I have to bring my husband some food. What chain restaurant will be open at 4 a.m.?" She coasted her black BMW convertible off the nearest exit.

"Not much," he lamented. "But I could use a bite myself."

"My husband, Peter, gets wrapped up in whatever he's doing and could care less about a meal. Sometimes I have to remind him to eat." She pulled into a Denny's where she spotted an aproned waitress through the front window serving a lone customer.

Rick held the door open for Diana to go inside. They both read a menu at the counter.

"The roast beef sandwich with mushrooms and onions," Diana said to the tired-looking woman. "Two to go."

"I'll take one, too," Rick said.

"Something to drink?" the waitress asked.

"Coffee," they said simultaneously. "And make them large," Diana added.

Johnny handed Tonya back her music. He wanted to find out about her mother. But how? Perhaps asking about her mother's death would be too personal. Just like he wondered if she had a boyfriend. In both cases, it was none of his business. The important thing was that Tonya's mother must have had a generous heart to donate her liver. And by meeting Tonya, he would remember the philanthropic family who had done it.

Tonya pulled clusters of hair between her thumb and index finger, studying Johnny's face when he wasn't looking. "My dad should be here soon. He's had a long trip. All the way from South America, to Birmingham, and now here."

"You haven't seen your father since your mother died?"

"No. He was working in Peru. My mother was alone at home, on Pensacola Beach and she had to get out of there because of the hurricane." Tonya's eyebrows lowered; she didn't think she could go on.

Johnny inched one seat over and briefly touched her shoulder. Tonya's mouth puckered as if she would cry. "She drove off the island with our dog, all packed up, and got creamed by another car. That was it. She went into a coma from all the injuries."

Amelia made eye contact with her brother after listening to Tonya's explanation. She had wrapped her hoodie into a make-shift pillow, ditched reading, and turned off the table lamp. Johnny shook his head and all three teens sat silently.

Diana and Rick left the smell of roast beef in the elevator when they exited on the second floor. "The waiting room is right around the corner," Diana said.

They passed the shelf of artificial plants and Rick doubled his pace on seeing his daughter. She sat with a male teenager, long and lanky, but sturdy in the shoulders. The boy rose with Tonya.

"Dad!" She fell into her father's arms as he wrapped her tightly then planted a solid kiss on her forehead.

"Dad, this is Johnny," she said, "and this is Amelia." She pointed to the couch where Mel had swung up to a sitting position.

"Nice to meet both of you," Rick said. "And this is Diana."

Diana shook Johnny's hand. "I'm the pilot who just flew back and forth to Birmingham," she said and looked at Tonya, "and brought your dad back with me."

"Dad's so lucky you had space," Tonya said.

Diana put her bag on a chair. "I'll be right back. I'll check if I can pull some strings for us to sit and eat more comfortably." Diana walked through the automatic OR doors and stopped at the front desk where no scrubs were needed.

"Hi Mrs. Devlin," a woman said. "Your husband is working hard back there."

"As always. Can you send a message to him that I'm here and I have food? No hurry."

"Sure. They're getting started though."

"No problem. And I'm with some people affiliated with his patient. Can we sneak into the doctor's lounge for a table?"

"Absolutely. Use it for an hour or two if you need, before anesthesiologists and surgeons start rolling in for a regular day."

"Thanks," Diana said. She went back to the waiting area and motioned to Rick, Tonya, Johnny, and Amelia to follow her.

Chapter 12

Jennifer's vital signs displayed reassuring numbers on a variety of monitors before the anesthesia team put her to sleep for the surgery. Blood pressure, heart rate, cardiac output, central venous pressure, pulmonary artery pressure, and oxygen saturation appeared next to red, yellow, blue and white wavy lines. Peter processed them all quickly in his mind: 120s over 80s, rate in the 60s, 4.7 liters per minute, CVP 10, pulmonary pressures 22/8, and oxygen saturation 99%. During her surgery, he would use Jennifer's baseline vitals to trend improvements or deteriorations.

He scanned and recorded everything one more time as Sukhdev Bhagat and Arnold Morris acknowledged their patient on the table and nodded to Peter their readiness. Peter titrated a small dosage of an IV narcotic, fentanyl, to begin Jennifer's general anesthetic.

"Good night, Mrs. Barns," Kevin said, injecting pentothal into Jennifer's central line. The anesthetic dispersed to her brain quickly so Jennifer didn't feel Peter hold pressure on the anterior cartilage of her neck to prevent regurgitation of stomach contents into her lungs. For safety, she hadn't eaten in hours, but it served as a precaution. Kevin followed it with anectine, a muscle relaxant, while Cindy held the face mask of oxygen. Peter stood at the right side watching vitals, ready with the endotracheal tube.

In a minute, Cindy tilted Jenifer's head, slid open her mouth, inserted the laryngoscope and slid in the tube while the vocal cords were wide open due to the muscle relaxant.

Sukhdev, Arnold, and the resident scrubbed their hands outside in the sink. Dr. Morris came back inside, gowned and gloved in sterile fashion and sat towards the base of the operating room table at his own draped metal table to work on the new liver. With latex gloves, Arnold extended the liver.

The trim donor had given them a beautiful specimen. Dr. Morris scanned instruments and quietly began teasing away a small amount of yellow fat around the posterior liver's layer. He began clarifying the ligaments. Finally, he chiseled perfect the hepatic triad of the portal vein, hepatic artery and bile duct, being careful to identify the perhaps unique anatomic pattern of Karen's liver. Everything had to be nicely defined to be sewn into the target areas left after Dr. Bhagat finished the hepatic phase of his surgery.

Peter remembered the first things he learned in med school physiology about livers. He had recited the three points many times to residents; that at rest, the liver receives twenty-five percent of a person's cardiac output, the most of any organ; and weighs over three pounds in a normal adult; and liver or hepatic oxygenation is shared equally by hepatic arterial and portal venous blood, in defiance of veins carrying only unoxygenated blood. Livers are underappreciated organs, Peter thought.

A nurse and Cindy each inserted a different temperature probe into Jennifer; one in the rectum and the other in the esophagus, then the nurse slid thin tubing into Jennifer's urethra and extended the tubing between Jennifer's legs to the Foley bag which Kevin hung under the table. Peter made an extra line in the anesthesia record to monitor the volume per hour of Jennifer's urine output to help monitor her fluid status. The basic physiology was elementary; a normal equilibrium exists between what goes in and what comes out.

Through the high pressure arterial line, Peter aspirated blood samples to get baseline starting values on every important lab they needed to know and follow. Christina, an OR nurse, washed Jennifer's abdomen with a bactericidal solution then Peter and Cindy hung drapes, the surgery/anesthesia barrier, across to opposing poles and secured them with hemostats. Kevin told Cindy he'd be back in an hour since they had completed the start.

Dr. Bhagat, now masked, gowned and gloved, stood beside the table and glided a scalpel for a long abdominal right upper quadrant incision. His bleary-eyed but attentive resident stood across from him, as well as the scrub nurse and her tables of instruments. Peter wrote *0447* on their anesthetic record for *surgery start time.*

"Dr. Devlin," Christina said standing alongside the anesthesia machine, "the front desk called. Your wife is here with food."

"Thanks, Christina. Good timing. I have to run the TEG."

Cindy nodded as Peter left for the adjacent lab. He placed a small sample of celite-activated blood into a prewarmed cuvette, lowered a suspended piston in and watched it move in an arc back and forth. The forming clot began transmitting its movement onto the suspended piston. The strength of the clot would be displayed graphically over time - the characteristic pattern like the shape of a cigar. But if Jennifer formed weak clots, the clot would stretch, delay the arc movement of the piston, and would graph as a narrow TEG. With a strong clot, the piston would move in synch to the cuvette movement, creating a thick TEG.

Peter peeled his eyes away. How he loved his specialty. The enormous scope of being an anesthesiologist had fired him up in residency when he wanted to be an airway expert and render anesthesia; and practice basic internal medicine, pulmonology, cardiology, and hematology in the OR. He performed mini-surgical procedures and even practiced obstetrics. He continued with regional techniques for laboring patients after residency and had twice delivered a baby. There was nothing else Peter would rather do than practice anesthesia.

––––––––––

Upon seeing Diana and ripping off his face mask in the doctor's lounge, Peter's dimples smiled like craters. He kissed her lightly and squeezed her hand. "You've had a long night. What are you doing here?" he teased.

"Killing time." She smiled.

"Just can't keep away from me, can you?"

"Steady, Romeo. First off, the hospital was closer than the house so I'll borrow your call room key and take a nap. Secondly, I brought you a sandwich because I bet you need it. And thirdly, I gave Rick here a ride."

Peter glanced across the table and shook hands with Rick.

"Rick was in Birmingham," Diana said, "because of his wife, who was the organ donor. He's going to Indianapolis for funeral services so he flew up with us, making his trip north a lot easier."

"And I'm so appreciative," Rick said. He now sported an unshaved look as dark hair had sprouted above and below his lips.

80

"I'm sorry for your loss" Peter said. "We have a very sick lady on the table. She will hopefully live quite many years due to your wife's thoughtfulness."

Diana handed the sandwich to Peter as he sat.

"I recognize you two from upstairs," Peter said to Johnny and Amelia. "Your mom is asleep. The nurse anesthetist is with her while I step out for a few minutes." Peter smiled at them and unwrapped the sandwich.

"So the surgeon is already taking my mom's liver out?" Amelia asked.

"No. It will take time."

"And this is my daughter, Tonya." Rick said and sipped the last of his coffee.

"Hi," Peter said. He took off the top of the roll and peeked inside. "Have you all been up all night?"

"It seems like I haven't slept in a week," Amelia said, rolling her eyes.

"Waiting here isn't going to help your mom. Why don't you go home? They'll call you if you're needed."

Mel looked at Johnny. "We could come back later."

Johnny inhaled through his nose. His sinuses felt plugged like an eardrum in a plane. He could use a decongestant and, if they went home, they could use some sleep.

"What are you two going to do?" Johnny asked Rick and Tonya.

"We shouldn't do the drive right now." Rick said. "Maybe we'll get a hotel."

"Why don't you both stay with us? We're just across the river."

"That's too kind of you. We couldn't impose."

"Really," Johnny said, "we don't mind at all and my mom would want that."

"I have bunks in my room," Amelia said. "Tonya could stay with me and our couch is to die-for comfortable."

"Dad?" Tonya chimed, her eyes growing like a fawn's.

"All right," Rick conceded.

———

In the hallway, Peter unfastened the safety pin from his scrubs and handed his call room key to Diana. "Thanks for the sandwich," he said. "You better sleep. You're going to be hung over on Monday for your regular job. I don't know about these weekend excursions you do."

"I'm not the only one burning the professional candle at both ends, Dr. Devlin." She clasped the key, eyeing the growing shadows under his eyes.

"Page me when you get up. Maybe the case will be finished and we can leave together."

Diana nestled into his wiry frame and gave him a kiss. "Later, handsome."

Peter expected the abnormal TEG graphic display. Jennifer Barns had a coagulopathy going into her surgery and Peter had to stay on top of the situation and know what she would require. He'd monitor the status of her blood as carefully as a sure-footed mule on a Grand Canyon trail.

"Platelets and FFP," Peter said to Kevin on entering the room, based on his evaluation of the TEG. Jennifer's vitals sank as oozing on the surgical field increased. Arnold had finished refining the donor organ and now helped Sukhdev from the other side of the table.

Peter and Kevin each connected a bag to the IV's and hung them on a pole as Sukhdev darted his glance to the monitors.

"Severe adhesions," Sukhdev scowled.

With the wide bore tubing and IV's, the contents disappeared within a few minutes. Peter nodded to Robert, who immediately delivered the ratio of 300 cc red blood cells, 200 cc fresh frozen plasma, and 250 cc platelets by the RIS. Jennifer's numbers popped back up and Peter proceeded to gather another battery of labs. Kevin charted and readjusted the forane vaporizer. The room took on everyone's silence as the background noise of beeps and instruments took over. Arnold turned his attention to cannulating the left femoral vein in Jennifer's groin, which along with cannulated portal vein blood, would return blood to the left axillary vein.

Caffeine-spirited OR staff bustled through the outside hallways beginning their day. A few peeked in the windows to see the early case jamming up an OR. Shuffling of morning cases was the routine, but curiosity over who was doing what in the middle of the night would nevertheless make the morning chatter more interesting.

––––––

The hours passed. Several premature ventricular contractions, irregular heartbeats, pranced across the EKG and Jennifer's blood pressure sank again. The surgeon's left side leaned heavily on Jennifer's right thorax, irritating Jennifer's diaphragm and causing arrhythmias.

"Sukhdev," Peter said smoothly, "please ease off resting on the patient."

Sukhdev faced the foot of the table. His head shifted up, then stayed motionless. "I'm having trouble here. Don't tell me how to stand."

"If your patient's PVC's and hypotension don't improve when you ease your weight off her chest, then resume standing any way you want."

Arnold poised his instruments and Kevin held a bated breath. PVC's tumbled across the screen. Sukhdev adjusted his posture, making less of a dent in Jennifer's chest. Finally, a normal sinus rhythm pranced across the screen. Peter sighed.

"Thank you, Dr. Bhagat."

"Humph."

––––––

Peter's eyes narrowed as he scanned the room. He had been so occupied, he failed to notice Arnold exiting from his partner's case. Stage one, the preanhepatic phase - from putting Jennifer to sleep to the complete dissection of the hepatic vasculature - was finished.

Sukhdev was now alone for stage two, the anhepatic phase, the most difficult part. With Jennifer's hepatic circulation interrupted, her liver would be removed and the donor liver implanted and reperfused. Arnold had secured the veno-veno bypass system with his cannulation work, but unlike coronary artery bypass, he didn't need to heparanize Jennifer. Peter and Kevin stayed acutely aware, watching for any sign of thromboembolism, or air embolism, in Jennifer's pulmonary or cerebral circulation.

Cindy carefully picked her way over, mindful of the cords on the floor. She swapped places with Kevin after his full report.

"Getting to reperfusion of the graft at the beginning of stage three is going to be a slow crawl," Peter said to Kevin. "Close your eyes in your call room if you can."

"Plus, we've got spillage hitting ground," Cindy added. Blood trickled from the field along the blue drapes and plastic, onto the floor, and the surgeon's brown plastic boots as Sukhdev worked on the lower caval anastomosis.

Peter manipulated the syringe to shoot a cardiac output - 3.8. He opened the cooler and grabbed another bag of red cells and FFP. "Robert, she needs more volume. Hit us with a couple of hundred." Peter tossed the used blood product bags to the floor behind their anesthesia equipment where they accumulated in a messy pile.

"I'll get an entire round of labs," Peter said as Cindy quickly jotted more units and tag numbers on the clipboard sheet. He lowered the vaporizer and began aspirating blood samples. He handed them all to the circulator except for the TEG, injected an insulin and glucose preparation to keep Jennifer's serum potassium normal and hurried to the adjoining lab. This time, the tracing was no longer a cigar shape; it looked more like a skinny cigarette.

Either piss-poor platelet function or crappy platelet numbers, Peter thought. Either way, he grimaced, because it was so profound. An exaggerated coagulopathy, Peter figured, and we're hours behind where we should be in a liver transplant.

"Urine output is worse than the last hour, Dr. Devlin," Cindy said when Peter returned and squeezed between the two carts. "Want to start dopamine?"

Peter nodded as she hung the newest addition and pushed the pump dosage at 2.5 mg/kg/min. He drew up more calcium chloride to inject through the stopcock and readied more epi and sodium bicarb for boluses as he also lamented over Jennifer's temperature. Both the esophageal and rectal temperatures had drifted down half a degree.

From around the corner of the ventilator a nurse handed lab values to Peter. He scanned the acidotic arterial blood gas. Not good. He also guessed that on the other side of the blue anesthesia/surgical drape, if the ischemia time of the donor liver wasn't a problem yet, it would be soon. He peered over, catching the indecisive surgeon's hands in Jennifer's abdomen while the surgical resident watched his teacher with a growing expression of fear.

Peter's alarm escalated. The drapes hanging over Sukhdev's side of the table were a causeway to the floor. It was raining blood.

Barbara Ebel

Chapter 13

Putt-Putt's nose sniffed up in the air, caressing a fresh mixture of smells that didn't make sense: the conflicting odors of nearby bay water, the torn bark of trees, and the contents of refrigerators. He tasted the molecules in his nasal passages and detected the presence of dead fish and small animals. What had happened to his world? The noise outside had abated and the wind had stopped. The groaning sounds inside the building had stilled but, underneath him, water crept into the room.

After the days of darkened skies, light finally surrounded him, pouring in from behind and to the left where a slice of the roof and the corner of the office had been smacked by a fallen live oak tree. Plastic prescription bottles, veterinary books, and dog supplies lay strewn in the aisle from the cabinet at the end. The wall behind him and to the left seemed displaced forward and shelves and their contents pitched forward. Wood panels and a backboard rested on a dog's crate and glass and bandage supplies littered his surroundings.

Straight across from him, the Weimaraner no longer stood gracefully but took shelter in the rear debris-free area of his pen, a gash evident above his eye. Next to him, a heavy-weight boxer sniffed at items within his premises, examining every tidbit for something to eat. Two pugs housed together on the other side seemed less fazed, comforted by each other's company. All the way over and across the aisle, a tall vertical crate was covered with blown material. Putt-Putt saw two cats in there before the worst of the storm but now he heard only one cat's distress call and no response from her cellmate.

Somewhere close, human voices came into range. "At least most of the building is still here," Susan Ricker said, sounding disheartened.

Her husband Phil pushed a scraggly bush out of the way from the live oak to evaluate the size of the hole in the building. He wore work boots and more easily stepped through the debris than his wife. Several dogs barked announcing their presence.

86

"Thank goodness we hear some of them," Susan said.

"Hopefully, you haven't lost any," Phil said, surmising the damage more closely. "But I don't have high hopes for the immediate viability of your practice."

Susan sidestepped to the right, frowning with despair. They made it into the front office after Phil stopped to unfasten plywood off the front door. The place was in more shambles from the one-sided damage than their home at the western end of Gulf Breeze. She climbed over a tree limb and the storm enlarged doorway, to her customers' kenneled pets in the back room.

———

With fascination, Putt-Putt watched the man and woman open each crate. Susan examined each animal while her husband swept out their floors with a dust pan and brush. From two waist holders, Phil took water bottles and rationed a drink in an aluminum bowl to each dog.

"I'll have to sedate him," Susan said, running her thumb along the Weimaraner's upper eyelid. "It has to be stitched." She picked over packaged supplies on the floor for what she needed.

Putt-Putt drank hastily when Phil placed water in front of him. He said thank you with his eyes but Phil walked away to the first crate. His tongue again lapped up water as fast as he could hold and swallow it and it helped fill a void in his belly. It definitely tasted better than the small amount of warm, dirty water he sipped from the seepage on the floor. When he finished, the Weimaraner stayed still before Karen, breathing rhythmically, and Phil held a motionless cat in his arms.

"One of 'em's dead," Phil said to his wife. "I'll put it in the front room."

She nodded at the feline and made a funny noise with her tongue. While Susan waited a few more minutes for the big dog's advancing sedation, she reached her hand to Putt-Putt, stroked his back leg, and edged him away from the wall. "You're fine, little boy," she said.

Quickly Putt-Putt gave her hand a tongue swipe and she rewarded him by massaging the back of his ear. He relaxed his muscles, a swath of security finally enveloping him, and he slumbered while she cleaned and sutured the aristocratic silver-grey dog and talked to her husband with words he didn't understand.

The clutter immediately around him diminished over the next few hours like the disappearance of human leftovers placed in dog food bowls. Susan and Phil formed a clear path in the room, examined and fed each dog, and leashed and walked the other dogs in pairs.

Susan and Phil put a happy hound and gentle mutt back into their pens. "I'll go cut away what I can," Phil said.

"Come on boy," Susan said, hooking Putt-Putt to a leash. "We'll see how you handle a walk."

Putt-Putt lopped up one more mouthful of water. The building was no longer cool like it was on his arrival; humidity hung in the air like damp clothes hanging to dry. When they made a left out of the room, he walked on top and around pieces of sheetrock and boards and office supplies. He tested his strength and degree of pain; he ached so minimally, perhaps he could trot off to search for Karen.

The water on the floor cooled the pads of Putt-Putt's feet and made him think of his last encounter in water, when Karen and Tonya had let him frolic in the bay where the water stretched a long distance - shallow, clear and nonthreatening, unlike the gulf which switched its temperament at will. His two female owners had sat at the water's edge, their toes testing the softness of the sand and the water's temperature, while they took turns throwing his rubbery toy. With a playful zest on land or in water, Putt-Putt had darted back and forth and around them. When the salty water weighed on his coat, he stopped and fervently shook himself, the spray causing Karen and Tonya to squeal and shout his name.

———

Outside the half-shattered building, he encountered further disarray, the neighborhood scarred from the dreadful wind. He concentrated on his most important task but he was unsteady on the debris to lean over with one back leg hung in the air, so he squatted instead. Finally, his bladder began to feel much better.

"I don't know how you held all that in," Susan said. "You sure are a good boy."

Behind a concoction of jagged paneling, a tire, and a twisted bicycle, a lady carrying a dog walked towards Susan and Putt-Putt. Little black eyes stared straight ahead from the bend in her elbow.

"Are you the vet?" the woman asked.

"I sure am," Susan replied.

"I found him hanging near what's left of our home. We'd don't have any way to take care of a dog."

The dog is small as a cat and the woman pushes it straight into Susan's right arm. Retying the yellow scarf she's wearing around her head, the woman spins around and walks away, her face a canvas of morbid disbelief at the storm's aftermath.

———

For the next ten days, the number of dogs swelled: some had been left at their homes, abandoned by owners because they couldn't fit them into packed cars or they were left behind because they wouldn't be allowed where the evacuees were headed. Some owners assumed they would simply be gone for a short time and would return in two days and left their pets available food. But after the hurricane passed, the canines found it easy to escape the surroundings where they were hunkered down. One national guardsman brought in a border collie that he found chained and standing on his dog house roof with nowhere to go - flood waters surrounded him, lapping at the edges of his perch.

No owner who had received vet services and subsequent boarding for their dog prior to the hurricane came for their four-legged friend, but if they were trying to reach Susan, hard-line telephone service still remained a wishful necessity. Giving owners the benefit of the doubt that they would come for their pet, Susan continued their basic care; a struggle because daily living had become more and more problematic.

Even though the acuity of the disaster was over, the aftermath brought new problems and discoveries by the day. A temporary nailed-down tarp was on the roof of her practice, the water on the floor had been suctioned dry, and the wet dry wall removed. Many supplies, too wet to salvage, had been thrown into the dumpster hauled to the front of her business. Veterinarian supplies diminished so she reordered what she could by cell phone but found out packages couldn't be delivered by ground freight companies and there was no mail delivery. The make-shift post office held accumulating mail, but most mail was lost, late or never to be seen.

———

Days later, Susan couldn't contain her giddiness as she came up behind her husband and put her arms around him. He stretched his neck from a crouched position, where he was pulling moldy baseboard from the wall, and eyed her suspiciously.

"Finally, help is arriving from out-of-state Humane Society volunteers," she said, letting go of her embrace.

Phil sat back and ran his hand over his forehead, displacing small beads of sweat.

"They're coming to vet's offices and shelters, picking up all the lost, abandoned, and stray dogs and cats, and making a central station to catalog, crate and see to their needs. Then they're transporting them to other states to be held there or adopted. Each animal's picture and description will be put on a web site for searching owners."

Susan plopped down on the floor next to her husband. "And in lieu of this, we're taking tomorrow off from this place." She looked questioningly at her office assistant, who had managed to get back to work within a week. "That is, if you can hold down the fort for me, Ruth?"

Ruth nodded affirmatively and squeezed her hand into a pocket for her mobile phone. "If you let me call your cell if I need to," she said, waving her basic Nokia.

"We'll be at the house just switching priorities around," Susan said. "I'll leave any paperwork for the dogs and cats to be picked up by the Humane Society. Dogs that are staying here will be in the back aisle. And if any walk-in customers show up, just tell them I'll be working a half day on Saturday."

———

Putt-Putt arched his left leg forward and raked the back of his ear with his paw. It had been a long time since he'd had fleas. Perhaps that's what the problem was because something bugged him back there. He could use a bath, too, because his coat had turned to a sour white. Perhaps if someone scrubbed him, he would get real attention, too. Like the days when he lived with Tonya, Karen, and Rick.

Although he sulked for his old family, he came to rely on a familiarity from Susan and Phil. Early in the mornings they took every dog out first thing for a walk when the quietness of the neighborhood made them more attuned to the odors coming from the dumpster. Later, other distractions began which suited the dogs just fine, causing some of them to make a mad pull on their leashes. The small brood of workers arriving on the scene to tarp roofs, take and estimate insurance claims, give contracting estimates, or slowly start work on houses, thoughtlessly tossed fast-food scraps and left-over garbage wherever they liked.

Today, however, the newly acquired routine changed. Putt-Putt's stomach growled and his bladder stretched. He waited longingly for Susan and Phil to arrive at seven, pacing the narrow aisle with a terrier and a diabetic Irish Setter. Most of the post-storm strays had been crated with other dogs, so Putt-Putt felt pleased to be free inside. The dog's docile manner and obedient nature had kept Karen from lumping him in with a cellmate.

At eight-fifteen the dogs barked in unison at someone's entry up front and, several minutes later, Ruth clasped the three loose dogs to dingy leashes and escorted them for a short walk. Putt-Putt balanced himself near a shrub pile long enough to empty half his urine. The big tuft of gritty weeds nearby would suffice next, but instead, Ruth yanked all three dogs back inside. She stopped at the counter to finish half a biscuit loaded with eggs and ham and then slipped them into the back room.

"I'm going to stack all the files. The Humane Society is coming this morning for most of you," Ruth said when she'd finished with the last dog.

———

Barbara Ebel

"We're gathering dogs and cats like they was giving 'em away at a fire sale," the male volunteer said close enough for Putt-Putt to hear. He looked through the doorway at the muscular elderly man named Jerry. A younger woman stood beside him gathering paperwork from Ruth. She wore pale blue scrubs with dog pictures splattered all over the top and smelled of lilac. As far as Putt-Putt could see, they didn't appear to bring any new canine friends into the office and he wagged his tail happily when they all trudged his way with leashes.

"The loose ones won't go anywhere while you move the others," Ruth said. She unlatched a crate, allowing a graying Bassett hound to step out. The short dog sniffed the heavy scents on the man's shoes while they hooked him up and readied his golden retriever neighbor. Both dogs disappeared outside. With so many people available to walk them, Putt-Putt's back end swung back and forth in anticipation.

In the front of the building, the volunteer set several crates out from a small truck onto the grass. The man kept the bigger sized ones up inside and with the back door open, steered the Retriever up a small ramp and into a cage.

More dogs left while Putt-Putt waited as patiently as he could. The young woman clapped her hands on entering the room. "Last call for a ride," she said and patted the top of his head. She led him, the terrier, and the Irish setter on leather leads into the bright sunshine and pranced them toward the street to do their business. Putt-Putt had little time after she spun him around. He was gently pushed from his hind quarters into a plastic topped dog kennel lying on the ground slightly underneath the truck. Next came the scramble of the terrier's nails on the floor of the crate next to him.

In the crate's front lip near the door, Putt-Putt detected the previous presence of another dog. He couldn't mark the former resident's odor; his surroundings were too small. The uncertainty of events made him whimper but no one paid any attention, not even the two people talking above him in the truck.

"We're almost full," a man said, "so no sense stopping at the other vet before unloading these dogs north of Pensacola."

92

"Yes, we have enough," the woman said. "I'll go get some extra water inside to put in our empty bottles and I'll be right back."

She jumped off the back and trotted inside while the man sat on the end of the truck, dangling his feet and lighting a cigarette.

"Nice morning for that cigarette break," came a voice.

Did Putt-Putt's ears deceive him? Familiarity with the man's voice made him stand and peer out through the aluminum wires. He couldn't see up because of the plastic roof but he saw the man's legs and sneakers as he passed in front. It was that man, the one who had kindly picked him up when he hurt, the man who had allowed him to ride in his vehicle's front seat and had brought him here; the man who seemed friendly enough but who had passed him on to someone else like a careless mother ignoring the runt of her litter.

"Except for the sky," Jerry said, "Ivan made a mess of things, didn't he?"

"My wife says it's not an accident the hurricane was named after a man."

"Hmm. She's got a point. He was worse than Erin and Opal." Jerry flicked his cigarette to the ground and slid off the back end.

Jim Kent continued on with his mission and went inside. "Hi," he said to Ruth. "I promised I'd pay the bill on a stray I brought in before Ivan. Is the vet here?"

"She's taken a much needed day off. What's the name?"

"Kent."

Ruth thumbed the files listed under clients. "Here you go. Looks like $145 and she charged you for three nights of medical boarding. That's all."

"Guess I asked for it. How'd the little fella do?"

"Let's see," Ruth said as the Humane Society's female volunteer passed them from the bathroom with two bottles of water. "Little fella? I guess so; compared to some of the giants Doc Ricker gets in here. Hmm. He should be outside so you can take a look. He's going to a mega dog shelter where he'll eventually get lost in the shuffle or euthanized." She grinned, unhappy with telling him the truth.

Jim put his hand in his pocket and pulled out a checkbook. He scribbled the amount, and his signature, and slipped it across the counter. "What a shame. More like a bucket of sadness. Wish you hadn't of told me that."

Ruth shrugged her shoulders.

When Jim stepped into the panhandle's dazzling sunshine again, the sides of the truck were loaded full and dogs barked with their precarious placement, some crates stacked on top of each other. He scanned the howling hounds but there were no familiar faces. The volunteers stood alongside the left side of the vehicle, the young lady jotting notes on clipboard sheets. As the man loaded a dog and cat and came back, Jim skimmed the kennels under the vehicle.

———

Putt-Putt smelled Jim close by and yearned to give him an excited hello. A dark blue sneaker planted itself in front of him and a head appeared almost upside down.

"Well, well," Jim said and broke into a smile. "We meet again." Putt-Putt squealed with delight while his nails danced loudly on the metal floor pan.

Jim looked at the busy man. "Can I take one off your hands before you haul him off to a foreign state? I was the one who found him and brought him in for repair," he chuckled.

"You'd be a dog's blessing in disguise," Jerry said, hoisting a soda can to his lips.

Putt-Putt couldn't pounce on Jim's thighs or run to and fro inside the cage. He wanted desperately to give him a proper greeting. After listening to Jim's conversation to someone on his cell phone about "coming home with that little white guy," Putt-Putt almost burst when the door latch slid open.

"You enjoy him," Jerry said to Jim. "And thank you. You can keep the leash."

Jim took the red leash, but instead of buckling him, he picked up the good-natured dog and squeezed him. Putt-Putt squirmed with excitement and when his four paws hit the earth again, he dodged around Jim. Walking to the car, Putt-Putt peed every last drop. Jim opened the dirty maroon door, picked him up, and put him on the car seat. "Don't want to stress that healing injury."

As they pulled away, Putt-Putt eyed the last crates being hoisted into the truck that held more dogs than he'd ever seen in a vehicle.

Chapter 14

The screen door banged behind them and Johnny turned to Mr. Puno. "I'll get a pillow and blanket for you," he said, "and the bathroom's the first door on the right." He selected linens from the closet and while he spread the sheets on the couch, the girls disappeared into Tonya's bedroom.

"Thanks for your hospitality," Rick said. He suppressed a yawn and dropped his things on a chair. "And our thoughts are with your mom."

"We should be thanking you. My mom's in good hands and soon she's going to enjoy life again and teach full time."

After stumbling to his room, Johnny stripped to boxers and got into bed. Silence came quickly; the house stilled as if vacant. Johnny closed his eyes with his arm under his head and his breathing slowed. He was glad they'd come home and thought about their house and neighborhood and knew sooner or later he'd have to move on. If it weren't for Jennifer's illness and their lack of money for a more prestigious college, he'd be enjoying dorm life with teens his own age. When and if his mother recovered from her liver transplant, it would be better for her to live without him; to get used to his absence. As his thoughts turned to his mother's surgery, sleep swallowed him, and he fought to ward off invasive dreams that his mother was drowning.

———

Rick awoke with a start, alarmed to be in yet another strange bed. Or couch, as he surmised. He took his cell phone off the table and checked the time - after eleven. He padded to the kitchen, turned on the coffeepot, and slinked out the back door. Rick checked on the status of Karen's transportation arrangements, talked again with the Indiana funeral home, and alerted more relatives and friends. A bleary sky hung over downtown Louisville and a long barge steered a midline course between the two shores.

When Rick came back in, Johnny and Tonya sat transfixed on the couch watching television. They glanced at Rick, then back to the screen, as Rick aborted his stroll to fetch a cup of hot coffee. A field reporter broadcasted from a helicopter and conversed with the anchors in the news channel studio.

"In all my years of weather-related coverage, this powerful image tops it all," the man said. The chopper flew over a huge choppy body of water as the camera aimed at the distant shore-line and then followed the large southern east-west interstate as it turned into the I-10 bridge over Escambia Bay in Pensacola, Florida. The two separate masses of concrete, one for eastbound and the other for westbound traffic, surmounted to a peak then sloped down where the eastbound highway abruptly plummeted into the bay. After a large gaping hole, a tractor-trailer dangled over water on the edge of the other side of the concrete interstate.

"Tom, explain to our viewers where you are," asked the suited desk reporter. "This is water damage from the hurricane far from the gulf?"

"Todd, we are flying twenty-five miles north of the Santa Rosa Island or what locals call Pensacola Beach. That area was practically flattened. The gulf created over fifty foot waves and a surge kept crashing north, through downtown Pensacola, through the Pensacola Bay, through Escambia Bay and through the East Bay. Destruction from water continues to inland areas, homes and communities north of here. But the sheer force and magnitude of the crashing water that severed these concrete foundations and interstate bridgework in Escambia Bay in half, is beyond any destructive power I've seen from a hurricane."

The footage panned over the wreckage below. The newscasters remained silent. With fear in her eyes, Tonya searched her father's face for solace as he lowered himself next to her. Her heart ticked louder in her ears and pressure mounted in her face as she breathed through her nose to stifle the tears and despair and sickness welling within her. "Dad, I think we've lost everybody and everything."

Rick's arm encircled his daughter and he pulled her tight. What would Karen say to Tonya right now? He didn't know yet how to be a solo parent to his daughter; his beautiful girl who had matured and become a young woman right under his eyes. For the first time as an adult, she cried and looked only to him for the answers. He missed the security of his wife and how she expertly handled things.

As Rick kissed Tonya on the forehead, she couldn't bear the images or listen to any more. She slinked out the back door and sat on the step before the grass and rocky slope.

Johnny waited, but not too long, to follow Tonya. When he lowered next to her, he maintained an adequate space between them, and slouched forward, side-by-side with her.

Tonya's left hand rubbed her eye. She brought her knees up and wrapped herself tight. "I can't believe this." Her sobbing caused her to speak slowly and in a whisper. "How can I talk to my mother on the phone one day? How can I have this to-die-for house on the beach? How can I have a blast living at college and have a dog that adores me? And in one day it's all gone?"

Johnny's shoulders rounded as he leaned over his knees and picked up a pebble. He glanced sideways into her eyes and furrowed his eyebrows. "You may never know why. You may never understand why. And you can never change what's happened. But don't let it sink you because things will get better."

She blinked several times and took a deep breath. "Hmm. I've had it ten times fancier than you, and here I am complaining. Your mother's been critically ill, your family probably can't pay the medical bills, and you'll probably be in college debt for years."

"It shows that bad?" He managed a faint smile.

Tonya's lips parted, showing a sliver of a smile.

"But thanks to your mother," Johnny said, "my mom now stands a chance."

The door cracked open and Mel stood there looking fresher than the rest of them. "The bathroom's free," she said. She finished using a brush and stuck the handle into her long shorts. Her hair was damp and tucked behind her ears.

"Guess we need to make a plan," Rick said to Tonya as he came out beside them. "The funeral parlor will call after they get your mom today."

"Dad, don't you still have calls to make and don't we need someplace to stay in Indianapolis?"

Rick nodded as Tonya continued. "Can I go with Johnny and Mel to the hospital again before we have to leave?"

"You don't have to do that," Johnny chimed in.

"But I want to." She looked down. "It'll keep me preoccupied."

"Mr. Puno," Johnny said, "you can use our phone, even catch up on more sleep."

"Okay," he said, realizing he was outnumbered and rushing north wouldn't accomplish anything. "I'll shower after you three leave."

———

Peter, Kevin and Cindy were armed and ready for the most dramatic changes during Jennifer's liver transplant: the beginning of stage III, the post anhepatic phase. With the new liver in place, Jennifer's partial hepatic circulation would be restored. Sukhdev would unclamp the inferior vena cava and portal vein to decrease the warm ischemia time of the donor liver. They knew the events to occur would be more dramatic than usual due to Jennifer's hemodynamic roller coaster ride.

There were other factors which Peter had to face. The donor liver had been conserved for some time in an organ preservation solution which would wash out into Jennifer's circulation - causing abnormalities in the electrical conduction of her heart. Liver cells deprived of normal amounts of oxygen would also bolus her bloodstream with extra potassium.

Peter swept the monitors and squinted in serious thought. He plugged calcium chloride, epinephrine and sodium bicarb into the nearest stopcocks and glanced at Robert, who needed an assistant for the frantic pace of his job. Next to Peter, Kevin whispered another cardiac output to Cindy, which she charted, and then put down the clipboard. Kevin's hair along his temples looked grayer than when they started.

Dr. Bhagat straightened. He rested his bloodied gloved hands on the field and looked toward the head of the table. "Dr. Devlin, if you're prepared, I'm going to start unclamping."

It wasn't easy to cower behind a surgical mask, but Peter detected Sukhdev's flinch. And for once, the surgeon's apprehension radiated through his jet dark eyes.

"We're as ready as we can be." And even that possibly wouldn't save Jennifer Barns's life, Peter thought.

Sukhdev's hand disappeared into Jennifer's open cavity.

Numbers sagged on the monitors despite Peter infusing bursts of epinephrine and calcium. Cindy speedily aspirated blood samples and a nurse ran them to the lab. Kevin and Robert had blood products going in so fast and furious, that the sturdy clear bags piled up like autumn leaves.

Peter's eyes narrowed as Jennifer's steady *beeps* from the EKG machine malignantly slowed across the monitor, her heart slowing to almost a standstill. Peter injected more stimulants and eyed the anesthetic vaporizer which was turned off. As Cathy shot a dismal cardiac output, the nurse left Jennifer's lab work on their anesthetic record. Peter and Cathy shot a glance at the barely decipherable urine dripping into the Foley bag and Cathy's eyes glossed over. Peter pulled blood from the hanging packed cells into a fifty ml syringe, turned the stopcock, and shot it into the central line over and over again until his fingers ached. He injected atropine, but the bradycardia didn't let up.

"My anastomosis of the hepatic artery will be pointless if you let the patient die," Dr. Bhagat said, not looking up.

The remark hung in the air as if it floated without a boat. Kevin inched shoulder-to-shoulder with Peter and whispered. "Yeah, if he wasn't so excruciatingly slow on a patient with a bleeding disorder."

Within fifteen minutes, Jennifer's dramatic changes began to subside, but the next quarter hour required more trickier management.

"Hmm," Peter hummed. Cindy and Kevin continued their pursuits, listening attentively to Peter. "Now's the point not to be too overzealous. High pulmonary artery pressures and high central venous pressure. We'll ease the rapid volume and not tax her heart. And it's time for another TEG so we can try and fine tune her coagulopathy."

With the small syringe in hand, Peter walked to the adjacent lab room. For a second, he allowed himself a quick thought about his anesthesia team. For the last thirty minutes the three of them had demonstrated such synchronized teamwork, they were like independent clocks ticking in unison.

———

Johnny and Tonya stepped out the front door while Mel lagged inside, grabbing a light sweater and throwing a few granola bars into her canvas bag. Johnny pulled the door handle and the garage door noisily opened. His basketball rolled from behind the door and he unenthusiastically pitched it overhead into the basket.

Tonya lurched to catch it. She bounced it, ran off, turned and also sailed it through the hoop. After dribbling it when it hit ground, Johnny circled Tonya and threw it again. She maneuvered in front and caught it.

"Are we going, or do I need standing room tickets?" Mel said, yanking up her shoulder bag.

Tonya stopped and handed the ball to Johnny, who raised his eyebrows. "I'm a Bulldog," she said, tugging her hair. "On the Butler women's team."

"Is there more to that story?"

"Partial scholarship. After they saw how good I could play."

"Nice," Johnny said. He placed the ball, they slid into the car, and Johnny cranked the ignition. "I'm driving a female who probably shoots hoops better than I do."

———

In the hospital, Johnny went through the automatic doors to the OR front desk. "Can you tell them in Jennifer Barns's room that her kids are here?" he asked.

"What's taking them so long anyway?" Mel said when they went to the waiting room. "How long does it take to remove a diseased organ and simply put in another that's normal and healthy?"

Johnny put two fingers on the bridge of his nose and massaged. "I don't know, Mel, but we knew it wouldn't be quick. Someone will be out soon to update us." He turned towards Tonya. "I bet you don't have Ohio Valley allergens in your Pensacola air."

"Breezy salt air washes over our decks from the Gulf. No pollution."

"I'm envious."

A woman in scrubs, armed with a concerned look, approached them. "Johnny and Mel Barnes?"

"Yes?" Johnny asked.

"They finished your mother's surgery. The surgeon will be out to talk to you both but it will take anesthesia and the nursing staff some time to get her ready and transported."

Johnny wrung his hands and Mel sat closer to her brother while the OR nurse walked away.

———

Diana Devlin opened her eyes and turned over to check the call room clock, the red numbers of 1:57 p.m. obvious in the darkened cubbyhole. Sweeping the fogginess from her eyes, she sat straight, wondering why Peter still hadn't come in to wake her. If he's still doing the same case, she thought, that speaks buckets about his patient's condition, and how tired her husband and staff must be - even the transplant surgeon.

She rinsed her face in the adjoining bathroom and ran fingers through her hair. The sleep had done wonders. She looked and felt refreshed. When she stopped by the OR, they told her that her husband's case had finished and would come out shortly.

"Hello," Diana said to the three teens as she rounded the room partition. "They should come by soon." She took a seat. "I'd like to wait."

"Yes, finished at last," Johnny said. "I can't believe this will be all over."

"But what are you still doing here, Diana?" Amelia asked.

"I just woke up. Have you been here long?"

"No," Johnny said. "We just arrived."

Voices from inside the OR filtered out as the doors opened and closed. Dr. Bhagat strolled in and stopped before them. He had changed into fresh scrubs and had removed the boots over his sneakers. He rubbed his eyes and took a deep breath while Johnny and Amelia rose.

"Your mother's surgery is finished but her liver was extremely diseased and her bleeding was excessive. I made sure she was amply transfused, but now, it will be a waiting game to see how she responds to the new liver. I'll watch her closely. She's still unstable."

"When can we see her?" Johnny asked.

"Will she be awake?" Amelia asked.

"Because of the anesthesia people, she'll still sleep for a few hours. But like we discussed, she won't be talking to you soon because of breathing on a ventilator. Once anesthesia isn't involved, I'll decide when to remove the breathing tube. Barring any other unforeseen problems, I'll have you all talking with each other by tomorrow."

Sukhdev's eyebrows sagged yet further when he noticed Diana sitting to the side.

"Dr. Bhagat," she said, acknowledging him.

Sukhdev cleared his throat. "I didn't know we were still in need of a plane."

Diana refrained from blurting out her first thought and then said, "I believe it's not against the law to wait for my husband."

It seemed odd to Sukhdev. He wasn't aware that Diana's husband was getting surgery. She hadn't said anything about it on the flight to Louisville. He stood speechless, a bewildered look on his face.

"My husband is Dr. Devlin," Diana said. "The anesthesiologist doing your case."

What a coincidence, he thought, two bad apples from the same basket. He quickly ignored her and shifted his sight to Johnny and Amelia.

"The nurses in the ICU will be quite busy getting a report on your mother and managing the orders I'll be writing. Please give them enough time. You can wait in the ICU waiting room. They'll call you in when they can."

"Thank you," Johnny said. "I mean, we don't even know how to thank you enough."

Amelia nodded in agreement. If she thought it appropriate to genuflect, she would.

Tonya studied the surgical giant. Hopefully he'd been as gentle with her own mother. Dr. Bhagat turned and headed to the ICU before his patient arrived. Johnny turned to his sister and gave her a hug but Amelia fought to keep from crying. "He just saved Mom's life," Mel whispered.

———

The noisy equipment announced their journey from the OR. Jennifer had been transferred to a large ICU bed, IV poles clumsily being pushed by personnel and Kevin squeezing the Ambu bag, breathing for Jennifer in route. The oxygen tank, the portable EKG machine, extra drugs and charts lay at the foot of the bed. Cindy jotted some en route vitals on her scrubs and helped intermittently squeeze a fluid bag. While nurses, orderlies and his team trudged ahead, Peter kept his eye on the whole situation, scrutinizing for any problem. Jennifer's eyes were closed, still taped to help prevent the possibility of a corneal abrasion, and clean white sheets covered her up to her neck. The multiple pumps attached to the two IV poles managed drug infusions and twice the group had to stop because the wheels of one pole needed fine adjusting to correlate with the pace of the pushed bed.

Johnny, Mel, and Tonya watched with concern as Jennifer passed. Diana and Peter's eyes met. Peter's OR mask dangled below his chin and his dimples seemed to mildly smile at his wife. The code of respect lingered as the troop made its way to the staff elevator.

On the third floor, the team pushed and pulled the equipment over the separation between the elevator and hallway. Johnny, Amelia, Tonya, and Diana arrived to see the team disappear inside the automatic doors of the ICU where the waiting staff signaled OR personnel and anesthesia into the fourth room.

Chapter 15

Jennifer's pale face blended into the lifeless equipment all around her and her eyelids stayed flat and closed. Monitors were suspended from the wall and danced with numbers and graphs. Drip infusion pumps beeped intermittently, fused with the other high tech sounds.

After they gave report for the benefit of the ICU nurses and their admission record, Kevin and Cindy collaborated with each other over the endless pile of blood bank slips and anesthesia paperwork. Peter stayed for thirty minutes and finally swiped the shabby OR bonnet from his head and floated it into the garbage can. He dabbed his temple; yes, he still had hair after this harrowing case.

"Considering what Mrs. Barns has been through," Peter said, "I'm pleased she's this stable." The ICU nurse listened but still adjusted tubing, rushing from one end of the bed to the other. Peter slipped the official anesthesia record from the stack. In addition to writing the OR anesthesia end time, he made a note. *No apparent complications from anesthesia. Stable in ICU. 15:12.* He turned and dragged himself away. Kevin and Cindy eyed each other, left their paperwork neatly with the chart, and hastily tailed behind him.

"Won't we all crash like babies?" Cindy practically whispered.

A pregnant pause hovered over them. Peter put both his hands on their shoulders and patted. "Change out of those scrubs, go home, and assume the fetal position."

The three of them stepped through the ICU doors where Peter made eye contact with Diana leaning against the wall with Johnny, Amelia, and Tonya.

———

Sukhdev Bhagat approached his gold Lexus on the physician's ground floor of the parking garage. A slight breeze flowed along the direction that cars drove up the cemented incline, as if it knew the way out. The ill-lit enclosure made it seem like early evening. He checked his watch; it was still early enough to make a business phone call. He dug his hand into his creased white doctor's coat, pulled out his key remote and pressed.

Sukhdev opened the driver's door and rummaged through the console. He restocked his portable humidor several days ago with three fine Havana specials. He selected a Bolivar Belicoso Fino and also grabbed his guillotine cigar cutter and lighter. His important call would have to wait. Puffing on this baby, at least some of it, came first. It always came first, even before a woman. He knew that a fine cigar satiated a needed longing much more than most women, because with women he couldn't count on their talents. Fine cigars never let him down.

He pushed the door closed, leaned against the body of the car, and peeled the band. Cutting the rounded edge of the cigar was an art and, being the connoisseur that he was, he had lots of practice. He maneuvered the cutter with more precision than a scalpel and took off - not too much and not too little - and lit her up.

A third of the cigar disappeared a little too hastily as Sukhdev appreciated its earthiness with a tasty tinge of honey. An oversized white SUV drove slowly then pulled into an empty spot at the end of the aisle while he contemplated making his call. Two doctors' voices emanated after the elevator doors opened, a discussion or heated disagreement about administrative politics. He avoided such matters if they didn't directly involve him.

Before smoking the exquisite final third, he pulled his cell phone from his lower right coat pocket and searched for the number he had for the big suburban hospital in Philadelphia where their administration wanted to begin a transplant service. There were two surgeons already hired but they needed a third with more experience. With his three years of proficiency, and flexibility to make a major move, maybe he could finesse it. The respect, responsibility, and salary increase would be staggering.

Sukhdev placed the call and held for a woman in the recruiting office. He moved the phone away from his mouth, enough to wrap his lips around the chunky brown cigar and take a pull. A lone physician trudged down the middle of the aisle headed for his car and glanced his way. Sukhdev turned sideways to shield his view of the anesthesiologist. No sense in dealing with him any more than he needed.

––––––

Peter slowed while he nodded at the group behind his wife. Diana hastened over to her husband and they kept going down the corridor to the elevator. The silence broke once Peter pressed the down button.

"Thanks for waiting for me," he said.

"You're welcome but your case took a hell of a long time, didn't it?"

"You could say that. But she's alive and may pull through all this."

The elevator door opened. A young girl and a woman brushed by and Diana and Peter entered.

"You should go home now," Peter said. "I'll be right along."

Diana grasped his left elbow, leaned towards him, and kissed the side of his mouth. He smiled, pulled her close, and softly said, "See you there. I love you."

––––––

In the men's room, Peter tossed his scrubs into the laundry basket and pulled on his casual clothes. Although his skin was grubby, the lightweight pants and Henley shirt felt like they were fresh out of the dryer. He splashed water on his face and dabbed it with a towel. He gathered his overnight bag and briefcase and tossed his OR shoes into his locker.

"Joan, I'll see you tomorrow morning," Peter said, entering the anesthesia lounge. A few nurse anesthetists and doctors came and went while Joan raised her head from her schedule and stared hard at Peter.

"I heard it was a roller coaster in there," she said.

"You could say that. Luckily, I had a good anesthesia team."

"Okay, now get out of here and go get some sleep. You never know what I'm going to give you tomorrow." Joan grinned and waved him away.

––––––

Outside, the fresh balmy air hit Peter as sharply as a crisp winter day. He took a deep breath. Now he wanted to forget Jennifer Barns and shake off the unpleasant memories of her case. If it hadn't been for the hurricane down south, too far south for Kentucky residents to pay much attention to, Jennifer wouldn't have had her lucky transplant. But her surgery had been a hell of a stormy course – there was more than one time when he thought they would lose her. And, she wasn't out of the woods yet. It was still possible that her body rejects the new liver or has other post-op complications.

Peter jockeyed his case and bag into one hand and fumbled in his pocket for his car keys. He continued to pass the back ends of parked cars and approached a gold vehicle. A man leaned against the driver's door. Peter looked sideways to see Sukhdev puffing on a cigar. He still wore scrubs and flattened hair by the many hours of wearing an OR bonnet. His dark eyes followed a wispy cloud of smoke. As Peter passed, the surgeon faced the cement wall.

Now Peter's overactive, sleep-deprived mind couldn't stop thinking about the liver transplant … especially with Sukhdev outside the hospital, not even in the same building as Jennifer Barns. If he were a surgeon, he wouldn't dare be that far away from a patient who had just been moved to the ICU in critical condition. But who was he to judge? Most of the time, a physician should not 'police' another physician, especially if they aren't in the same specialty.

By the time Peter arrived at his car, he smelled the earthy aroma of cedar coming from the surgeon's unhealthy habit.

———

Johnny, Amelia and Tonya filed through the doorway as if they rode the same rip current. "Thank you," Johnny said to his mother's nurse, "for allowing Tonya to come in, too."

"Be extremely quiet," the nurse said, "and stay for only a few minutes. I'm going to be right next door." He adjusted Jennifer's emptied Foley bag hanging off the side rail and pushed a chair in their direction.

Amelia softly fell into the chair. She barely gazed at her mother and the surrounding technology; more gadgetry translated into a more ominous condition. She hesitated to touch anything, including Jennifer.

Johnny sat on the edge of the bed, making sure that not one plastic tube lay beneath him. He placed his hand on top of his mother's. After moments of silence, he realized he breathed in unison with the noisy ventilator; realized he breathed simultaneously with his mother's rising chest. His eyes filled with moisture as he thought. For all these months, he had given her necessary gifts – support, faith, and the sustenance to hold on to hope. How important his mother was to him his entire life.

How meaningful everyone's mother is, he thought. That one single person who nurtures the first nine months of life, an irreplaceable bond, besides the offspring inheriting half of her DNA makeup. Had his mother transmitted her feelings? He'd been told how loving and proud and excited his mom had been during her pregnancy. Perhaps because of her, his natural nature was to be optimistic about most situations.

———

Tonya had only been in a hospital twice to visit anyone. And nothing she'd seen looked like this room or this patient. Did her mother have substantial knowledge about what was entailed in becoming an organ donor? How involved it was? Do people actually get better after going through all this? Tonya's new friends seemed as shell shocked as she was.

Tonya closed her eyes. Until a few days ago, her biggest problem was if her roommate had left a clearing on the floor, enough for her to walk to her desk. Now her best friend was gone. Her nurturing mother who had always protected her yet didn't smother her. A Mother who had never pried deeply into Tonya's personal relationships or school life; a Mom who answered and elaborated on questions exactly when Tonya had needed it; a Mom who was the sustenance to her father. Even though her dad was a very capable man, it was her mother who had been his backbone for success and self-esteem. And how he had loved her.

Now she didn't know how her dad would continue or how they would address all their tasks: arrangements and a funeral, work and her father's necessary travel, and a house and belongings on an island which may not have survived a hurricane. And Putt-Putt? She loved that little dog. She stopped her mind from visualizing the disastrous plight he might be facing. But he could be dead. And dare she think it? He probably was dead. She gulped and wanted to cry but how could she do that in front of Johnny and Mel?

———

"Johnny." Amelia tapped his right knee. "The nurse is back. I think he needs for us to leave."

Johnny sniffled and slipped off the bed.

Jennifer's nurse turned a dial on an overhead machine. "Come back during the next regular visiting hours. Your presence is as significant as anything we're giving her. She most likely senses your presence even though she's asleep, sedated, and in critical condition." His tone was sympathetic and assuring. As he lowered his arm, he grimaced at a red light flickering at a bedside pump.

Johnny nodded to him. "Thanks, I bet you're right."

Beyond the nurses' station, Johnny paused for Tonya, who followed a few steps back. Their eyes met. As if his hand was waiting for hers, her fingers slid straight into his palm. Johnny's long fingers wrapped around her soft, smooth hand and they exited from the beeps and alarms of the sterile ICU environment.

———

Peter slowed down as he passed the hedges of their property and turned at the top of the asphalt driveway looking down a long hilly entrance to their home. He drove down between the summery landscaping which they paid a yard service to maintain. Beyond the magnificent home, no other houses were visible further down, only stately oaks and pine trees far away. Bushes dotted the entrance to the house as well as a few tall black light poles.

Peter pressed the remote and slid his Toyota next to Diana's car already in the garage. He took his things from the back seat; if he didn't take them, he would end up returning for something he needed. He grasped the doorknob and went in.

As if she'd heard him in the garage, Peter and Diana's cat sat on the dryer waiting to greet him. Diana had named her Silver for the prominent silver-gray in her tortoise shell coloring. Her big green eyes glared at him as she let out two quick successive "meows." When Peter extended his free hand to pet her, she stood, arched her back, and circled around, letting him run his fingers along her spine. She jumped down in front of him and stayed with him.

The blinds were half drawn in the kitchen, an unopened pile of mail lay on the center island, and the red light for phone messages blinked the number 7 on the wall phone. Peter left his briefcase on a chair, poured some juice, and sauntered through the great room to the other side of the house with his duffel bag and the glass. He entered the high pitched ceiling bedroom as Silver jumped up on the bed and pounced playfully on the bulging comforter over Diana's hip.

"You awake?" Peter asked.

"Yes," Diana purred, "waiting for you."

"Nothing like sleeping at odd hours." He took the last sip and set down the glass on his dresser. The rich mission-style bedroom furniture had been his selection, giving the bedroom masculine warmth. Better yet was the richness of the room when his wife was in it, or when they both were home, a rather rare event.

"I'll join you in a minute," Peter said, and went into the bathroom. He turned on the shower, brushed his teeth, and peeled off his clothes. He stepped into the glass enclosure and soaked and lathered. The overdue shower not only rinsed him off physically but rewarded him psychologically, like washing the last twenty-four hours of stress down the drain. He stepped out, dried, and put on briefs. As he left the bathroom, he threw his dirty laundry into the basket.

Peter recalled a marital promise when he entered the bedroom. All the major stress of their professions should be left outside. For Peter, that meant thinking about the extremely sick patients, the demanding surgeons, and the high volume of cases he staffed. And for Diana, that meant the FAA regulations, the demands from the company, and the aggravating last minute schedule changes.

When Peter approached the bed, Diana had turned under the covers and faced him. But as he walked around to the other side, she switched to face him again. He peeled back the bedspread and sheet and slithered in. Silver meowed, unsure where to go, and sat up.

"Here girl," Diana said, reaching for her. As Diana rose off her pillow and took the cat, the covers fell away, exposing her soft skin. Fleeting goose bumps ran along her arms and her small, firm breasts.

Diana closely embraced the cat. She cupped her tiny head into her and kissed above her squinting eyes. "Okay, now. Settle down." She squeezed her again tenderly then let her go. "Time for my husband," she said. Silver quickened away between them and settled at the end of the bed, facing the doorway, as if she was a Doberman pinscher guarding the room.

Peter pushed his pillow closer to Diana's, closing a small gap. He reached for her right shoulder, guiding her back down into the warmth of the bed. His arm went around her back and he tugged her close, her head nestling into the base of his neck.

Diana's chin felt the closeness of her husband's chest hair; she put a small kiss where her lips rested. She draped her arm along the side of Peter's chest and her fingers slid along his skin; firm from the occasional work-out with machines, slightly damp after his spotty towel drying. She ran her fingernails over the area once and then stopped and massaged.

Peter smoothed his left fingers through Diana's silky hair, while aware of her breasts pressing into his chest.

"What are you doing to me?' Diana whispered softly. "Do you know that's the path to heaven?"

Peter gently tugged her hair while bringing her head back, and looked into her almond shaped eyes. "Massaging your scalp?"

"Anything you do to me."

Peter draped his mouth over hers, lingering over the contour of her lips. She kissed him back when he stopped, and draped her right leg over him. He squeezed her hard and when he let go, he hummed, "Nice to be home."

"I missed you this weekend," she countered.

Peter wanted to take his wife right then but he knew that, although they both stirred for each other, their energy was sapped. Making love always meant more than simply going through the motions even if they hadn't seen each other for a few days. Besides other reasons, it was what made their love so special. There was a connection; about everything. They'd fall asleep in each other arms and neither one of them would stir or mind the other person's breathing body up close, or mind an appendage draped over them, or mind their spouse's hair if it tickled their skin.

No, they would make love when he was not physically and emotionally fatigued - when he could better shake off an OR day when he came home. He hoped that would be tomorrow.

At the bottom of their feet, Silver curled into a ball and gave up her watch.

Chapter 16

Tonya scooped rice on her plate from the Chinese take-out they bought on the way home from the hospital while Rick passed broccoli and beef to Mel.

"Dad, I put the food on my credit card," Tonya said. "Johnny and Mel have been kind enough to let us stay here."

Rick stirred the food on his plate. "You're thoughtful like your mother. I mean, the way your mom was."

A flicker of a smile crossed Tonya's face. "Did Mom tell you that I started a little job near school?"

"No. I didn't know."

"A part-time job at the barber shop. They call me when someone can't come in or they need an extra hairdresser, but I won't do it around exam time."

"Good, make sure your studies come first."

Tonya studied her father's face. The handsome man she knew, the man who always had a likeable appeal and an irresistible smile, wasn't there.

"We must leave in the morning," he added.

Tonya glanced at Johnny, who grinned. They all ate in silence until Mel cleaned her plate and put down her fork. She turned to Tonya. "You know, there's somebody around here who's been dying to make his hair shorter, but doesn't have the guts. Do you do house calls?" She looked towards Johnny and chuckled.

Johnny lowered his eyes. "Mel," he scoffed.

"Sure," Tonya said. "If you want me to, Johnny. But don't get mad if I do a lousy job."

"You can't make him any worse than he already is," Amelia said.

Johnny tapped his index finger on the table while the girls waited. "Okay, I'll find the scissors. I had it cut recently but I'm ready to do the big butcher cut on it. We can go to the back if Mel will clear off the table."

"I shouldn't have opened my big mouth," Mel said.

————

Johnny stopped in the bathroom to pat down his hair with water and grab a hand towel while Tonya waited outside the door. They went to his room and he turned on a dim bedside lamp. He shoved school books toward the back of his desk and put down the scissors. "Will you be able to see enough in here? Without scalping me?"

"This is fine," Tonya replied. "You want it short, right?"

"Kind of, but try and give it a style," he said. He sat on his bedroom chair facing the desk and put the bathroom towel around his neck. Then he reached past his schoolwork and picked up a small drug store bottle. "Sorry," he said. "Allergies. It's like living with a brick weighing down my forehead all the time." He popped one white pill and gulped.

"No water?" she asked.

"I'm adept at the dry method. When I'm out, water isn't always available."

"Ouch." She took the comb he'd given her and ran it through his hair. Not too thin, not too thick, she thought. Straight with a healthy sheen. "I can spice up a short haircut; make it Ivy-league in short layers. Wait'll you see what I can do to it."

"Less boring than what I have now?"

"You and your hair isn't boring, Johnny."

"Nor you or yours," he said arching his head back and smiling.

Tonya took the scissors and started to snip on the right side. She worked her way around to the back and tipped his head forward and worked in silence. She enjoyed his closeness and had a better appreciation of the width of his shoulders. He sat tall in the chair while she ran her fingers upward to test the shaping layers.

————

Tonya's body so near to Johnny's made his heart pound. She wore navy drawstring sweatpants and her white T-shirt stopped an inch above her pants. The small amount of exposed midriff was flat and toned and right behind his shoulders. How come she smelled so fresh? Like walking through country woods in pine needles and evergreen cones.

During high school, Johnny had dated as much as anyone else. Several times, he had been the favorite of more than one girl for a dance, especially for special occasions like a girl's junior or senior prom. They'd eye him in class or watch him play basketball after school. The girls he attracted knew he was down-to-earth and wouldn't play games with them, like stringing them along by not calling when he said he would. And going out with Johnny was strictly Dutch treat. Most students dated Dutch but there were still the boys from well-to-do families who tended to pay when taking girls out, especially if they weren't star athletes or good-looking. But luckily, most of his dating had been casual and hadn't cost him or a girl much at all.

For Johnny's senior prom, he had taken Sue Barrington, who sat next to him in English class. They had proof read each other's term papers, giving each other enough objective criticism and suggestions for change to propel their papers to two As. Johnny, however, had more commitment at home than other students, and he never peeled away from his responsibilities enough for a girl to monopolize his time, so relationships stayed neutral. Besides, he never liked them as much as they liked him.

———

The hair style Tonya continued to whip up for Johnny took on a life of its own. She had only been cutting hair for a few months, but she owned an innate sense of pairing the correct face shape with the most flattering style. She more often pleased young people rather than older clients because the elderly would rarely attempt a brand new look. Johnny had a thin face, especially a narrow chin; a thin upper, but a puffy lower lip. His eyes gave him a wild-eyed bad boy look, and they were dark, like his hair.

Tonya cut the back and sides in very short layers but increasingly left a longer length as she moved across the crown and the top of the head to the fringe area. "Any mousse around?" she asked. "And a blow-dryer?"

"Beneath the sink in the bathroom," he said. "But I won't have to do this regularly, will I?"

"If you leave in conditioner or just use the mousse, I think you'll be able to recreate what I'm doing. But I'm going to show you how to fix it the best way."

Tonya padded off with her shoes off and when she reappeared, she carried a hand mirror as well.

"No looking at the back until I'm finished." She lathered mouse in her palms and quickly massaged it into his hair, bringing her fingers into his scalp. For seconds, which seemed like minutes, the massage was sheer bliss. Then the warmth of the blow dryer whizzed upward from his forehead as Tonya used her fingers to comb his hair and separate it and blow upwards to maximize the volume of the cut. He had never felt so relaxed and mesmerized by simply getting a haircut.

"Ta-da," she exclaimed, handing him the mirror. "The top looks messy, fashionably messy, like you just got out of bed. I like it." She widened her eyes. "I really like it."

The next morning, light moisture hung on the driveway from a nighttime mist and a pinkish hue of midlevel clouds began to disappear. Rick had whisked up almost a dozen scrambled eggs for their breakfast and had gone to put on fresh clothes and pack while Tonya went outside with Johnny. Johnny opened the garage door and grasped his basketball, then followed her to the trunk of her copper colored Civic sedan where she dropped in her backpack.

"How about shooting hoops before you leave?" Johnny asked with a grin on his face.

"I don't know," she stammered. "After giving you such a cool haircut, I wouldn't want you annoyed at me when I leave."

"Ha. That won't happen, even if you squeak by with a few decent shots."

"Okay, you're on."

They both trotted to the head of the driveway, where Tonya clutched the ball. It rose along the open zipper of her jacket and off her right shoulder as her knees dipped down. Johnny waited midstride as the ball rocketed off the rim and sailed behind him, where he caught it after the bounce. He spread his fingers on top and held it underneath with his left hand. He jiggled it while Tonya spread her arms in front of him. Johnny jumped and sank a shot, landing flatfooted behind her. But Tonya pivoted and turned, caught the basketball, and sank one one-handed.

"Wow!" Johnny exclaimed as he kept moving. "I've never seen a girl do that."

"I have a skilled coach," she sputtered.

Johnny and Tonya's arms and legs got closer as they scrambled for the ball, but Johnny outmaneuvered her, caught it, and softly lifted it. It behaved and dropped through the center of the net, leaving the rim untouched.

Tonya made no comment and managed to get possession of his prized toy. Her hands wiggled it nervously in the air while her feet were planted like stakes in the ground. She ducked around him and threw, but the ball ricocheted off the rim.

Johnny stopped to wipe a bead of perspiration from the top of his forehead and run his sleeve across his nose. The front door opened and Rick came out with his suitcase.

Rick's movements weren't as slow as the night before and the good night's sleep had left him looking less tired. "Are you ready to go, Tonya?" he asked. His daughter nodded. He paused near Johnny and they extended their hands and shook. "I hope the transplant makes your mom healthy again. I'd like to call in a week or two and ask about her."

"Thanks," Johnny said while nodding.

Rick stepped away quickly and Johnny and Tonya stood facing each other. Johnny took a step closer. "I'll call your cell later, if that's okay with you," he said.

Tonya nodded. "I'll call later, too, if I haven't heard from you … after we're in Indianapolis and you've had a chance to see your mother."

Johnny and Tonya's faces neared. Tonya exhaled while Johnny breathed deeply. Their bodies advanced again, they closed their eyes, and gave each other a quick soft kiss.

———

"I'm rushing into the ICU before going to the OR," Peter said at home before dawn the next morning. "I'd like to see the transplant patient, Jennifer Barns, before staffing my cases."

Diana tightened the belt on her robe and poured two cups of southern pecan coffee. "If that family needs anything, get a little involved, okay?"

Peter cleared his throat. "So says my philanthropic pilot wife who should've gone into medicine."

"No. I'm right where I'm supposed to be." She pushed a mug toward him. "It's not decaf and I'm probably going to regret that. Your rattling around already woke me up."

Peter sat on a kitchen stool, fingered his mustache which needed trimming, and took a sip. Diana halved a piece of toast and nibbled. She slid the other half to him as Silver materialized and slinked around her feet.

"Actually," Diana said, "I'm glad to see you this morning. I'm leaving mid-afternoon and doing short Louisville to Knoxville round trip flights all week."

"Maybe we'll get to pass each other tomorrow morning," Peter commented.

"I hope so."

Peter finished, rinsed his cup, and kissed her good-bye. Diana headed back to bed as Silver loyally followed, pouncing after her open-back pink slippers.

———

Peter changed into OR scrubs, donned his white coat, and worked his way upstairs to the ICU. Hadn't he just done this? Time in the hospital seemed to be growing. The familiarity of the OR rooms and hospital units seeped into his blood, the many walls without windows, the unnaturalness of it all. Sometimes when he stepped away from it at the end of some days, he felt exhilarated to have fresh outside air hit his face. But here he strode again after only going home once in the last forty-eight hours to sleep.

Since anesthesiologists' days start earlier than most practitioners, Peter didn't expect many other doctors making ICU rounds. Most would arrive later, after their coffee and before their office hours at 8 or 9 o'clock. Sometimes surgeons made rounds early as well and, if they had surgical cases, they would show up for their OR cases which were being prepared by anesthesia and wheeled into the OR. So it was to Peter's surprise that he saw a small man standing before the main desk outside Jennifer's room looking at a chart.

"Dr. Liu," Peter said approaching him from the side. "Good morning." He noted the bulky chart of Jennifer Barns.

"Good morning, Peter. I rarely meet you men and women behind the masks except on rare occasions when you dart into the doctor's lounge or pop into a quarterly staff meeting."

"Well, it looks like we're both interested in the same patient. Are you Jennifer's internist?"

"I'm the one. I originally steered her to the transplant center, so I have a vested interest. You were her anesthesiologist?" Peter nodded. "From what I can gather in the notes, that was a very rocky course. Peter, I know your group intently slogged through it. I need to be very involved now as I think she's deteriorated in the last few hours. All night, the nurse tells me, they called Doctor Bhagat and he kept ordering more blood products." He grinned at the lab work done throughout the night. "I just don't know," he said softly.

"Dr. Liu," Peter said, concerned, "then while you're still evaluating the chart, I'll step in to see her."

Peter turned and crossed into Jennifer's room while her nurse, Jackie, scurried in as well. The overhead florescent bulbs inside the ceiling's plastic covers winked out for a second. Peter rubbed his eyes. The EKG's tracing and high-pitched sounds hastened along on the monitor, faster than they'd been the day before.

"Dr. Devlin," Jackie said, "it's been catch-up on blood products the last few hours. I called Dr. Bhagat and explained her tachycardia, told him the labs, and about her low urine output." She pointed to the Foley bag then pushed her jacket sleeve several inches up her forearm.

"That's all for how long?" Peter asked, looking at a trace amount of pinkish urine.

"Three hours."

Peter swallowed hard. He walked along the side of Jennifer's bed as an arrhythmia pranced across the screen.

"She's got a fever, too," Jackie added.

Peter listened to Jennifer's chest and heart and placed his hand on her. He wasn't sure, but was there some rigidity? "Is her temperature rising and is she getting any muscle relaxants?"

"Temperature was 100.5 an hour ago. When I checked it ten minutes ago, it was 101.1. And no, we've not given her any Norcuron."

"I want you to ask respiratory to hook up an end-tidal CO_2 monitor to her tubing," Peter said. "And I'll go check her labs."

At the desk, Dr. Liu sat inside the circular area scrawling his note in the chart. When Peter rolled a chair beside him, Dr. Liu stopped, flipped the chart to the lab work section, and slid it a few inches so Peter.

"Potassium is creeping up," Peter said. "We treated acidosis all along in the OR but, since she's been here, that's getting worse, too."

"But there aren't any new labs ordered for this morning," Dr. Liu said. "Maybe Sukhdev is going to order some when he comes by."

"I'm concerned, though," Peter said.

"Yes, I agree. I'm going to order some Lasix. She should be making more urine. You know, by all indications, I think she's had enough volume to pee like a race horse."

Peter hoped the IV diuretic would work, too. "Okay, and are you ordering a whole set of labs before the surgeon comes in?

"Absolutely."

"I will take a look at them as well. I'll try to run up from the OR by noon."

"That's thoughtful of you, Dr. Devlin."

Peter patted his medical colleague's shoulder. "Nothing that you wouldn't do." He started to leave, but hesitated. "May I add something?"

Dr. Liu pushed him the chart and Peter leaned over. He unclipped his pen from his upper pocket and wrote on the physician order sheet:

Urine for myoglobin.
Plasma creatine kinase and then every 6 hours for 24 hours.

121

Peter Devlin, M.D.

Doctor Liu arched his eyebrows and thought. He didn't really understand why Peter ordered what he did, except that if the results were higher than normal, it would suggest something askew with the patient's muscles, like a muscle break down.

Peter left the nurses' station, and popped his head around the corner of Jennifer's room. "Jackie," he said interrupting the update of her nursing notes. "Dr. Liu ordered a list of blood and urine lab work. Would you put pressure on the lab department for results?"

Jackie looked up and down quickly. "Anything for you, Dr. Devlin."

————

Downstairs, Peter rushed into Joan's office where anesthesia providers were coming and going and he grabbed a walkie-talkie from the charger. "Dr. Devlin," Joan said, "I saw your blue scrubs rushing out of the locker room before. Now if you're ready to get to work, hurry yourself over to OR nine. Patient's in the room. The surgeon ran in here and announced that EMS brought a patient straight up with a ruptured aortic aneurysm."

Peter zigzagged through the three people plugging up the doorway while Joan got up and followed him, spilling out the details. "You'll have to get a history from whatever notes they jotted down from the scene. Since then the patient has been non-responsive."

Peter pulled his OR hat from his pocket and slipped it on his head. With each step, his stride grew longer. He pulled a mask from a box over a hallway operating room sink and stopped outside OR nine. He placed the blue cover over his mouth and tied the strings in the back of his head. "And that's all I know," Joan said, turning around. She waved her right hand. "And save another life, Dr. Devlin."

As Peter peered inside the window over the sink, EMS was rolling their stretcher away from the table. An early shift nurse anesthetist who had just beat Peter by three minutes scurried at the top of the table to get the necessary bare minimal materials to rapidly and safely put the patient to sleep. The circulating nurse scrambled to help put on monitors.

Peter took a deep breath. This patient was white as a ghost from where he stood; a dying patient whose abdominal aorta had ruptured and was spewing out his entire circulation into the gut of his belly, no doubt. He opened the swinging door. A momentary look of satisfaction crossed the faces of the nurse anesthetist and nursing staff, who both looked his way.

Peter bridged the space to the patient's surgical table. "Throw me an A-line kit," he said, grasping the patient's right forearm as a surgical nurse poured betadine on the man's abdomen to scrub. "Cycle the cuff on the other upper arm."

For one more second, Peter's thoughts grappled with Jennifer Barns's condition. Although she was no longer under his care, he'd keep his eye on her. She'd come this far…

Chapter 17

Cool air wafted over Putt-Putt's shiny black nose. As Jim drove along the bay street, Putt-Putt inhaled the salty scent of beached seaweed already starting to decay. Green dumpsters sat scattered along the street and, like the vet's neighborhood, roofs and walls of houses were yanked in different directions and tree roots were heaved from the ground. An awning was embedded between two trees, its aluminum gnarled and twisted between the tree trunks.

Yet, Putt-Putt recognized this street to be the original one he ran on after the accident. He reversed his direction on the passenger's seat to look backward instead of forward - to look towards the direction of the car crash. Beyond it, on the other side of Santa Rosa Sound, was home. Had Karen woken up from her unconsciousness in the car, that scary sleep which he didn't understand? Had she looked for him? If Karen wasn't near the base of the bridge, then he assumed that his owner was on the island. Safe at home, maybe she was putting his food bowl on the floor, waiting for him. He would get back to her if he could. He wanted to make her smile when she woke up in the morning, keep her warm in bed when Rick was not there, and wag his tail at Tonya when she came home.

———

Jim used three fingers to push his stiff-brimmed cap further back on his forehead while his four-legged passenger whimpered. The little dog's head rested over the seat, his eyes glued to the rear. "I couldn't do it," Jim said. "Leave you there or wherever you were going. No telling where you would end up or what would happen to you." He shuddered while thinking of stories how euthanized or dead dogs became dog food ingredients.

"What's back there, boy?" Jim said, viewing Putt-Putt's direction of concentration. He slowed, turned into their driveway, and eased the vehicle to the back in front of the brick garage. "Speaking of 'boy,' I wish I knew your name. We'll have to think of something now that you're part of the family." He walked around the car, carried

Putt-Putt out and placed him on the grass, away from strewn branches and shingles.

Jim went into the house and patted his trousers. Putt-Putt followed, recognizing the place as a recent memory, where he had sought safety below the front porch after the accident and during the thunderous wind. While Jim set down his car keys, the dog explored, his nails clicking on the kitchen tiles. He found some toast crumbs and, to his delight, he pawed a peanut from under the lip of the corner cabinet.

Janet spoke from the dining room before they saw her. "Guess we've got another mouth to feed." She leaned over at the doorway where Putt-Putt met her halfway. She petted the crown of his head, buried her fingertips behind his ear, and massaged. "Now don't you go breaking my heart," she said, his eyes as big as saucers staring into her soul.

Jim turned away. Years has passed since their last dog had died. His wife then made every attempt for them not to get another. "I'm not ready, I just can't do it," she said every time Jim mentioned another pet.

Janet straightened and attempted to close the lower button of her blouse, but the fit was too snug. "We lucked out while you were gone," she said to her husband. "The neighbors arranged for a roofing business to tarp the roofs of six or eight of us at a time. Seems like we've beat other areas to it because we're giving them a bulk order."

Jim smiled. "And at least we only have a little hole under those blown off shingles and garage."

"No reason to smile yet. Who knows how long it will take them."

Putt-Putt sat perfectly straight and locked eyes with Jim. Janet passed a cereal bowl from the dish drainer to Jim and he filled it with cold water. "I'll have to go back out and buy some dog food," Jim said as the dog lapped the water he put down.

"Jim, please also stop at the drug store. They have someone filling prescriptions and I've asked for refills on my heart medicine."

Jim picked up his bulky keys. "How's your blood sugar? Do you need any supplies while I'm there?"

"I'm staying under control and I don't need anything else."

Jim leaned over Putt-Putt and planted a kiss on his wife. "You get the honors."

"What honors?"

"Of naming this little fella." They watched and chuckled as the dog gazed up at them with water dripping off the sides of his mouth.

———

Janet took a cold drink from the refrigerator and went into the family room. She felt guilty about their good fortune because they had been wise on their house purchase years ago. Trying to make it on Jim's job selling insurance and her part-time receptionist's work in the nearby attorney's office had given them a decent living, but they hadn't been foolish with their incomes. Knowing the area's history of disabling hurricanes, they had purchased the solid, yet small, brick home, on an elevated area from the bay, and close to a health care facility. The hospital nearby meant that their home was in the same power grid and Gulf Power always needed to establish the hospital's power first. Jim and Janet knew about this special arrangement when they purchased and now they enjoyed quickly reestablished electricity - the fruits of their smart planning.

Janet turned on the television where all the noon broadcasters spoke about the gulf coast. The need for establishing electricity in Pensacola and the surrounding towns was so great that trucks and manpower were pouring in from electric companies all over the southeast, but the rate limiting step for some of them was the removal of debris across major inbound roads to Pensacola. FEMA had one hell of a task on its hands.

After sipping her sugarless iced tea, Janet decided on her next task. She bused the clothes basket into the laundry room and loaded the washing machine while two bright eyes followed her every move. She went back inside, slightly short of breath, and sat in a maroon recliner. When she rubbed the dog's shoulder, he jostled on the floor belly-up, exposing himself in all his glory so she rubbed his chest. Putt-Putt's front legs danced in midair, his head upside down leaning on her sneaker. His eyes still managed to talk to her besides his body language.

"Don't you try and make me fall hard for you. That'll only get me in trouble, like the last time."

Putt-Putt slowed his air-swinging paws. His alert eyes didn't let go of her. She stroked him lighter and studied his coloring; an albino-like delicate pink skin with faded spots underneath his white hair, too camouflaged if she didn't look closely. Although he had stark white fur, the large round spots on either side of his spine were a yellowish-brown, as if he wore suntanned circles.

"You're white like the emerald coast's sugar sand but have tan areas like Alabama's beaches." Janet scratched under his neck. "What if we call you Sandy? Yes, that fits. You and I will try it out before Jim comes home. We'll see if you like it."

―――――

Sukhdev turned the ignition off. He shoved his cigar case, which he restocked the night before, into the console, and jiggled his briefcase and white coat towards him. He stepped out of his Lexus, left foot first. Perhaps it was because of the blood baths he often encountered in the OR resulting in the ruination of multiple pairs of tennis shoes, but he'd developed a fastidious obsession over his non-OR shoes. His right foot followed and he scrutinized it as well. He had buffed the soft leather shoes almost a week ago and, since he wore them only while not wearing scrubs, the mahogany colored shoes looked as if they'd been pulled out of a Fifth Avenue shoe store window.

Expensive shoes, he believed, not only spoke a certain language to a patient when he met and evaluated them and family members in his office or in the hospital, but they made a certain sound. Shoes of his caliber echoed along the corridors announcing his professional entrance and the shined hospital floors worked synergistically with his step to create a perfect sounding accent.

He beeped the car's remote and made his way across into the hospital. He already performed surgery at a smaller satellite hospital where the transplant team had privileges. He'd removed a patient's kidney due to a renal cell carcinoma. Now he would round on his Good Samaritan patients. The ICU had called him several times overnight about his liver transplant patient, so he wanted to visit her first and see if the internist had documented anything today. He hoped to see a robust note saying how the patient would now have a miraculous new stab at life. Because of him, of course.

In the elevator, Sukhdev slid into his doctor's coat and adjusted the collar. He stepped languidly into intensive care. He thought twice about placing his leather case on the desktop, so instead he placed it on the floor adjacent to the inside end of the nurses' station. Health care workers sometimes put a dirty glove or two on the top. Better to keep his briefcase as clean as possible.

Cynthia, the morning shift nurse, followed Dr. Bhagat into Jennifer Barns's room. "Good morning, doctor. I was about to beep you. I was wondering if I could up the dopamine before you showed up."

Sukhdev sank a first impression on the status of his patient. Despite the information he received overnight and the continued treatments he ordered by telephone, there continued to be a sagging of blood pressure, resulting in a need for more vital drug support. He took a large sigh. He'd been working on this patient's case for what seemed like days. Didn't he deserve an intermission, like watching a play, where he could come back in and the plot changes for the better?

"Can I?" the nurse asked again.

Sukhdev startled. The experienced RN waited for an answer. He waved to go ahead, listened to Jennifer's lungs and found no answers there, and sulked out to gather her morning paperwork. He studied the unbound sheets of lab work protruding from the chart. Quite dismal. In addition, some oddball values were included; perhaps those labs were orders on another patient and were mistakenly labeled or filed as Jennifer Barns's.

The unit secretary, a sun-weathered middle-aged woman, rolled her chair toward Sukhdev and put down a piece of paper. "Here's another one," she said pointedly. "I need to bind them. Leave the chart there for me, if you would please. In any case, Dr. Devlin should be by soon to see some of those."

"Dr. Devlin?"

"Yes sir." She wheeled back to her original spot.

Sukhdev sucked in the fleshy inside of his cheek and ran his tongue along it. He flipped the pages to the *orders* tab and searched towards the back. That confirmed it. What gave the anesthesiologist the right to meddle in his case, or the authority to write orders on his patient when his role in her care was over? That anesthesiologist, Peter Devlin, had officially and postoperatively signed off on her case after the first hour, as is normally the case. Sukhdev, as the admitting MD in charge, had not requested a consult or anything further from him.

He needed coffee. That would simmer his brewing thoughts. Actually, the ICU personnel brewed the stiffest java in the hospital. And they went through more of it than the ER. It always made Sukhdev think that the darker the roast and the larger volume of coffee consumed went hand-in-hand with the most wired departments. You couldn't separate them. Those department workers were the movers and shakers, maybe not always the brightest, but the ones that couldn't sit still, the adrenaline junkies.

He wondered if he went into the wrong field, he thought as he got up. Perhaps he should have been a psychiatrist. They drew respect from their knowledge of what lurked in peoples' minds and, suggestively or pharmaceutically altered their patients' behavior. Well, forget it, he thought, repositioning body parts was still what he wanted to do.

In the adjacent kitchenette, Sukhdev poured coffee into the largest cup, drizzled a blue packet in, and stirred. He sipped while leaning against the counter and admired his shoes.

"I put Mrs. Barns's X-ray jacket in the viewing room," a technician said passing in and out with a stack of radiology jackets under her arm.

"Better late than never," Sukhdev said to lost ears. Careful not to spill confectioner's sugar, he took a bite-sized donut from a box, and washed it down with more coffee. He placed the x-ray up on the view box in the little side room and saw no adverse lung developments or any forgotten surgical sponges in the upper abdomen.

He slid the film back into the brown paper jacket, relieved over Jennifer Barns's pulmonary picture, and his thoughts fell mightily on

Peter Devlin. How dare he? To meddle in his patient's care was to belittle him, the most skilled, highly accomplished physician on the whole hospital staff. After all, who else removes major organs from almost dead people, keeps those organs viable, and hooks them into another human being successfully? Let alone to keep the transplanted patients alive in the short and long-term postoperative period after their sentence would have been an underground brown box? Well, his partner, Arnold Morris, transplanted organs, too, but Arnold sometimes made mistakes like doing surgeries on riskier patients that Sukhdev believed wouldn't make it. And Arnold flew through his surgeries in a lot shorter time, so he probably wasn't as thorough.

Yes, Peter Devlin. What a prick. Come to think about it, so was his wife. No, anatomically that's not what he should call her. She was definitely a bitch. What had she said when she had stopped their plane from departing? Something like him thinking he was God but to shut the hell up in her plane. And then leaving Birmingham, she was highly insulting in the cockpit because he called the hospital using his cell phone. She had even alluded to the fact that she was totally responsible for everything and everyone to do with the flight operation.

Which is the way he viewed his transplant case. He was in charge of Jennifer Barns, not her anesthesiologist husband. Yes, totally in charge. All Peter Devlin ever did was put tubes in people's throats and turn on the anesthesia vaporizer. Big deal. Sukhdev shot his glance to the floor, where his shoes seemed to sizzle, a steamy cloud between his eyes and his excellent shine job. The blood flow in his neck quickened, he heard it in his head like standing near the runoff from a waterfall. Now he hated both of them.

———

Peter trudged to the doctor's lounge knowing Joan would hunt him down quickly to tell him his next case. He sidetracked past the docs in conversation and went into the rest room. He urinated, washed his hands, and removed the OR bonnet. He glanced in the mirror. His mustache had gotten a little darker compared to his sandy colored hair. Or maybe his hair was graying, making the mustache seem darker. He went out and poured a half cup of coffee. The lunch platters of fresh cold cuts, breads, and two hot entrees of spaghetti and stir fried zucchini were on the counter.

"I'll let you have lunch before handing off more cases on you."

Peter spun around and grinned at Joan.

"Thanks. But I'm heading to the ICU to check on the transplant from yesterday."

Joan put her hand on her hip. "Don't ignore the opportunity, Dr. Devlin. But being conscientious about eating isn't your thing, is it?" She smiled, stole an apple, and walked away to another anesthesiologist.

Peter finished the black coffee and exited the lounge. The morning's aortic aneurysm patient had gone like clockwork. His other case, removal of orthopedic hardware, proved more difficult due to the seventy-four year old's hypertension.

He rode the elevator in front of a somber looking couple and stepped out briskly when the elevator stopped. He straightened the uneven stethoscope hanging around his neck and went straight into Jennifer Barns's room.

"I was just charting," Cynthia said. "Here, Dr. Devlin." Jennifer's nurse tapped the chart on the tray table.

Peter faked a meek smile. The high tracing and elevated numbers on the end-tidal carbon dioxide monitor he had asked for on Jennifer's respiratory tubing had him concerned. He looked at the Foley bag. "When did you last change it?"

"There's been nothing to change, because her urine output has dropped down to nothing."

Peter squinted and opened the chart to lab values. His heart thumped when he viewed the arterial blood gases, a combined metabolic and respiratory acidosis. The significantly elevated potassium made him gulp and when he saw the ten-fold increase in catecholamine levels, he knew what he must do. The creatinine kinase levels were high but those he needed to trend over the next day. Jennifer's charted temperatures were elevated and he spied a ventricular arrhythmia prancing across her EKG.

"Get respiratory and a lab tech to draw blood in here stat," Peter said. He walked to the ventilator and increased Jennifer's minute ventilation to eighteen while he snapped his walkie-talkie off his belt. "Joan, it's Dr. Devlin up in ICU."

"I'm here," Joan snapped, knowing Peter's soothing calm voice was absent.

"Send up the malignant hyperthermia cart stat with the anesthesia tech and send me an additional pair of hands."

Chapter 18

Johnny and Amelia sat disheartened in the waiting room after the ICU staff told them they couldn't see their mother. Apparently nursing personnel had their hands full. Johnny tucked the drawstring into his sweatpants and tightened the shoelace on his sneaker. He glanced around. All the waiting rooms were beginning to look the same: plastic plants, maroon cushioned seats besides upholstered couches, and clumps of children's toys in brightly colored corner containers.

"Sounds like something's going on," Mel said.

Johnny heard voices filled with alarm and the rolling of equipment. He watched his sister's slim figure hustle to the hallway, where she peered towards the ICU doors and saw two young women with surgical hats pushing a red cart. The cart jostled over the lip of the doorway mat as items on the top bounced.

One woman said, "We're going to do the emergency drill we practiced for over and over again."

"But still," the other young woman replied, "doing the real thing is different." She grasped the corner of the cart as they flew around the turn.

Amelia settled back into the chair next to Johnny. "Those hospital people sure are in a hurry. There must be an emergency."

———

Peter made sure the central lines he put in Jennifer the day before were still fully patent; he needed to depend on them once his help arrived.

Cynthia moved all paperwork from the cart tray and asked an assistant outside for a forced-air cooling blanket like Peter had asked for. She squeezed in her question before the anesthesia tech and nurse anesthetist made it through the doorway. "Dr. Devlin, I don't understand. A few years ago there was an ICU patient in here with neuroleptic hyperthermia from antipsychotics. He had muscle rigidity and a fever like Mrs. Barns. But this is different?"

"Yes. This is not neuroleptic malignant syndrome. This is malignant hyperthermia precipitated by certain anesthetics. It is an extremely rare genetic problem."

"I don't get it. She isn't getting any anesthesia."

"You're correct, Cynthia. It's rarer to have it postop after the discontinuation of anesthetics, but it can happen. Jennifer Barns is not our typical patient."

Peter turned the volume up on the EKG machine, increased the size of the tracings on the monitor, took off his jacket, and draped his stethoscope on the door handle. They stripped the outer blanket off Jennifer and laid the new cooling blanket over the sheet. Audrey, the anesthesia tech, and Robin, the anesthetist, arrived with the cart and the three of them rummaged through the drawers.

"Did you bring the sterile water?" Peter asked.

Audrey nodded and set bottles of dantrolene on top. Robin grabbed big needles and syringes from the cart. Peter did the dosage mathematics quickly in his head and then spoke out loud. "2.5 mg/kg. We'll use 140 milligrams to start."

"To start?" Cynthia asked, staying out of their way.

Audrey and Robin began as Peter also started one preparation. Peter knew minutes mattered for Jennifer's life. The dantrolene, with mannitol included, needed to be dissolved in sterile water, a preparation difficult to mix, and the tedious task would require time. But the skeletal muscle relaxant was the absolute sole therapeutic treatment to prevent further calcium release from skeletal muscle cells.

Peter pulled and injected through the different bottles ignoring Cynthia's question. After he mixed a workable solution he squeezed to the top of the bed and began injecting into the central line in her neck.

"Cynthia, we'll repeat a dose if she doesn't respond in thirty minutes. But this isn't going to reverse contracture. It should prevent further muscle contraction." Peter glanced up as an irregular heart beat pranced across the screen. "Tell them to call the lab again. I need blood work from the A-line on a regular schedule."

Cynthia dashed out as the respiratory therapist dashed in. "I changed some settings," Peter said. "Hyperventilating her. Check the

134

other parameters and evaluate if there's anything else you can do to maximize her oxygenation while we wait for the next ABG's."

The therapist scanned the machine then stood near Peter and ran the suction catheter through the endotracheal tube and into Jennifer's bronchi. A small group stopped outside and peered in from the doorway; the patient's diagnosis in room four had circulated among health care workers. Talk at the bedside abated as everyone skillfully hurried to reverse Jennifer's ominous condition.

———

Sukhdev poked his head back into the kitchenette and spied the open box of donuts. He stepped back in and with his index finger and thumb, he removed another bite-sized donut and popped it in his mouth. Always at their best when they're fresh, he thought. He put his foam cup into the microwave to zap the remainder of his coffee and turned around. Outside the glass window, people were moving faster than normal as if a code were in progress. That's strange, he thought, realizing it was his patient's room gathering the attention.

The buzzer sounded after ten seconds and Sukhdev removed the cup. Perhaps it was just family visitors making a fuss in there, or nurses talking about a party, or nursing students with faculty making some kind of rounds. They could use his patient as a good teaching example. In any case, he would be the first to know if Jennifer Barns coded, and fat chance of that.

A lab tech holding a plastic container, with a tourniquet dangling off its side, zipped past the unit secretary. In his other hand he waved a piece of paper. "Stat results for Barns," he said.

The woman waved him over to room four. "Bring it in there to Dr. Devlin."

What the hell? Sukhdev tried putting down the coffee on the edge of the sink, but missed, and it toppled to the floor. That meddling, arrogant, know-it-all insignificant doctor was at it again, he thought. He took one step but stopped. He was going to play this right. His stance was unequivocal; he must tackle the anesthesiologist ruthlessly. Peter Devlin belonged in the operating room, not in his patient's room. He was going to shred him to bits. In front of everyone.

Sukhdev marched over, his rage mounting upon seeing a red cart with a pile up of bottles, sterile water, and syringes. It clearly was not a crash cart.

"Devlin!" Sukhdev yelled loudly and abruptly at the doorway.

Peter popped off a needle cap to inject the next dantrolene syringe into the central line and almost stabbed himself upon hearing the booming irate voice at the door. He startled like standing next to an unexpected shotgun blast.

"Yesterday you signed off on my patient," Sukhdev shouted. "You are no longer a treating physician on my case."

The lines around Peter's eyes squinted so tight, he could barely focus. And he was trying to see the lab sheet lying in front of him while he injected the syringe's contents.

"It's my duty to intervene, especi..."

"Duty? You think I can't handle my own patient?" Sukhdev regretted the statement. Why should he play into Devlin's hands and be defensive?

"Most doctors are not trained in this diagnosis," Peter interjected quickly while watching the syringe, "and aren't trained to handle it."

Sukhdev didn't know what Devlin was talking about. The longer he stood there, the more he was going to look like a fool.

"You continue to touch my patient, it will be considered assault and battery."

Peter's pulse quickened with Jennifer's emergency and now his blood felt like the first water bubbles to boil in a pot. He tried to put the aggravating surgeon out of his mind and note the time - to allow thirty minutes for the initiation of dantrolene's therapeutic effect.

The silence between the two physicians deafened everyone in the room. The respiratory therapist held the suction catheter in mid-air not knowing what to do. He looked stealthily at Audrey but she gave no clues. She was too busy feeling her lunch settle upwards into her throat.

"You have a skewed idea of misdemeanor felonies," Peter sharply retorted. "There is no criminal intent here, unless following emergency malignant hyperthermia protocol qualifies."

Sudhdev tried to recall medical data not surgically related, from medical internship days. Hyperthermia, yes, something inched forward. Heat stroke. But he could only think of muscular male athletes overexerting themselves on a football field. He also recalled something about hallucinogenic wacko patients strung out on psychiatric medicines. But this was a failing end-organ liver patient with a transplant and there was nothing which tied her to those problems. Hyperthermia? Maybe a spiking fever due to an infectious source. Even he knew about that. Perhaps she had acute meningitis. Did Dr. Devlin stop to consider that? Which brought him to the same conclusion – to get the damn anesthesiologist away from his patient.

Sukhdev's dilemma searching for a response gave Peter a second to glance at his watch and realize his other continuing predicament. Robin and Peter needed time to catch up. Robin helped him all along but not one intervention, dose, time, temperature, or arrhythmia had been recorded. Lawyers in a courtroom wouldn't give a damn if he was trying to save a patient's life. Everything had to be "documented" or it "didn't happen" and remembering every small detail after the fact was not easy.

Peter realized in this type of situation that another person was needed to just write. But then again, that person would have to be a health care worker. And that individual would be responsible for taking care of someone else, and what if something happened to their patient in the interim? The catch-22 medical-legal aspect of practicing medicine and anesthesia made him unhappy more than anything else.

Peter wiped his forehead and slipped under the ventilator's tubing while the therapist stepped aside. He patted Robin and escorted her to the back counter with anesthesia record paper. "Let's get a record going," he said softly. "We'll work on it together while I keep my eye on her and the lab work which will be streaming in."

It only took the surgeon three steps. Blocking anyone else's view of what he did, Sukhdev's right hand gripped Peter's left bicep. His fingers pushed deeply into flesh, inflicting pain.

Up close and for Peter's ears only, Sukhdev's words were clear. "Consider yourself ruined. Your wife, too."

"Johnny, I'm missing Mom," Amelia said sullenly in the waiting room. "And we don't even know if she's opened her eyes yet."

"I know. I want her back the way she was. She didn't deserve hepatitis." Johnny turned towards his sister and frowned. "I'm learning we can't pick and choose certain parts of our lives." He pinched the bridge of his nose to stall a sneeze.

"God bless you," Mel said.

A man limped past them and dropped a cafeteria plastic cup in the trash. When he went past them again, he cushioned himself into the couch and fidgeted with a *Courier-Journal* newspaper. The headlines and front section pictures still centered on the ravaged gulf coast as well as the area's humanitarian groups gathering resources to donate to the victims or Red Cross, or to schedule trips for emergency services.

They weren't the only ones with troubles, Johnny thought. Tonya had it even worse. He wished she lived in southern Indiana. He wanted to call her later on; he found her easy to talk to, even easier than his sister. He liked her big brown eyes, spirited walk, and interesting choice of school subjects. She was smart but sporty.

Johnny and Amelia heard the automatic ICU doors out in the hallway, then someone clumping out like a Clydesdale horse. Dressed in street clothes, Dr. Bhagat turned the corner rather abruptly, and stood before them after being told the teens were outside.

Johnny and Amelia got up; something about Sukhdev looked more anxious. For one, his eyebrows were held higher, like he drank a pot of dark roast Jamaican coffee. And why the fiery glow on his cheeks? Johnny's stomach turned somersaults. Something dreadful must have happened to his mother and that's why all the commotion. Mel's hand touched his forearm, alerting him that she felt the same way. Sukhdev signaled Johnny and Mel a few steps over from the adjacent man who'd given up on his newspaper.

"I'm glad you're both here," Sukhdev started. "Your mother's new liver just needs more time. It's a waiting game. Ultimately, however, I think we're going to be satisfied with the transplant and, so far, I'm happy with my surgical results." His thoughts toyed with his forthcoming words while he plastered a smile on his lips.

138

Johnny relaxed his posture and Mel let go of his arm. Sukhdev peeked around to check who might be nearby. "Unfortunately," he said, "it appears the anesthesiologist has some complications. Medications, or in this particular instance, anesthesia, can have side effects. If patients have reactions to prescribed medications, doctors are supposed to stop them immediately. Your mom has gotten very ill from drugs which no one should have given her."

Johnny's metabolism slowed, except for his heart which thumped against his chest, causing him to grasp for air. Mel felt light-headed.

"What does this mean?" Johnny stumbled. "Can we see her?"

"Even if you could, she's still not awake. And the anesthesiologist is giving her potent drugs to try and reverse what he did to her."

"You mean from the anesthesia yesterday?" Johnny said.

"Yes. But better late than never." Sukhdev gave Johnny and Mel his most practiced empathetic expression. "I hope she lives through this, well, negligence." He patted Johnny's shoulder, turned, and was gone.

―――――――

Sudhdev had trouble keeping patients and families straight. How could he always remember which patient was married, which family member always took grandpa to see him in the office, which children were medically-legally responsible for an elderly parent? His job was the surgery and the rest was simply a facade. On his way to the OR, he wondered. He hoped Jennifer Barns had a caring spouse, or significant other, or that the son was old enough to take matters into his own hands. Who knows? Maybe the boy was headed to law school. Hopefully, however, someone in the family has ties to a shark malpractice attorney. A malpractice suit was one major inconvenience for a physician – both personally and professionally.

He would love for legal action to begin after today against Peter, the anesthesiologist, Devlin.

Chapter 19

At Janet and Jim's house, Putt-Putt trotted down a hallway and found two bedrooms to explore. It would be fun to hunt around for new and interesting smells. He could tell if there were dogs there before him or if food was nestled in unseen places. Perhaps little people had played in one of the back rooms. They always left fresher scents like the newness after a spring rain, not like the sour smell of old people with aged skin. Not that he preferred the young over the old, he liked them both, but his built in curiosity came from his DNA.

He found no trace that little humans had been on the beds in either room. He was slightly disappointed for the time being because he had lots of energy and, when that happened, he loved to play ball with youngsters or frolic in the bay or run with them. But if he wanted to take a nap, or get stroked until he fell asleep, then best to be with the humans with the wrinkles. He had experience with all of that.

From the living room, Putt-Putt heard Janet. "Sandy, come here, boy."

Who was she calling? Strange, because Jim was not home and there was no one else in the house. She called someone, but her tone was like when a person called over a dog. He backed out of an open closet with uninteresting shoes and went to investigate who may have come in the door. When he entered the main room, Janet gleefully smiled and opened her arms.

"That's a good boy. Sandy. You're smart and earned that new name." She leaned over and ruffled his head.

Not again. This seemed very familiar. He had a name in the very beginning. He remembered a man doing the same thing - calling him something over and over - at which point Putt-Putt realized it was him that the man wanted.

Putt-Putt plopped his hind quarters down in front of the couch and spread his front paws forward. His head followed and he closed his eyes for a long time. But he didn't dream. The past came back in bits and pieces; he didn't understand how the past played in his head like the humans' movies. Sometimes it made him feel sad to replay his life; other times what he remembered was sheer joy.

———

Putt-Putt remembered being brand new. At that time, he was such a small round ball that he could tuck between his mother's legs and suckle her milk. Next to him, there were two more puppies and, although paws tangled in each other's faces, and heads rested on each other's stomachs, that time had been the most comforting and secure he had ever known. They lay squished together under a clump of bushes deep in a field and his mother often licked them with her tongue and religiously gave them her teats. Each day she left them for short intervals to forage for her own food and, when she reappeared she was full and tired but delighted to see them.

———

Putt-Putt's sister greedily sought their mother's milk and attention; she had been the one to more slowly get up on all four legs and hobble under the bushes. Compared to her brothers, she stayed physically close to her mother like a marsupial staying in her mother's pouch. But each morning in the coolness of the shade, Putt-Putt and his brother and sister rolled around and pranced on each other outside their leafy covering. They nipped at each other's throats and ran short distances after sparrows and lizards. They stepped on newly blooming little flowers and experienced the sting of fire ants hiding in sand bubbles under the springtime grass.

For what seemed like a lifetime itself, this immunity against life's harm continued. But one day while their mother had gone for her last excursion of the day, a little girl with shaggy red hair and worn sneakers stumbled past the bushes and found the three pups. She stopped humming when she saw Putt-Putt play bowing in front of a tree frog that had frozen in his spot with its legs tucked in and eyes shut tight. The little girl also liked the grassy-green creature but finding the three puppies turned her previous make-believe games into a spectacular real life discovery.

One by one, the puppies were swept between the legs of the girl as she sat on the grass. Putt-Putt felt her hands around his belly as she swung him in the air. She nuzzled her face into his and smacked her lips at his nose. Her hands had no fur and she stroked through to his skin which felt as comforting as his mother's nudges.

As the day's brightness began to diminish, and their stomachs began to growl, they heard a human voice approach from the direction past their nesting place and shrubbery.

"Misty, where are you girl? Misty?"

The little girl pushed the dogs out of the way and jumped up. "Daddy, look what I found!"

A long, tall man with sneakers and stubbly growth on his face pushed his way through and hovered above them with a look of surprise. "They here all by themselves?"

"Yup. They's just babies, see?" She proudly picked one out and nudged Putt-Putt's brother toward her father.

"Well, we gotta go. And get ourselves some dinner." The man named Bobby picked up the littlest one and frowned.

"Can we keep them?" Misty pleaded.

Bobby looked all around and pondered. His daughter had only the next day, Sunday, for visitation with him before going back to her mother and on weekdays he worked for a heating and air conditioning company making service runs.

"Daddy, they mustn't be hungry. They can have my dinner."

"Oh, all right. We'll figure this out. I'll carry two of them and you take that one near you."

A huge beam spread across her face as she stood up. "Be careful Daddy, they's delicate."

————

Since his ex-wife lived in what had been Bobby's home even before he had married her, he had rented a trailer east of Gulf Breeze in a neighborly trailer park. Bobby had planned on taking Misty for a hamburger, but when they got back with the pups, they warmed canned ravioli and green beans for themselves and then turned their attention to their live stuffed animals.

Bobby placed a bowl of milk by the door and placed newspapers on the other side. Along with his siblings, Putt-Putt sniffed the milk. The strange liquid was similar to what he drank from his mother, but not as fresh, and not as thick. Sure enough, after swiping his tongue along the top of the bowl, he decided to wait it out. But why were they there and where was their mother? They needed her and she would be frantic searching for them.

"Misty, we'll have to name them something," Bobby said while reaching into the refrigerator for a Budweiser. He sat on the kitchenette seat and rubbed his short beard. "Think of a name for the little girl."

"Cream," she said emphatically.

Bobby thought of Irish Cream while he snapped open his beer can. Might as well make them a liquor series, he thought. "Okay, and how about the other two? Bud and Whiskey?"

"Okay," she said, patting Putt-Putt. "This one's Whiskey." She petted and hugged the three dogs until she tired, then changed into pastel pajamas. The dogs didn't see her the rest of the night.

Bobby unlocked the door and carried the three pups outside. They were supposed to pee on the grass but the dogs sniffed around for their mother instead. Finally, Bobby scooped them back up because they were too little and wobbly to climb the two steps.

That night, Whiskey, Bud, and Cream huddled together tighter than ever on the strange flat floor. They whimpered and cried; scared, alone, and in the wrong place. And mostly, they missed the familiarity, warmth, and milk from their mother.

———

It was impossible. Bobby tried to housebreak the three dogs. Leaving a pile of newspapers allowed Whiskey, Bud, and Cream a place to relieve themselves, but then how would he train them to go outside when he was gone for ten hours at a stretch? And how old should they be to not pee in the trailer? Plus, Misty had only visited on the weekends and now she wouldn't be coming for three weeks because she had summer vacation time with her mother.

———

Misty sat on the wooden step and enticed Cream with a white sock she and her father had dedicated as a toy. Bobby playfully nudged Whisky with his shoe while scouring the grill. He cooked his daughter and himself an early dinner of plump chicken breasts and corn on the cob and now the time had come to put the subject of the dogs behind them.

"Misty, we've talked about the dogs, how Daddy can't keep 'em." He stopped nervously cleaning and crouched to her level. "While you're on vacation with your mom, I have to find them a good home."

Misty was only six but she had seen sad stories about animals on her mother's TV. Although she wished the three dogs could have a happy home with a fenced-in yard, she wanted the three dogs to belong to her forever. She wished she was a grown-up because then she could keep them no matter what. She wanted to be mad at her father, but she couldn't. He had brought the pups home when they may have died by themselves, and he had tried his best to look after them.

In one hour, Misty's mom pulled off the dusty road and onto the front strip of gravel, while Misty gathered her belongings and then sadly hugged Whiskey, Bud, and Cream good-bye. "I love you. I'll never forget each of you," she said, nestling her head into their growing bodies. She climbed into the front seat of her mother's sedan, buried her face against the window, and allowed droplets to form in the corners of her eyes.

After his daughter was safely out of sight, Bobby cleared a tool box and bucket from his pickup truck. He took pride in keeping the bed clean, especially since the dark green vehicle was only three years old, and as the second owner, he'd bought it with only twenty-one thousand miles on it. He depended on the back end for occasional air conditioning or heating parts for customers. But for the last four months it had worked fine for the occasional trips he took with the dogs, just for the fun of it.

He believed he would miss the dogs as much as Misty. He thought a great deal about his decision, especially in the evenings when Whiskey, Bud, and Cream rested around his feet or followed him all around the trailer, bonded like the polar bear and cubs he enjoyed at the zoo with his daughter. Although he had asked around at work and in the trailer park, no one was in the market for a new dog, let alone three of them. The general consensus was for him to

144

take them to the pound or local shelter where someone would adopt them. Fat chance of that, he thought, after checking on the statistics. Why, the euthanasia rate hovered around ninety percent.

One by one, Bobby put the three dogs in the back of his truck. He headed west and then north over the three mile bridge. Within fifteen minutes, he pulled into a parking lot in a community complex with a sports building, outdoor swimming pool, and a large fenced-in dog park.

———

Whiskey enjoyed the balmy breeze whizzing past him in the open back of Bobby's vehicle on the way to the community complex. He loved the routine of Misty coming and going but, this time when she left them, it seemed different. Sometimes he wished he could go with her and be with Bobby at the same time.

Whiskey's brother and sister stayed alert within a paw's reach. Simultaneously, they stretched their necks into the air and wiggled their noses full of the salt air as they crossed the bay. Cream let out a little sneeze then buried her muzzle under her front paw. Whiskey crawled closer to her and licked her forehead.

When Bobby's vehicle stopped they heard voices calling out names and the discord of several barking dogs. Bud and Whiskey extended themselves onto the back wheel inside rim and saw more dogs together than they'd ever seen. Some ran and fetched with their humans close by, others ran after each other or sniffed at trees, and another drank from a bowl where water dripped from a faucet. There were giant dogs and little ones with short hair; it appeared to be a place for dogs to play. Whiskey and Bud's tails whipped faster. They slipped off their perch and Cream quickly took Whiskey's spot.

"Who's coming?" Bobby asked after getting out of the front end. He slipped his keys into his pocket and grabbed Cream, the closest dog.

As Bobby turned without getting the other dogs, Cream's eyes locked onto Whiskey's and held. The distance between her and her brother lengthened until Whisky no longer saw the alarm on her face.

Twice Whiskey and Bud poked to the top of the bed from their perch and looked past the chain-link fence. Bobby sat on a park bench and Cream tolerated a nosy Cocker Spaniel sniffing at her tail. Several couples and dogs left the area, car doors slammed, and the park thinned down to fewer than a dozen people. When Whiskey checked again, Cream stood by a friendly Labrador retriever and a teenager and, strangely enough, Bobby had pulled his rarely worn baseball cap low on his forehead and was latching the gate behind him. He quickly jumped into the driver's seat and started the engine.

Whiskey's heart panged as Bobby backed up and left the park. He barked as loud as he could over the loud engine while Bud imitated his brother's example. He wanted to yell in human talk that his sister was still back there. He barked and barked until his throat gave way to hoarseness and he could only yelp in intermittent spells.

Bobby stopped again. Maybe he would turn around. Whiskey and Bud shivered with alarm for what had happened to Cream and stood flank-to-flank against each other. Their solemn-looking master again got out of the driver's seat. This time he picked up Bud, whose feet dangled against Whiskey on his parting exit. Cars stayed still and others came and went, and people went by with strange silver baskets that rolled.

Whiskey peered over the top, this time more often. Bobby stood still at the front of a huge long store but Whiskey barely saw his brother hidden in Bobby's arms. When no people were around the entrance, Bobby stealthily put Bud on the ground, and disappeared from the dog before anyone noticed. Bobby walked down a different car aisle and was at his front door in a jiffy. With all his might, Whiskey tried to jump to the top of the bed and over. All he could see was his frightened brother glancing from right to left as the pickup truck took off again.

Whiskey didn't want anything to do with the truck ride anymore. Terrorized as to what may happen to him, he couldn't hold the contents of his bladder and peed like a running faucet. The yellow stream ran between the long floor bumps and towards the back door. Helpless, he held his position against the front end.

This time Bobby drove over two bridges and, after a while, he slowed and threw coins into a pocket in some kind of lane. In a few minutes Bobby stopped again by a building that smelled like the barbecue chicken he made at home. The people walking around here wore less clothing and their skin was darker than Whiskey's. They laughed quite a bit and even bumped into each other when they walked.

As Whiskey tried to make sense of where he was, Bobby grabbed him and swiftly carried him to the back of the lot. An oversized canister stood on sandy-colored sugar. Lots of it. Bobby put him down and trotted away. Whiskey followed him, but not fast enough, and Bobby went into the restaurant. The inexperienced dog didn't like the two cars which rolled by while he waited outside the door. They could have hit him, so he trotted to the end of the building but stayed near the front of a parked car. Over at the next business, bright lights glared down on people hitting a small ball on green material, sometimes into holes. The people laughed and patted each other and walked away after their small swings.

It seemed like an eternity that Whiskey waited. He watched two small children like Misty play with the little white balls. They saw him through the fence and one of them approached but their Mother yelled after them. Later, two men and two women talked at length in one spot and a lady in a white and black uniform asked them to resume their play and move to the next hole.

Although Whiskey never saw Bobby come out of the restaurant, the next time he looked at the spot for Bobby's pickup truck, the vehicle was gone.

––––––

Before full darkness set in, the sky turned a pinkish blue, which is what the beach heavens often did to herald its unique glory to the island locals, or visiting tourists, or mainlanders drinking beer and Margaritas. Whiskey, however, didn't care anything about a gorgeous sunset as he shied away from the rowdy, tipsy customers leaving the Wings Restaurant and pulling out of their tight slanted parking slots. He cowered to the back side of the monstrous green dumpster where more fire ant mounds existed than around his trailer home. Behind the tank of garbage, hidden paper wrappers, beer cans, cigarette butts, and various other tossed items poked out of the sand or lay on top waiting for people to dispose of them properly.

What was he to do? Bobby wouldn't be coming back for him; he sensed that as sure as he'd witnessed the dumping of his brother and sister. He backed up too far and experienced prickly cactus plants against the chain link fence, a barrier he knew about from earlier in the evening. He heard the friendly banter of people on the miniature golf course next door and cowered between two small Sego palms.

"You can't hit worth shit," he heard a young man say. The man's daytime sunglasses were perched on his head and his arm muscles were hard like rocks. He leaned over and picked up a little white ball and brought it over to a top-heavy woman with tight shorts. She pressed against him and said something, and then they moved on.

A man with two women showed up next. The younger woman with trim legs and big brown eyes put her ball down and putted. She contemplated her shot while she pulled her hair behind her right ear.

"Way to go, Tonya," said her father, his accent unlike others and his voice soothing. His wife stood next to him and for a few seconds he massaged the middle of her back.

"This isn't fair," said Karen Puno. "You are far too superior to be playing with us mere mortals. I didn't know excellent basketball skills could somehow weasel their way into a family miniature golf outing."

"Mom, you won't have me around next fall when I start college, so enjoy my talents while you can." Tonya said it halfheartedly. Jesting about leaving her parents to go to Butler University up north wasn't exactly a pleasant subject. She placed her left hand on her hip while her mother dropped a ball at the flat top of the hole with the pirate treasure house. Her father, Rick, paid close attention to his wife.

Whiskey watched Tonya walk away from her parents down an incline where she stopped before a sign, 'The Pirate's Chamber.' She took her eyes off the ball and spotted Whiskey.

The puppy relaxed his muscles and stood up. He pushed his nose between the chain links and wagged his tail. He had to know if this human would acknowledge him and his situation, or make things right, or at least the way they were. Somehow, this girl seemed like the one he needed to tell.

"Why, hello little boy," the girl said. She took three steps in her flip-flops and crouched down. She peered underneath him and nodded her head. "Boy is correct, although you sure are pretty. What's your name?"

Whiskey is what he wanted to say if he could talk like her. But he jostled his body back and forth instead and swiped her hand with his tongue as best he could through the silver mesh.

Karen Puno finished her shot. Her daughter was nose to nose with a dog on the far right side so she carried her club with her as Rick began his turn. "Tonya, you know you shouldn't be messing with a stray."

Whiskey's stark whiteness stood out in the dim artificial light by the bulky dumpster. He excitedly plunged at Tonya, his paws dancing in the air and making contact with the fence.

"Woe, boy," Tonya exclaimed.

Whiskey finished his greeting and panted from the humid island air. Tiredness was setting in, as well as thirst. He gave a scarce wag of his tail when the man followed in his family's footsteps.

"Hmm," Rick mused. "Not a safe place for a dog. Does he have a collar?"

"No, Dad. And we can't just leave him here."

For Karen, it was love at first sight, but she held her tongue. "Except for those brownish areas," she said, "he's as white as paper. But the killer is that he has a little face like a seal." She shook her head. "Somebody's going to be missing him."

"Come on ladies," Rick said. "Perhaps his owner is close by." As they returned to Tonya's next play, Rick had the liberty to peer back over his shoulder and watch the dog curl up under the green palm.

———

After Tonya, Karen and Rick left the adjoining lot, Whiskey licked between the webs of his front paw. He had been repeatedly stung by the miniature crawling beasts. What was he going to do? Fatigue gripped him like a python and he went to sleep dreaming of a car crushing his brother Bud in the parking lot with all the shopping carts. And in the morning, his legs twitched him awake after a dream about Cream. The last person to leave the dog park brought her home in their car, where the family let her live in their garage with a fluffy dog bed. He dreamed she was free to go and come when the family was home and left the side garage door open.

———

Whiskey's next day in the core area of Pensacola Beach rattled his nerves. No one put a bowl of Dog Chow in front of him like Bobby or Misty and no four-legged creature romped and enticed him like Cream or Bud. At least around some strewn trash, he found a half pack of peanut butter crackers and he ate a clump of old chicken wings with splintery bones. As tasty as gourmet delicacies, they satisfied his morning hunger, so he went in quest of water, toward the sound of crashing waves.

On the beach, the late morning sand felt cool to the padding on his paws and he chased little birds that ran faster than him. He darted back and forth with the enticing water that wanted to play with him and stopped and play-bowed with an armored creature making holes. It snapped it claws at him when he got too close. He ran up to two women sitting on blankets with two children like Misty but the women screamed about sand and shooed him away. One little girl ran after him, got scolded, and aborted her play.

Whiskey tasted the salty water. Even though the water stretched out forever and it would be there for him whenever he wanted, it didn't appease his thirst. As two more hours ticked by, his energy was drained from the heat of the sun and the temperature of the sand.

A huge vehicle unlike any Whiskey had seen before, came sliding along the sand with a great noise. The black tires were almost as wide as a doorway and they came straight for him as he lay in a divot in the sand. His mind scrambled to flee but his body froze. Which way should he dart? Between the two huge tires was a space in the middle.

"A dog!" shouted the teen lifeguard driving the Island Patrol.

Whiskey still hesitated as the bottom of the ATV was upon him. Running either way, he would be crushed into the sand like being underneath a bulldozer pouring asphalt.

Abruptly, the homicidal piece of steel stopped. A girl with a white-creamed nose stood and looked back and forth from Whiskey to the bronzed boy next to her. "Lucky we saw him at the last minute, camouflaged like that."

"Get away," she yelled. "No dogs on the beach." She waved a yellow scarf similar to the one hanging as a flag on their truck – signifying the water safety color of the day.

Whiskey safely scurried up the sand dune to the wispy sea oats as the teens waved at him from their seats in the truck. "Shoo, shoo, shoo," yelled the girl again, "before you get scoffed up by animal patrol."

Whiskey loped his way back to the core, drank dirty water dripping off an air conditioner, and by early evening ended up back behind the dumpster.

————

"I wondered if I'd see you again."

Whiskey opened his eyes. He was too tired and thirsty to bolt. The voice and the girl were familiar. The female, wearing a mango cotton blouse and coral beads, petted him all along his back and then cupped her hands alongside his face. He pushed the length of his muzzle into her hands. His eyes longingly pleaded into hers.

Tonya's arm nudged him to get up, his face impossible to resist. "You're coming home with me," she said slowly. "It was a family decision if I found you here tonight." When she stood, she eyed Pirate Cove and the miniature golf games in progress. "We'll name you for where we found you. Not the dumpster, but for the game. Putt-Putt. What do you think, boy?" He didn't understand her slew of words but sensed a change for the better.

————

Putt-Putt sat in the front seat of Tonya's Civic sedan and ignored the half-open window. He smelled the air around him of the sweet girl beside him, her hair smelling like honeysuckle. Putt-Putt's eyes spoke. His sadness was replaced with hope.

Chapter 20

Peter left the ICU once to preop a patient for the next day and then told Joan to keep him out of any afternoon cases. Other staff doctors would need to fill in for his absence. Most anesthesiologists would not encounter a malignant hyperthermia or MH patient in their entire career and caring for Jennifer Barns was his topmost priority. He gave Dr. Liu the basic information about MH. The intense doctor's expertise, especially for possible further complications like disseminated intravascular coagulation, would be extremely helpful.

The 7 p.m. labs correlated well for the trends Peter expected, solidly confirming his diagnosis. The creatine kinase levels continued to rise, the high serum potassium began to decline, and Jennifer's urine tested positive for myoglobin. Along with active cooling and attentive staff, he managed to reduce Jennifer's core temperature and her arterial blood gases also showed improvement. Along with two more doses of dantrolene, Peter made sure Jennifer received small doses of non-MH triggering medication to keep her sedated. If Jennifer slowly awakened to chaos and a life-threatening condition, Peter thought, it could make her condition worse.

Peter finally went in search of Johnny and Mel. "I don't think they're outside right now," the secretary at the ICU desk said. "Before, they said they were going to the cafeteria."

Food. Peter remembered he ate toast with Diana hours ago but nothing since then. He headed towards the ground floor cafeteria to look for the teens and grab a meal. When he stood in the empty hot meal line, he considered calling Diana, to hear his wife's voice and tell her briefly about Jennifer and his reportable case. But she was probably knee deep with flight preparations or already en route from Louisville to Knoxville.

Peter passed on the chicken cutlets which resembled sponges saturated in old reused oil. He asked for the beef in brown gravy and bet on the mashed potatoes and mushy carrots. As he filled a plastic cup with sweet tea near the register, he glanced in the next room, spotted Johnny and Amelia at a cluttered table, and walked over.

Johnny hunched over a piece of pie and Amelia's head was propped on her hand, her elbow on the table. Her dinner plate was pushed to the side.

"May I join you?" Peter asked.

Johnny looked up, surprised by a visitor, but Amelia had seen him coming. Johnny's muscles and jaw tensed and he didn't respond.

"May I tell you about your mother and what happened today?" Peter asked. "Some of it has a bearing on the both of you." He held his tray at waist height, waiting for acknowledgment. He felt a newborn iciness from both of them.

Mel moved her dishes to make more room for Peter's tray and gestured for him to sit and continue. Peter put down his food, drank some tea, and realized he had also ignored his thirst for hours.

"Dr. Bhagat told us about our mom's condition," Johnny said coldly.

"I don't know if I'm going to repeat what he said." Peter responded. "Do you mind if I continue?" He looked at Johnny with sympathy and glanced at Mel.

Johnny shook his head. "Please tell us. Did you give our mother a drug that she wasn't supposed to receive, jeopardizing her recovery, and placing her near death's door?"

Peter narrowed his eyes. "We gave your mom a balanced general anesthetic tailored for her critical condition. Lighter doses than for most patients because of her unstable vital signs and continuous bleeding."

Peter wanted that to sink in and not overwhelm them all at once. He sprinkled a dab of salt and pepper on the mashed potatoes while Amelia turned to her brother.

"Have either of you taken any genetic classes?" Peter asked.

"I have," Mel stated.

Johnny shook his head. "I had an introduction to it in a high school biology class and I'm taking a college course next semester."

"Good. That's a start. Your mother has malignant hyperthermia. It's an autosomal dominant genetic syndrome which affects skeletal muscles. She had anesthesia before this surgery without a problem. But that's what can happen. You can get it later, years after having a previous uneventful experience with surgery and anesthesia."

Peter sliced his meat and continued holding their attention. "The gas and the muscle relaxant we routinely use in anesthesia caused an abnormality of calcium control leading to contraction and contracture of your mom's skeletal muscles, which in turn, led to a domino effect of other system problems. But it didn't start until surgery was finished. And as you know, her intraop course was difficult in and of itself."

"So Dr. Devlin, she still has this malignant event going on?" Mel asked, becoming teary eyed, alternating looking at her brother and Peter.

Peter leaned back and offered her a napkin to dab her eyes but she declined and gestured for him to continue.

"At present she's under control. There is only one definitive treatment. And we gave your mother all the appropriate doses of that unique drug."

"So you're saying there was no way to know about my mom's DNA make-up?" Johnny asked. "That she would have responded like that?"

"There was no red flag in her surgical history but, now, there is a precedence for the both of you. The both of you need to be evaluated. There are several medical centers in the US that can perform the testing."

Johnny fidgeted in his pocket for a decongestant. He gulped down the pill with his remaining soda and set the glass aside.

"We'll talk again," Peter said, "but they must take a piece of fresh thigh muscle from you for what's called a caffeine halothane contracture test."

Johnny's eyes grew wide. "Ugh," Mel whined.

"It's important and it's not as bad as it sounds."

Peter pushed the carrots around with his fork. "Before I leave tonight, I'll check on your mom again and I'll keep a close watch on her condition tomorrow. She's not out of the woods yet. And I'm sure Dr. Bhagat will update you on her liver transplant and whether there are any signs of organ rejection."

"Dr. Devlin, what about that breathing machine?" Johnny asked.

"And do you think our mom will wake up soon?" Mel asked.

"She must be stable before I recommend the breathing tube comes out. And her lungs must continue to stay clear. And Mel, if she comes out of the seriousness of this MH, I believe she'll awaken, and we'll also decrease her sedation. Okay?"

"Thanks," Johnny said, "and by the way, you have a really nice wife."

Peter's smiled. "I'll second that. She's feisty, though." He lowered his voice. "She also has a temper." Mel giggled and Johnny put down his fork. "But she's a keeper. She also keeps me on my toes."

"I doubt that," Johnny said. "You two must be really smart."

"No, Johnny, not really. Our professions required a lot of studying and training, but it was manageable. Either of you can do it, too."

"Dr. Devlin, I think I'll have to look after my mom when she gets home. I don't know if I can finish college."

"You're very devoted to her, I'm sure, but go back to college when you can."

Peter stared out the glass windows to the parked cars, the bountiful concrete, and the street motorists hurrying to their destinations. He had a fleeting desire for a change of pace, a change of scenery, a break from the intensity of anesthesia in a big hospital. Like a vacation. He shirked off the feeling. Impossible, he thought.

———

At home, Johnny and Amelia went straight to their rooms. Jennifer had only been gone a few days, Johnny thought, and yet it seemed like weeks and, in a short period of time, their routine had turned upside down. Her liver transplant was what they had all hoped for but it had created more hurdles and obstacles.

Not only did Johnny think his mother would need assistance when she came home, but keeping up with classes and studying for the near future didn't seem feasible. He may need to take a school break like he mentioned to Dr. Devlin and, hopefully, resume classes again in the spring or next fall. And on top of that, he may be a carrier of the quirky DNA that his mother must have.

Johnny stripped to his underwear and absent mindedly gathered dirty wash and bused the pile to the washing machine for the morning. He went into the bathroom, brushed his teeth, and examined this new haircut. Tonya had been a refreshing surprise in all of this - an exotic American beauty. Besides being an eye catcher, she seemed grounded and mature, unlike most of the girls her age that he knew. He had loved the attention of her hands running through his hair. Kissing her had been even better.

He thought about kissing her again, went back to his room, and picked up the scrap paper with her number and called.

"Hello?"

"Tonya, it's Johnny. Am I calling too late?"

"No. My dad and I just finished a long talk. He went downstairs to find a vending machine. It's a good time. I thought about calling you within the last few minutes."

"Are you doing okay and how did your mom's arrangements turn out?"

"I saw her at the funeral parlor before they were going to embalm her or whatever they do. But my dad and I talked about everything. My mom told him a year ago that it didn't matter to her if she was ever buried or cremated. There's a family plot in town with some space in it but since everything was so tragic, we decided instead to cremate her. We are doing it tomorrow and we'll have a little church service the day after for family."

Johnny curled up on his bed. What could he say to her without making her pain worse? "So your dad won't have her laid out in the funeral parlor? Because of her accident and the organ harvest? Is that what you mean ... because of the way she looked?"

There was a small silence and Tonya caught her breath. "Yes. We can't remember her like that."

"I'm sorry. Maybe if she had not donated her organs, this farewell would be easier."

"No. That was the best gift she could give. And it was just like her. I'll get over this now but a part of her will live on in your Mom."

Tonya turned on her side on the hotel bed and propped her head higher on a pillow.

"But Dr. Bhagat gave us terrible news today. My mother's condition is a roller coaster."

"I'm sorry."

"And I've decided not to finish my semester right now."

"I'm not completing Butler's term either. Dad needs to resume work. Next week he must go back to South America for new business. Someone has to ego to Pensacola Beach and find out about our house and what needs to be done. That leaves me."

"Jeez. Your house may not be standing."

"I guess that would make it easy." She mounted a giggle. "But I'm only kidding. That would be tragic."

Rick knocked on the door and came in. The circles under his eyes had grown. He put a soda on the dresser, walked over to Tonya, and handed her a candy bar and soda and managed a fake smile. Wrinkles crinkled at the corner of his eyes. "Johnny, can I call you back in a little while?"

"Sure. I'm not going anywhere."

———

The hotel restaurant closed at 10 p.m. Tonya took up residence on the velveteen couch in the hallway after surveying the evening menu posted outside the locked doors. It touted their specialty steaks and Greek salads which made Tonya crave more than the sandwich she ate hours ago. The area suited her better than the lobby because there was less traffic into the bar. The nearest activity was by the elevator but, by lying down with her head on a throw pillow, she was hidden by anyone getting on the elevator.

Tonya stayed glued to the phone as she and Johnny talked about school and sports and favorite books. The hour hand on the clock passed midnight and they resumed talking about their problems.

"At present, I don't think my dad can handle everything," Tonya said, "and he is probably worrying about work, too. So I haven't reminded him again about our dog."

"You have a dog?" Johnny asked.

"We do, although I left him to go to school up here.

"What's his name?"

"Putt-Putt."

"I've never heard that one before. It's cute and original."

"Thanks. We found him on the island in the main core by the putt-putt golf course."

"That's terrible he was a stray. You took home a dog you didn't know?"

"Not exactly." Tonya edged her hair tightly behind her ear. She could distinctly visualize her first encounter with the Lab-mix through the fence. "My mom and dad and I were playing miniature golf one night. I guess that was the last time we did that as a family." She paused and took a needed breath. "We saw this pretty white dog with big black eyes and a friendly disposition all by himself. We couldn't resist him but we weren't sure where he belonged or if he had an owner."

"And? You adopted him?"

"No, not then. When I stopped at the restaurant the next night, where he had huddled in the shadows, I saw him again. There was no way I was going to let him stay an unwanted, homeless dog groveling for where his next scraps would come from."

Johnny heard the compassion in her voice. He visualized her lounging comfortably as she spoke to him, and he pictured her fine details, even the strings tied on her sweatpants across her textured, slim stomach. What a sensation it would be to touch and kiss the middle of her.

"What do you think?" she asked. "I guess I sound crazy."

"No," Johnny said. "Your parents just let you keep him?"

"They are suckers for a lost soul. My mom was so cool about it. And the dog, well, the reason I mention all this is because he was in the accident. We don't know what's happened to him."

"If he survived the crash, I hate to say this, but then he was at the mercy of a major hurricane and debris flying everywhere."

Tonya hated to admit it to herself, but Johnny was right. The odds were stacked against the little dog. "However," she said, "despite all the possible pessimism a human mind can think of, sometimes the reality of life can surprise us and give us different outcomes that we expect."

"I hope you're right." Johnny said. "For my mom and your Putt-Putt."

Tonya fiddled with the draw strings on her pants and decided to change the subject. "So, now that you've had time to live with it, how do you like your new hair cut?"

"I like it. The beautician, however, was the best part."

Tonya's cheeks blushed as she sat up. "Flattery will get you everywhere."

"Really. Then I hope we can link up again soon. Especially since school isn't on the agenda right now for either of us."

"Perhaps we can help each other out."

"My mom would probably love to meet you and know about your mother's contribution."

"If I can help with her recovery, I will. And maybe …?"

Johnny rolled flat and didn't mind waiting for anything she had to say. "Yes?"

"Do you know the steps people need to take if they have damaged property from a hurricane?"

"I don't have a clue. If my mom makes it, let's bridge your problem together."

Chapter 21

Gulf Breeze police officer Kent Milton leaned his thick-muscled frame over the substation counter and took the ripped note paper from a woman on the other side. He glanced at the traffic accident report number and her name and hobbled to the cabinet to searched under 'J's' for the paperwork filed that morning by the on-site officer.

"My insurance company wants it," the lady driver said. "Did it get wrote up yet?"

"Yes," Kent said. "I found it." He carefully walked the three steps over, disgusted at obeying his leg when he should be ordering his body. He handed her the information from the incident the day before when she had veered away from hurricane debris only to dent a man's sports car.

"Do you think you could fax it to them?" The short woman half-heartedly smiled and handed him a second piece of paper with a number.

"Only since it's easy to do with my right hand." He nodded towards his left arm in a sling due to a fractured humerus. He walked away again, dialed, and set the two pages on the machine.

"That will be two dollars."

"Just for that fax?"

"No. I threw that in. The fee is for the processing of your accident report."

"Oh." She rummaged in her purse for change and left briskly with another reminder of how complicated life was after Hurricane Ivan.

———

After processing a never ending stream of requests, Kent went to the back room for his brown-bagged lunch while another officer handled the desk. Because of continued bottlenecks and problems with traffic along the major thoroughfare between Fort Walton Beach and Perdido Key, there were more, rather than less, driving misdemeanors. The chief of police had reassigned him from patrol duty to the clerical desk job. Besides giving Kent the physical and mental 'break,' the staff in the sheriff's office annex building needed the extra help with citations, traffic, and accident reports.

Kent Milton unzipped his black thermal bag, slipped out a peanut butter and jelly sandwich, and unscrewed a sports drink. This day felt no different than the day before, or the day before that, or as far back as the day which he sped his police car across the base of the beach bridge. He wished that speeding southbound motorist headed for the closed island never showed up on that infamous day in his life.

He vaguely remembered the captain's radio call to stay put early that morning and watch over the last vehicles heading north. Then he was supposed to drive back over the bridge and hurry any stragglers but he never made it. He did remember gassing the foot pedal in pursuit of the car ripping through their barrier, despite the fact that the beach was officially closed. The next thing that happened - he ended up smashing a northbound CRV straight into a median post. Despite the blasted wind, white caps pounding the shoreline rock, and the distant crashing waves, that thunderous motor vehicle impact and screeching of metal was a minute forever carved into his brain.

Kent played it out a hundred times a day in his thoughts. He wished he left Gulf Breeze and drove to the toll-booth side of the bridge to alarm any remaining residents to leave. Or if he went in later for work that day and not early, perhaps the captain would have dispatched him somewhere else. Since the beach evacuation order was announced overnight, the first officers in were sent to where official changes had been made.

Kent rubbed his shattered knee where bone chips had been removed. His patella slowed him down but it was the least of his worries. Initially, the ER casted his left fractured humerus but the plaster was put on too tight, causing the skin beneath it to open and blister. They took it off and now the broken bone needed to heal in a sling. His orthopedic injuries caused him to use a bench in the shower; and microwave dinners weren't the exception any more, but the rule.

Those injuries had not kept Kent in the hospital after the accident. The impact of plunging forward into his steering wheel had caused a cardiac contusion. And as the ICU staff became weary due to a worker shortage after the hurricane, and when the machine monitoring his heart was turned off, and as his sedation was discontinued, the first officer and one of his colleagues at the accident scene told him all the gruesome details. What happened and to whom.

Kent gulped, even when there was no sandwich left to be washed down with his drink. A woman was dead because of him; a beach resident and a wife and a mother. She had done the right thing in a timely manner: she listened to her elected officials, left the beach, and properly planned her evacuation. She had rushed towards safety with her dog; and now she was gone forever.

How did he screw up so badly? Because of someone else's ineptitude, he was sucked in by the situation and had acted as rash as the person he had tried to stop. How did he manage to do such a thing? And how come fate was so cruel to the woman named Karen Puno? For every day of his remaining life he would think of the accident he caused and mourn inside his soul for the life he had taken.

It was more than self-reproach. He lived and breathed the force work like his father and twin brother; they cajoled each other that their profession was keyed into their DNA. And in their belief system, causing a mistaken injustice was as bad as being a criminal yourself.

After Kent ate a granola bar, he wiped his hands and took out his wallet. He pulled out the clipped obituary notice on Karen Puno from the *Pensacola News Journal*. It was dog-eared already so he promised himself he'd Xerox or laminate it later. He read it for the second time that day:

Karen S. Puno

Karen passed away in a Birmingham hospital on September 19th. She was 41 years old. Although a native of Indianapolis IN, she moved to Pensacola Beach, FL two years ago. She is survived by her husband, Rick Puno, and daughter, Tonya Puno.

Funeral arrangements are being handled by Cantrell's Funeral Home in Indianapolis. Expressions of sympathy may be made to the United Network for Organ Transplants.

The fact that Karen signed her driver's license and donated her organs made Kent realize she was a caring and philanthropic person and her death weighed on him even more heavily.

Also, in his line of work, it seemed as if good people harbored the worst luck. If someone was hurt in an accident, it was not the drunk driver, but the innocent bystander. If someone was injured in a store robbery, it was the unsuspecting mother walking in the door or dutiful father buying formula for his baby. If there was a drug bust, the conscientious college student getting out of his car got jammed in the middle of the sudden gunfire on the street corner. With Karen Puno's death, his view on life in general had turned dark, pessimistic, and bad enough to not warrant getting up in the morning.

From his wallet, Kent slid out another clipping, short and to the point - the article in the *Pensacola News Journal* the day after the accident. He hated reading the whole thing but the writer's sentence made him want to grab a shovel and start unearthing dirt for his own grave:

... Gulf Breeze officer Kent Milton broadsided beach resident Karen Puno as she and her dog left the island yesterday because of evacuation orders. Mrs. Puno was transferred from a local hospital to Birmingham where she is in critical condition and Policeman Milton is being treated for various injuries in Gulf Breeze Hospital. An investigation of the accident is pending and the officer will be relieved of active patrol duty for an unspecified time.

Kent shuddered to consider. What if his father saw and read that article, or his brother whose career had taken on more prestige than his own? They knew the details of his 'event' and tried to be understanding but, nevertheless, there must be a feeling of disappointment in the family.

He had to do something. Any amends or sacrifices he could make, he had to try. He turned around, transferred the desk phone to his lap, and dialed.

"Hello," came the deep voice of his friend and colleague, Tyrone, who was the first officer at the scene of his accident with Karen Puno.

Kent could hear the backup beeps of heavy equipment in the background, the now familiar dinosaur bulldozers moving debris in Pensacola. "Tyrone, I have another question about the MVA and maybe a favor to ask."

"Kent, you know we've been through it, man."

"I know. But this is something different."

"Shoot."

"The dog. The dog in the car that escaped. Can you give me mug shot details? Anything?"

"I don't think there was much space in the back of the packed vehicle to start with. On top of it, it was heavily dented which made it worse for me to crawl on top of everything to the driver. The dog paused near the body." A pause ensued and Kent grimaced. "I'm sorry Kent, I mean the lady. Well, then we passed each other; him out and me in. He was white as snow and a medium size. Like, you know, not an eighty pounder but no twenty pounder either. His tail was thick and he was scared as hell but friendly for me to be so close to him and his owner. Oh, and his face was the sweetest thing."

"Do you know for sure it was a male?"

"No Kent. Not sure."

"Did he seem hurt?"

"Not that I could tell, or not overtly."

"Do you have any clue which direction he went?"

"My guess is west of the wreck. My car and your car and emergency vehicles were either parked or screeching their way there, so the east side got jammed up. And I doubt he would've headed up the southbound ramp towards the core of Gulf Breeze which makes it more possible he headed across toward the bay street, or even back over the bridge." Tyrone stopped at a red light. He wondered about his friend's glum disposition since that day. "What are you thinking?"

"I did enough damage. If this dog is roaming around out there, it's the least I can do to find him, take him in, or reunite him with the rest of his family. After all, I killed his owner."

164

"Listen Kent, you've got to stop being so hard on yourself. Now, what's the favor?"

"I'm making a short list. Can we check on a few vets and a shelter in Pensacola before you drop me home after work?"

"Yeah. You got it buddy. See you around three-thirty."

———

Kent handed his crutches to Tyrone to wiggle into the back seat. The two wooden sticks were necessary items he needed when bridging more than a few steps.

"So where we going?" Tyrone asked.

"I already crossed off the nearest veterinarian's office. As I understand it, many of the vets have cages where they board a few dogs. So that's another reason, besides medical care, that one of them may have him."

"So why's the first one eliminated?"

"It's on the island. I tracked the doctor down earlier." Kent nodded for Tyrone to make a left. "The place is destroyed. Poor woman. She finished vet school a year ago and was getting her practice established."

Tyrone glanced out the window. News like that was commonplace among post-hurricane stories.

"We're headed to the Gulf Coast Animal Clinic," Kent said, "and then a few miles in the other direction to the Ivory Coast's Veterinarian Hospital. Then Pensacola."

"You're buying us subs tonight."

"No problem. Buying sandwiches will be like a night on the town." Kent figured it would be a change of pace for Tyrone as well, judging by the crumpled burger bag garbage on the floor.

"I hear there's only a handful of places serving limited menus in Pensacola, anyway," Tyrone said, changing lanes due to a pile of building lumber, a shattered appliance, and an upside down wrought iron chair.

Kent nodded. In a few minutes he narrowed his eyes which were the souls to his contemplative kindness. "That's it, up here. Place doesn't look too bad."

Tyrone parked right where they braked. Two other vehicles sat in the only cleared areas functioning as parking spots. "I'm coming around so you don't kill yourself."

"Then you're going to have to do a lot of that."

Tyrone slammed his door while Kent hastily opened his. "Shut that kind of talk up Kent." He shoved the crutches at him and monitored his buddy getting out.

As soon as they opened the office door, they met large-breed dog food bags piled in the middle of the floor. "Sorry," Ruth said from behind a folding table which served as the front counter. ""What can I do for you?"

"We're two Gulf Breeze policemen off duty," Kent ventured. "May I talk to the vet?"

"Sure. I'll get her."

Another female vet, Kent thought. He wondered how females carried great big dogs after sedation. But he was old-fashioned to think that way, he knew, and probably the reason he hadn't married. Women were too emancipated for him.

"You can step back," Ruth said, after ducking away for a minute. She tried to set a calico cat into a carrier, but the animal set its front paws on the door in defiance. She finally tucked its paws together and slid him in. She seized the opportunity to grab her cigarettes and go outside.

Kent and Tyrone passed her and, inside, Susan Ricker had a poodle mix on the table with her fingers sliding along his gums, examining its teeth.

"What did I do?" she asked. "I paid my one and only speeding ticket years ago." Susan threw in the jab; it felt good, no one told jokes these days.

"We thought we saw you on this month's most-wanted list," Tyrone shot back.

"Oh." Susan took her hands out of the dog's mouth. "Hah. Take me away. Life would be a lot easier right now in a cell."

Tyrone chuckled as she scrutinized the both of them.

"What did you do?" Susan asked, staring at Kent's arm and leg.

"Hurricane related," Kent mustered up. "It's nothing."

Susan grinned at him and scratched her patient's head.

"I'm searching for a dog," he said. "I thought I would start here. It escaped from an accident scene right before the hurricane made landfall. White, medium sized."

Susan puckered her lips before she spoke. "Strikingly white with two sandy spots almost up top? Probably a Lab mix?"

"Could be," Tyrone said.

"A man brought that one in. It wasn't his. The dog ventured onto his property here in Gulf Breeze. He didn't want him, but needed him fixed up." Susan paused, figuring out the timing. "And yes, it was when we were boarding up the place. The hurricane was imminent."

"How hurt?"

"Lucky fella if he scrambled out of an accident. But that would make sense; he only had an open gash in his back hip. I cleaned it and sewed him up."

Kent looked at Tyrone. "Sounds like him."

"I'd bet on it, Kent."

"Where'd he go?" Kent asked.

"I had more than my share of lost dogs. The Humane Society came in and picked up all the homeless strays. They took them up north. You can search the web where the volunteers posted photos and descriptions to help owners find their pets."

Kent glanced at the floor; another disappointment.

"I'm sorry," she said. "Was he yours?"

"No," Kent said. "But I wish he were now."

Chapter 22

Cool, dry air filtered into Peter and Diana's bedroom from the open windows, pushing out old September air like someone shoving away too much food. The room smelled fresh as Peter glanced over Diana's shoulder.

Although the numbers on the bedside clock illuminated 4:14 a.m., Peter stretched with renewed vigor. Whenever he could, he went to bed early at night with a nonfiction book or something related to medicine. Last night, he retired after cranking the windows out and bringing the latest *American Society of Anesthesiologist's Newsletter* into bed. He read as far as the pro and con letters to the editor regarding an article in the last month's edition.

The best possible evening scenario going to bed, however, involved Diana. If she wasn't flying or bunked down in another city, they sought their queen bed together where they basked in intelligent or frivolous conversation, or listened to each other's opinions on whatever current news blasted the headlines.

He did not hear her come home before midnight because she padded across the bedroom rug without even stirring Silver. Peter gave the coverlet over her shoulders a tender pat, wondering if he should get up, make coffee, and finish his *Newsletter* in another room. If he didn't wake her, she could sleep a few more hours.

Peter's foot felt a soft lump at the edge of the bed as he stirred. He propped himself on an elbow to see Silver, her head bobbing left to right eyeing the doorway, as if contemplating making another nocturnal sweep of the house. Instead of darting away, a lengthy meow came from her miniature mouth.

"Doctor, you shouldn't be awake." Diana rolled flat in the shadowy bedroom, her voice with a hint of mischief, and a tone laden with content.

"Nor should a slinky pilot who is earthbound and capable of stirring her lecherous husband."

Diana pulled her hand out of the covers and placed a fingertip on his face in the smiling dimple. "Capable of sensual arousal, but not lecherous."

"I'm skilled in granting your every wish before going to work," he whispered. Peter slid the sheet and covers off her lightly clad body, pulled her close, and moved his hand along her back. His fingers inched further while he deliberately kissed the top, then the bottom of her lips.

———

"Will you have any energy left to give anesthesia today?" Diana murmured after they finished and she closed her eyes.

"Plenty. There's nothing like good sex before getting up in the morning," he said, swinging his feet to the side of the bed. "And I'll be smiling, thinking of you all day."

"Your compliment is noted," she said. "And by the way, what's the update on Jennifer Barns and her loathsome surgeon?"

"You don't mince words. I'm glad I'm your husband and not your foe."

"With some couples, that relationship is one and the same."

Peter reached over and snapped off the alarm clock. "The malignant hyperthermia is behind her and although Dr. Bhagat didn't like it, I managed her course as peripherally as I could after that first big day. He may have been nervous about her condition because days later he wanted me to make the decision when to extubate her."

"So he finally did what was right for the patient?"

"Yes, lucky for Jennifer Barns, but I was worried how she would do without the ventilator. But listen to this. Yesterday the hospital staff president, Dr. Hamm, paged me. I go to his office where he's definitely perturbed. He called me in to chastise me for treating Dr. Bhagat's patient when I was no longer a consultant on the case and he also said that other doctors were as capable of extubating their patients as anesthesiologists."

"Wow. After Bhagat asked you to do it?"

"Precisely. He asked me to see about pulling her breathing tube out while I was going into an OR case and he didn't put it in writing on the chart. It seemed to me that he planned the whole scenario."

Diana sat up and slipped on the cotton tank top she wore to bed. "What a rat."

"My involvement with the family is not over; I told Mrs. Barns's kids they need MH biopsies."

"That Johnny and Amelia are going through a lot. Nice kids," she said. "Don't hesitate to ask them if they need any kind of help. We're short on philanthropy these days."

Peter shook his head at her and got up. "No. You're always helping out. And your energy is like a cell phone that doesn't need charging."

"I feel like I live here, Johnny," Amelia said, opening her fingers and letting the movie star magazine drop on the table. She slumped into a chair as Jennifer's nurse bobbed past the plastic plants and poked around the corner. Johnny's thin legs jolted him up and he bridged the distance to Cynthia.

"My sister's going to be dropping her sleeping bag here," Johnny said, "if our mom doesn't leave the ICU soon." He felt the same way and wished he could sleep inside Jennifer's room. If only hospitals would allow over-night visitors next to their loved ones in the ICU.

"You can both sneak in a little early. Overnight, they gave her no pain medicine or sedation." She turned and waved for them to follow.

Johnny turned to Mel, who stood next to him in a flash. They followed Cynthia but when the unit doors opened, Johnny's long stride overtook her and he entered his mother's familiar room and nestled on the left side of her mattress. Noticing no tubes or wires on Jennifer's right side, Amelia also perched herself alongside her mother.

Johnny took a swift glance at the room. Over the last few days, it had been decluttered. The ventilator and its associated tubing was gone and only one infusion pump remained. The counter space resembled a normal room with liquid soap, tissues, and nursing papers.

———

"Mom, we're here," Johnny said. "Just like yesterday, the day before that, and almost two weeks ago when you first arrived at the hospital." Johnny inhaled the medicinal smells of the ICU, his nose less blocked than normal. He swiped his hand over Jennifer's upper arm and contemplated how may skin colors she had worn: from a myriad of yellows because of her liver failure, to almost blue during the height of her resuscitation, ashen, and now almost a normal white with bruising from IV sticks.

"Your faithful kids are here coaching you to recovery," Mel said softly.

Quietly the teens listened to the conversations outside; the banter about patients and the telephone calls regarding doctors' orders. Jennifer stirred then stilled. Mel smoothed the knit blanket; her Mother thinner underneath than Mel could ever remember. Johnny's thoughts wandered to Tonya, their late night calls now a routine. Never before was he able to talk so freely and share so many feelings with anyone. Despite the obstacles in their lives, a sincere friendship and attraction had grown between them.

"Now, don't you see? That wasn't so bad."

Johnny startled from his thoughts. "What wasn't so bad?" he asked Mel.

Mel's pupils dilated in response because she hadn't said anything.

"Getting a new liver," Jennifer mumbled.

"Mom!" Johnny and Amelia both exclaimed. They leaned forward but Johnny let his sister caress Jennifer first and then he kissed her cheek.

"How long have the two of you been sitting here?" Jennifer asked. She licked her dry lips and her words formed slower than she liked.

"That makes no difference at all," Johnny said. "We would sit here for a year if needed."

"No. Both of you have lives to live, too."

"Don't worry," Amelia said. "We've only been here a few minutes. Today, that is."

Jennifer attempted a small smile. This was the most awake she had been and it warmed her heart to find them so close.

"So tell me what you know. They told me before but events have been a blur. What's the verdict on my surgery? And how have the two of you managed without me? And what day is it?" Jennifer paused between each question and Johnny and Amelia gave her plenty of time. "Do either of you know the answers?"

"We're so happy you're finally talking to us," Johnny said. "What a present!"

"Mom, a sport's architect built a roller skating pathway along the floor inside the house." Mel shot Johnny a mischievous glance.

Jennifer managed a tiny chuckle.

"And a builder reworked our previous garage into a basketball court," Johnny added.

"Now don't make me laugh," Jennifer said. "My side hurts."

"Sorry, Mom," Johnny said. "And we'll all tell you more about your transplant later."

Jennifer groped for their hands and wrapped her fingers around theirs as her emotion swelled. "I'm so glad you are both here and I love you both."

———

Busy carrying out Jennifer's routine care, Cynthia came and went during the next hour. She handed Johnny a cup of ice for Jennifer to suck on and she gave Mel a moist wash cloth to rub her mother's face or arms before she gave her a sponge bath.

Johnny and Amelia hesitated to tell Jennifer too much about her surgery or postop complications and noticed that Cynthia informed Jennifer of only minor events. "Dr. Bhagat will be here shortly on his rounds," she said.

"It's a miracle someone donated their liver which matched mine, when they did," Jennifer finally stumbled.

"Actually," Johnny ventured, "Mel and I met the donor's family."

Jennifer's expression perked up. "Did you give them a huge thank you from me?" She stopped after a realization sank in. "But their grief must be tremendous. Who was the donor?"

"A woman about your age," Johnny said. "She lived in Florida. That gigantic hurricane was on its way and she had a car accident."

Jennifer contemplated this in silence. Images formed in her mind of a car crash and perhaps a tormented spouse and children who survived. Her expression changed and Johnny realized he'd told her enough for the time being.

"Good morning, Mrs. Barns." Sukhdev stepped into the room with Cynthia at his heels. Johnny and Amelia slid off the bed and took a step back, giving the surgeon adequate space next to their mother.

"Your transplant was difficult but I buried myself in my work and it paid off," Sukhdev said.

Jennifer glowed and waved for him to come closer. "I trusted you. I don't know how to repay you or thank you enough."

"It's my specialty to save people's lives," he said triumphantly.

"It was my time. And you saved mine."

"Now everything is up to your body," he said, "which is now in charge. It can still decide to reject this liver, something out of my control."

Jennifer's sinewy, stark white hand clutched the sheet as if it would help pull her up to a sitting position, but she lacked the strength and tossed away the idea.

Sukhdev took the chart from Cynthia and scribbled notes and orders with a sleek silver pen from his breast pocket.

"Are you in much pain?" Cynthia asked. "And if Dr. Bhagat orders a liquid diet for today, do you think you can handle that?"

"My right side is uncomfortable but, no, I'm not hurting very much. I would like to try that."

Sukhdev placed the chart on the counter and turned to leave. "I'll stop by later this afternoon," he said. "We'll try to move you out of the ICU as soon as possible."

"Doctor Bhagat," Johnny called. "Are you going to tell my mom a little about the reaction she had?"

Sukhdev stopped at the doorway and glanced over his shoulder. "An anesthesiologist wants you to get a muscle biopsy to confirm some genetic code problem. His anesthesia was your life threatening crisis, not my surgery." With that, he stepped away glancing at his buffed shoes.

———

Jim slid Sandy's leash off the door handle. The morning routine of waking, walking, and eating breakfast had taken hold of Jim, Janet and the dog as if it were a way of life for decades.

"Come on Sandy," Jim said. Putt-Putt's new name had attached to him like rubber cement and he popped out from under the table in a hurry.

"I'll be here when you come back," Janet said as she sliced a halved banana over a small bowl of raisin bran. She spied Sandy's black nose in the crook of her elbow.

"Not a day goes by that he doesn't try to make you come along," Jim said, slapping his baseball cap on. "He's sure attached to you."

"Us," she corrected her husband, and smiled.

Jim clipped Sandy to his leash which he did as a preventive measure to guide him away from lingering debris which could cut his paws. They stepped out into the rising sunlight.

"She rarely smiled before you came," Jim commented to his canine friend. "You chase away her worrying about her medical problems."

Sandy trotted smoothly alongside Jim and peeked up with wonder in his eyes. What had Jim said, anyway? He peed on the feathery leaves of a crooked sego palm while Jim waited and evaluated their street. Progress had been made days before when two large trucks weaved through and workers took the biggest and most accessible garbage. Half the homes wore blue tarps and half the mature trees had seen their demise.

Jim waved at a neighbor standing by the crushed front end of his vehicle with his morning coffee and then he gave Sandy a gentle pull. Together they walked along areas of broken asphalt. Jim enjoyed the companionship and the new morning routine. He silently thanked their new pet for his morning walks and daily inspection of the neighborhood.

A lanky man wielded a chain saw and revved it up as Jim and Sandy passed. Jim gave a short wave as Sandy switched sides trying to avoid the racket. When they turned around and approached the back door at home, Jim unleashed the dog and Sandy scurried up the steps. The dog waited for Jim to let him in while his tail circled like a wind turbine.

"I know. I know. She's warming your treat." Jim opened the door not fast enough for his friend. "We're back," he announced.

"I made you some toast," Janet said. She placed Jim's plate on the table and then put two leftover pieces of bacon from the day before in the microwave. When it warmed, she tore them apart and mixed them into Sandy's dry dog food. The dog sat obediently in front of her, politely waiting as she put the bowl on the tile.

"Just for you," she said. Sandy thanked her with his eyes, his tail, and by being obedient, and then he ate the breakfast with several gulps. Janet went back to her arm chair near the living room door to sit and watch them both - a respite before washing the morning dishes.

Chapter 23

A drizzle fell from the cloudy sky while the intermittent windshield wipers swiped the front window. Tonya turned away from the departure lane and headed towards the Indianapolis International Airport parking lot.

"I wanted you to just drop me off," Rick said, adamantly shaking his head at his daughter.

The lighter than normal midmorning traffic allowed them time to spare. "Dad, you wouldn't park curbside and let me out if I were catching a plane. I don't know why parents think they should take a back seat to their children's proper behavior when it comes to them." She slowed and took the parking ticket which spat out of the machine. After circling several aisles, Rick pointed out an open space and Tonya parked.

Rick checked in, his luggage marked for Lima, Peru and connecting in Miami. After his sabbatical from work, Southern Telecommunications begged him to resume his consulting. His professional skills and knowledge of the technology, his influence, firm footing with locals, and fluent Spanish, made him their most valuable representative. His employer did not send one in his place during his absence.

But it was not only Southern Telecommunications which wanted him back on the job. Besides Tonya, Rick needed the day-by-day challenge of his business life to motivate him again. He knew it better than anyone but, he also knew that on past trips, he loved calling Karen and returning home to her. This would be the first time neither would occur and he must get that void over with. The only woman he had loved was no longer here. Still a difficult reality to grasp. The hole in his chest was like an empty pillow case which he needed to fill with artificial stuffing.

Tonya and Rick walked away from the counter and planted themselves at a coffee shop outside security. "Medium black coffee," Rick said to an employee behind the counter and Tonya ordered a cappuccino.

When they sat at a tall round table, Rick took the lid off his cup and stared blankly at the steamy coffee. "I know you'll need help down there once residents are allowed back on the island. But don't worry, your mom and I had everything stocked for such an event." He looked up, gloom written all over his face. "If the house is still standing."

"Dad, be optimistic, okay?"

"Yes, it's best to plan for the worst and hope for the best."

"And we've done a lot. I logged FEMA's information and all the insurance companies we contacted into one folder. And I checked again last night. Besides the normal leaseholder's pass to cross the bridge after a disaster, the National Guard is going to have a check point before anyone can go down Fort Pickens Road. They are expected to do that any day." Tonya sipped, mostly the foam from the top of her drink while a growing stream of business people formed a line at the counter.

"The beach has been unoccupied for quite some time," Rick said. "There must be other issues I haven't thought about. Like pilferage. I'm concerned. Maybe I shouldn't let you initially tackle this yourself."

Tonya tweaked strands of hair and paused her fingers behind her ear as if in thought. "Dad, as you said, you can't not work. Think of the huge repair costs if we have a lot of damage." She realized she hadn't used that incentive with him before, an angle which would work with her father. "Besides, Johnny offered to come with me if his mother continues to make progress. He's out of school like me."

"You mentioned that but that's a lot to ask of him."

"He volunteered. And geographically, he's led a more sheltered life. In some ways it would be an experience for him."

"It's going to be an ordeal for you, too. We've never been involved in a natural disaster." Rick dropped the contents of one sugar packet in and stirred. "You two must be talking a lot. Are you sure you are both compatible enough to take a trip and perhaps do some manual labor together?"

Tonya's brown eyes glimmered like fine amber. "Not to worry, Dad."

They finished and headed to the security checkpoint line. Rick embraced his daughter and kissed her on the cheek.

"I love you," she said. "Don't worry about a thing."

"I love you too. And don't forget," he added, picking his briefcase back up from the floor, "under the proper conditions, spread your mom's ashes and try to find Putt-Putt."

"I will, Dad. I will."

Rick and Tonya fought back displaying any tears. The only thing left to do was to divert their pain – her with Pensacola Beach and him with South America.

———

Although Tonya had talked with her counselor and had officially resigned from the semester's course work, she had not gone back to the dorm to remove her things. In the interim since being in the initial hotel with her father, Tonya and Rick had stayed in a short-term furnished apartment while they worked on the estate legal matters and contacts regarding the beach house.

Tonya knocked on her previous dorm room. She slid her key into the doorknob and swung open the door. Her spirits drooped upon entering, yearning for the short college life she experienced before her mother died. She wanted to read from bulky textbooks at her desk and smell the stale odor of college laundry. She wanted to stay up late on the simple bed and hear student conversations as they passed on the path below.

She jimmied her backpack off her shoulder and unzipped her brown hoodie. She placed desk supplies into the outside pockets of the backpack and loaded the biggest compartments with underwear and shorts and pictures. The last framed photograph she wrapped carefully in a Butler sweatshirt; Karen, Rick and her standing in front of the gulf, their bare arms around each other's shoulders, smiling profusely. The flat horizon and aqua-blue water sparkled behind them. Little did they know the perfection of that moment, Tonya thought. The foamy shoreline and the sand around them seemed like a mirage, especially since the present Indiana day reeked of dreary dampness.

———

The OR door swung shut behind Peter. He washed his hands and watched through the window as the surgeon made a small navel incision in the patient and inserted the laparoscope. Another gallbladder coming out, Peter thought. The nurse anesthetist faced Peter and nodded - patient doing fine.

The pager clipped to Peter's scrubs rang abruptly so he headed to a phone in the doctor's lounge. He recognized the voice immediately.

"Peter Devlin, how are you?"

"Better than I deserve. How did you and Ginger fare the storm and to what do I owe the honor of this call?" Peter always talked candidly to Fred, a dear friend from his church who had moved south with his wife to Navarre Beach three years ago. The couple had devoted their several retirement years in Louisville to philanthropy which had made Peter feel guilty for not getting involved with causes. Yet how could he? What Fred and his wife always needed from others was a commitment of time which Peter lacked. If helpful souls volunteered to work with them, then the silver-haired, spry couple could delegate tasks faster than Peter could rush to a code.

"We're fine and our brick home fared well, except for the garage which is being worked on. Life's a mess down here. The little things in life that you normally take for granted are now what you look forward to."

"Wish I could be of service."

"Then it will be easier to ask you. Many docs here have their own hurricane problems and are also swamped with patient care. I'm going to start a long-range endeavor of a free medical clinic but getting it started now is imperative. Being a personal friend, I thought I could rally help from you. You never leave that practice and you must have more days off owed to you than the number of toothpicks in a new box."

"I'm listening," Peter said as he nodded to a doctor muting the television volume.

"For eight months Ginger and I have been procuring the financial backing for a start-up. Almost all the money has come from a county grant, a bay group of successful entrepreneurial women, and private businesses and organizations. I have pharmaceutical representatives donating high blood pressure medicine, cholesterol and diabetes drugs, and antibiotics. Everything will be free of charge for the patient but we'll screen everyone for their eligibility ... for those most in need."

Fred continued, picking up verbal speed like a child animated with a favorite toy. "Since Ivan, there is a medical crisis. There are people here working in construction or services for post-hurricane repairs and displaced families who are out of prescription drugs who don't have previously established medical care. And there is a huge influx of Mexican workers." Fred paused then galloped forward. "A small office building became available to rent, the perfect price, size and location on Route 98. It suffered damage but it's ready now because of a trade. Three men worked on the place in exchange for free medical care once we open up. We have stocked enough basic medical supplies and one recently retired physician and a few nurses will help. To start, we'll be open for patients on Tuesdays and Thursdays late afternoon to early evening."

"Fred, it doesn't sound like you need an anesthesiologist."

"No. But you're an MD first. I'll be working on more stable recruiting but I sure could use you in the interim, as little or as much as you can do. You can stay with us at our home."

For Fred, Peter would do anything at all possible, especially after watching him for several years at church do over and above what he half expected from others. His leadership and role modeling skills headed the pack. After several more minutes of details, Peter said, "I'll see what I can do. I'll call you back with a simple yes or no."

—————

Peter made his way through the crush of jubilant new residents pouring into the lounge and down the hallway into the anesthesia office. From his briefcase, he took out his call schedule, the bible by which he lived. He glanced at the squares, date columns, and doctors listed with daily shifts and time off. His row was heavily stacked with pending vacation time.

———

Peter noted the green vitality of the bluegrass hills around the house as he pulled into the driveway. He took long deep breaths, exhaling the stress of the ORs left behind. The beauty and solitude of their home and property always made Peter thankful. The setting sun left a golden halo off the eaves and corners like a shimmering frame highlighting its subject. In the garage, he maneuvered his car next to Diana's and closed the door on the southern view.

Silver slinked across the kitchen floor towards the laundry room when Peter opened the door. She stopped and sat, not bothering to go any further. "You lazy cat," Peter said, and stooped to scratch her head. He left his things on a chair and went in the great room where Diana reclined with a stack of mail and an empty plate, her right hand nestled around a blush wine.

"How was your day?" Diana asked, her mood mellowed by a half hour of couch comfort and a glass of chardonnay.

"Fine." He pushed a tabletop book of *The Beatles* out of the way, sat on the cocktail table, and leaned over. "Mmm. Fruity," he said after giving her a kiss.

She nodded and smiled. "Here, finish mine and I'll pour some more in a moment." Silver jumped up and stretched her clawless paws. Peter nodded and took the glass. "I think all I drank today was coffee."

"Peter! At least I hope it was decaf."

"I switched mid-day," he said. "Guess who called today?"

"The lottery winner's office," Diana shrugged.

"That would make my dilemma easier. I could hand over my winnings to Fred. He's starting a free medical clinic on the Gulf Coast and needs a temporary MD right away to start seeing patients. He wants to launch the grand opening, especially since that will give him media exposure to lure in more volunteers to run the place. Eventually he wants an EKG machine and other equipment but he has so much already, including minor surgical supplies. The amazing thing is he has the initial capital and the local hospital is willing to do some free lab work and X-rays. It will all be need-based and they'll screen the patients."

"And he had all this in mind before the hurricane?"

"He did. It was in the works."

"And now God gave him a greater task. And he wants to borrow you for the time being. He even told you how you needed a break from the stress of big cases, big egos, and a big city practice." She narrowed her eyes and looked at him knowingly.

Peter marveled at Diana's perception. She wore antennae that grasped distant situations like a satellite in orbit tracking a weather pattern.

"You know I'm coming with you," she added.

––––––

Jennifer Barns read all the get-well letters and cards and the inscriptions on the flower arrangement notes that Johnny and Mel brought her from home. For almost two weeks she resided in a regular hospital room. She received phone calls from the principal, Mrs. Waverly, and teachers, students, and relatives; she spoke with Dr. Liu and Dr. Bhagat and the staff that came and went mostly on twelve hour shifts; and she had her vital signs checked and rechecked.

The blood work they took at first from her central lines and then her arm IVs became less and less. Finally, she didn't feel like a pin cushion any more. She never understood why, since her Hepatitis C was first diagnosed, so many vials of blood were needed. Why not test for everything from the blood in the single vial with the brown rubber stopper on it?

Her progress at physical therapy surprised everyone. Her slave-driver therapist with the ripped arms and bounce in his step had done more for her mind than her body. His theory, which he said was not emphasized in school, was to have the mental commitment and the unwavering resolve to make your body cooperate. Will your physical progress first, and then work your body like your life depended on it. He reinforced his mantras during every session. Jennifer's PT paled compared to other patients who underwent major orthopedic surgery. Day by day her endurance, balance, and strength crept a little further along.

She appreciated her room with a window overlooking I-65 and the busy trucks going north and south. It was no rural hospital with a manicured lawn and flower bed but the view instilled in her the desire to get back out into the busy world, better than before. And since the bed next to her had been devoid of another patient, her room had given her space and privacy when Johnny and Amelia visited. Her indispensable kids ... the real reason she wanted to put her life back together again and leave the hospital. She often doubted if she would have put herself on a transplant list if it weren't for them.

After a two hour nap, Jennifer swung her legs to the side and slipped her feet into a pair of slippers. In the bathroom, she combed her hair which had thinned since her transplant. She took a hard look in the mirror over the sink; an unknown woman stared back at her with a different pallor and sporting new gray around her temples. The hairs flitted through her hairline as if individually painted with a fine artist's brush. One more thing to get used to. She examined her smile and her lips. While she recuperated and gained strength back at home, she thought, why not start wearing some makeup like lip gloss and eye liner? What normal women did.

"Mom, glad we didn't wake you," Mel said, standing in the doorway.

"Hey, Mom," Johnny said behind his sister.

Jennifer took a step and hugged each of them.

"How are you feeling?" Johnny asked.

Jennifer motioned them into the room and sat down. "Pretty well. Good enough to continue with the discharge plans for tomorrow."

"We're so excited," Mel said. "Everything is ready for you at the house."

Johnny pinched his nose and sat across from her. Is it still okay if Mel looks after you and your appointments? And I can take off to Florida for a while?"

Jennifer reached for Johnny's hand and rubbed the top. "You must go. You must let go of caring for me. I'll be responsible for myself in the coming months, alone, as much as I can." She smiled lovingly at Mel. "Amelia will be in charge when I need the help and support."

Jennifer refrained from mentioning Tonya, the young woman whom she kept hearing about. She didn't want to butt in regarding

Johnny's relationship that had formed during her hospitalization. So far, she had nothing to fear regarding her son's judgment of people or for the family who had donated her golden gift.

Chapter 24

Peter rapped on the semi-open door to Jennifer Barns's room and entered where he said good morning to her and her children. Although he noted her loss of weight from her whole ordeal, her dark eyes had a soft glow.

"They are releasing me tomorrow," Jennifer said. "I'll see my internist and surgeon often but at least I'll be home with my daughter." The lines around her eyes twinkled as she wiggled her finger at Mel.

"Congratulations," Peter said, "and I have information for Johnny and Amelia about getting MH biopsies." Peter stepped forward and handed Johnny a brown envelope. "Wake Forest in North Carolina would probably be your best bet. Are you still out of school?"

"I am; for the semester. But Tonya Puno is driving in today and I'm going with her to Florida. She and her father have not gone back since the hurricane. All they've seen are aerial shots of the beach and pictures on the internet. They aren't sure about the damage to their house and her dad has to work."

"That's nice of you. How are you both getting there?"

"We're driving down in Tonya's car."

Peter could already hear Diana criticize him if she found out the two young adults were headed in the same direction as them and they hadn't offered to pool their resources. Jennifer waved him over to sit on her bed.

"Perhaps we can all do the trip together or combine our endeavors," Peter said, unbuttoning a lab coat button. "Where is Tonya now?"

With heightened attention, Johnny pressed forward in his chair. "She'll be here this afternoon. We're leaving tomorrow."

"Perfect. Why don't you pack your things and the two of you stay with us tonight? Diana can brainstorm this but, the way I see it, I can arrange for your biopsy the day after tomorrow in North Carolina. We can drive there and then to the coast. My wife can bring Tonya, fly that is, and we can regroup down there. Between the four of us, we'll have an airplane and one car."

After his surprised look abated, Johnny broke the silence. "But Dr. Devlin, we can't ask you to do that."

"You're not. I'm already going down there to assist with the opening of a clinic. Besides, it will be an adventure outside the OR, something I'm not familiar with these days. Having a hectic personal life is more Diana's territory. And maybe you'll need some help with the Puno's house."

"Don't you think you should ask your wife first?"

"Are you kidding? I can already visualize her assigning Tonya tasks in her plane and having you help with tonight's dinner. Are you up to it?"

Johnny looked back and forth between Jennifer and Mel. Jennifer nodded with support and Mel spoke up. "Johnny, I'll take care of Mom. Get the test and go to the Gulf Coast." She impishly added after a pause, "And you're overdue for a girlfriend."

———

Jim scrubbed his face over the sink, grabbed the hand towel, and briskly patted himself dry. When he ambled out, Janet was pulling a floral blouse up her arm while sitting on the bed. Between her two feet, Sandy nestled on the carpet looking like a regal sphinx guarding his favorite temple.

"Don't you two make a sight," Jim quipped.

Sandy popped his head up from the floor, his ears more attentive, and he followed Jim's movements towards his wife. Jim waited as Janet buttoned slowly and then gave her his hand. She wrapped her finger around his bumpy knuckles and rose with a warm smile. "I'm going to go check my sugar first and take my blood pressure. And then I'm going to fry some bacon for you guys while you're out."

Sandy wiggled side to side with glee. He advanced quickly in front of them to the kitchen, stopped, and made sure they were following. Jim reached into the kitchen drawer for his usual coffee measuring spoon. He unraveled the folded ends of a generic breakfast-blend coffee. When he set the pot to drip, Janet sat on a chair peering down at her glucose monitor, her automated blood pressure cuff draped on the table. "You okay?" Jim asked.

"I'll be alright." She put the accu-chek monitor on the wooden table and patted the furry white head in front of her. Sandy nuzzled her hand and wiped it several times with a robust pink tongue. "You are the sweetest little thing I ever met," she said softly, her eyes glowing back at him.

Jim removed the pot and cascaded some coffee into a mug. He sipped while planning what needed to be done after a dog walk and breakfast. The water which had penetrated the garage ceiling now left its grimy footprint. He thought about mixing a diluted Clorox solution into a spray container and then starting to tackle the fuzzy mold which was forming like black sod on the white paint. It was doable, he believed, or at least he'd give it a shot. Perhaps it would take him most of the day, especially if he needed to give it two washings. But each day he saw progress and the only way to think of it was one day at a time.

"I do believe coffee tastes better on some mornings," he said. " Would you like me to bring you some?"

"Sure," Janet replied. "Please put a little milk in it and set the bacon out since you're going in the fridge."

Jim stirred in whole milk the way she liked it. He placed Great Value bacon on the counter, slipped out a frying pan, and left it on the stove top. He placed Janet's cup on the table and walked away.

"All right," Jim said enthusiastically. Sandy turned his head and darted to him, brimming with energy. The dog smelled the cold bacon and now had two reasons to be excited. Jim retrieved his leash and hooked him up. "See you soon," Jim said as he opened the back door. Janet nodded once to herself.

———

Outside, although he couldn't see it, Jim heard the loud annoying backup noise of a big truck. Probably around the block, he thought. He walked down the driveway noting the solid high gray clouds. Sometimes sunshine day after day got old; plus, he accomplished more around the house when it turned to weather that northerners were used to.

Sandy pushed against his collar to sniff a cluster of pebbles then lifted his leg. The spray also hit a clump of grainy dirt where fire ants zoomed along their own established trail. "Take better aim at those stinging little bastards," Jim said.

Jim paused at the end of the driveway as two pick-up trucks passed slowly, the second one piled with construction material in the flat bed. He recognized the first driver as the popular contractor for many of the area residents. The second man's window was open and the occupant yelled out, "Handsome dog." Most of the damage on their street had occurred far down to the right, the western end of Gulf Breeze, the houses facing the water. So most mornings, it was the popular direction they all went.

Jim and Sandy restarted. "Dogs," Jim said, shaking his head. "Social lubricants. That guy wouldn't have said a word otherwise."

Three properties from Jim's house, he noted his neighbor's mail box. A new post had been planted in the ground and the glossy paint made the box shine like a new penny. A red flag hung horizontal and the house numbers were already nailed into the wooden post. Another sign of progress since their last walk was the picked-up fence pieces from a neighbor's yard, all accumulated and stacked neatly in a pile on the edge of his lawn. Sandy squatted and did his business and Jim used the small plastic bag from his pocket to pick it up; something he was conscientious about. He dropped it into a garbage bin further down on their walk.

Jim walked extra, thinking if it rained later, he would have given Sandy a better than usual walk allowing his bladder to last longer. He couldn't always figure out the dog's needs. Sandy never made demands and acted content whenever Jim did or didn't take him. They finally turned around and heard a car start and a woman's voice yell good-bye.

Approaching their house and confident the area lacked dangerous materials for Sandy's paws, Jim let him off the leash. The dog extended his front paws quickly onto Jim's jeans as if to thank him or hurry him up and trotted along the lawn edge to scrutinize for additional aromas. He ran up and down their driveway in play, hurried ahead and around the corner, and then fully shook himself on the back step. A flurry of white hair danced off his trunk.

188

Jim caught up. He ran his hand along the dog's coat pushing away the excess hair and then solidly patted his side. Sandy could hardly wait, his mouth now open, and his tongue dangling. "My goodness," Jim said, "hurry on in to see her." He opened the door. The dog also anticipated the smell of frying bacon, the imagined molecules already rolling around in his mouth.

Sandy darted in. He did a quick loop of the kitchen, his nose arching high to the untouched package on the counter. The frying pan sat where Jim had left it and there was no concentrated aroma of bacon fat or cooked long brown strips laid out on a plate.

The dog sprang over to Janet. She sat in her favorite green armchair but still did not acknowledge him. Sandy bumped his nose into her legs, pushed his head into her lap, and nudged her arm on the armrest. He repeated the process but her hand didn't reach to pat him and, oddly enough, her upper body didn't extend to kiss him on the head. Nor did she tell him what a good dog he was or ask about Jim.

Sandy edged further into her lap. Janet's lower legs were exposed from three-quarter length pants; they seemed unnatural and still. He managed to nuzzle into her breasts and attempted to reach her face and give her a wet kiss to waken her like he did most mornings. But this time was different. Why wasn't she moving and why didn't she say anything to him?

Jim stopped to take an extra bag from his pocket and hang up the leash. Another cup of coffee was what he had in mind as well as bacon and eggs but he didn't detect any cooking going on. Putting distance from the door and looking ahead, he saw Janet and Sandy. The dog whimpered and his head firmly rested on his wife's lap. Jim's eyes enlarged with concern as he hurried over. He leaned over her, saying at first, softly, "Janet?"

Placing his hand on her left shoulder, he nudged her. "Janet?" he said louder. Her head slumped slightly, her eyes were closed, and her lips parted. Jim knelt on the floor, extended his arms into her. "No. Janet, no." He kissed her dangling left hand, a cold wedding ring also brushing his lips. Her arm fell into her lap when he let go. He ran his hand along her cheek but she didn't respond. Jim's heart strings pulled and he ached all over.

Alongside him, Sandy whimpered again. Jim took a moment to wrap the little dog's face in his hands and look him straight in the eyes. "Sandy, Janet's dead. She left us when we went out together for a walk."

———

Johnny scooped up the clean laundry and carried it into his bedroom. He sorted the items and began folding, his backpack suitcase on the floor ready to hold the clothes. When he finished and zipped the largest section, he gathered toiletries from the bathroom and stuck them in the outside pockets.

As Johnny attached a better luggage tag Mel poked her head in. "Car just pulled in," she said.

Johnny got up off his knees. "I'm feeling a little guilty for leaving you and Mom," he said as they walked to the front door.

"Why? One of us has to have that biopsy. You're doing me the favor so I'm not the guinea pig."

"Yeah, right," he frowned.

Johnny wrapped his hand around the doorknob and tried to act calm. Seeing Tonya again felt a little intimidating. Talking on the phone was easy; their conversations flowed like water in a stream. In person, body language spoke for itself, and what you didn't do physically was as important as what you did do. What should he do when they came face to face outside? Should he offer her a hug or keep a distance? When he came right down to it, he was no jock and he was not good enough for her. It was their mothers' circumstances which caused them to cross paths, he thought. If anything, it will be a long-term friendship and there's nothing to be afraid of.

"Bring me back some of that sugar white sand they talk about," Mel said, "so I can dream about wiggling my toes in it someday."

"What else can I do for you?"

Johnny knew his sister was trying to divert his attention but he felt his heart pound faster as he opened the door. Tonya stepped out of her sedan and dropped her keys into a pocket. Her rosy complexion and big smile put him at ease but he took a few deep breaths nevertheless.

"Hey," she said.

"How was your drive?" Johnny asked.

"No problems. It wasn't a long drive like driving to Florida."

Johnny put his bag in her trunk, they sunk a few baskets, and said goodbye to Mel. The Ohio River shimmered as they drove across the bridge to stay with the inspiring couple who had been involved with their mothers' medical plights.

————

In the Devlin's kitchen, fat crackled and sizzled in the pan like red hot logs in a cookout pit. Diana took tongs and rotated the bratwurst then set her utensil on a saucer to the side. Johnny and Tonya perched themselves on kitchen stools and Peter placed a stack of napkins on the counter.

"You leave me little wiggle room in my own kitchen, Silver," Diana said, looking at the floor. "She didn't escape fast enough before the two of you sat down. So she's stuck in here. You know how cats avoid visitors in their own house?"

"I've never had a cat," Johnny said. "My mom avoided animals even for herself because I always had allergies." He poured the other half of a cola into his glass and smiled at Tonya. "Tonya has a dog, though. He's lost in Pensacola and we're going to try and find him."

"I hope Silver doesn't provoke you into a sneezing fit," Diana said.

Johnny grabbed a napkin, split it in two, and blew his nose. "I'll be fine," he said. A loud pop broke from the frying pan causing Silver to announce her distrust of the pan above her. She took her chances and sprinted out from behind the kitchen island.

Peter reached into the open closet door and pulled out a box of tissues. "Here you go," he said, sliding them across to Johnny.

"I'm glad I pulled these Johnsonville bratwursts out of the freezer this morning," Diana said. They make a fine back-up dinner plan." She gave the brats a spin, zipped to the cupboard, and grabbed four plates.

"For everyone's trivia knowledge, did you all know that the sausage company is located in Wisconsin? That's basically the bratwurst capital of America."

Peter narrowed his eyes. "Really? Wisconsin is also one of the hot spots for malignant hyperthermia."

"What do you mean," asked Johnny. "What's a hot spot?"

"I didn't tell you. There are three geographic clusters in the US where there are more concentrated cases of MH. Wisconsin is one of them."

"So maybe an association exists between eating bratwurst and getting MH." Diana said.

"Ha!" Tonya chuckled. "That means we can eat Johnny's share and save him from a possible episode."

"Hey," Johnny said, "whose dinner side are you on anyway? We may be knee deep in sand together soon."

"Not to mention," Peter said, "you two may need to cram a lot of college material in together before you both go back to school for a full semester."

Diana opened the refrigerator and, after a hard stare, settled on a can of beer. "The perfect thing with brats," she said. "I should have cooked them in this."

"Actually, are bratwursts some kind of hotdog?" Johnny asked. He made another pretzel disappear as Diana smiled and leaned against the counter.

"No way. It's a German sausage made by stuffing a casing with pork, beef, veal, or a mixture; and they put in pepper and caraway seeds and other spices. People make them all different ways. These happen to be the Italian sweet ones." She rolled her eyes. "Heavenly."

"I don't think my mom has ever made them," Johnny said, "but I ate one at a fair once."

Tonya cleared her throat and tugged her hair. "You can fry 'em, smoke 'em, bake 'em or grill 'em," she said methodically, imitating Forest Gump when he told his friend about cooking shrimp.

Everyone smiled. Peter took a seat and stroked his mustache. Diana turned the sausage to its last uncooked side. They waited, as if for Tonya to continue.

"Not only that," Tonya obliged, "but one of the oldest things recorded as far as cooking goes, is sausage. And bratwurst is considered one of the world's first regulated foods."

Johnny threw his tissue away and glanced at Tonya with dismay.

"No kidding," Tonya said. "Thuringian bratwurst - that's a German region, Thuringia - was made 600 years ago. And the sausage makers had to use the best and freshest meats or they could be penalized a whole day's wages or get fired."

"Making it a Middle Ages consumer-protection law?" Peter queried after relaxing his open-mouthed expression.

"Exactly. There were actually committees in German markets that were assigned to monitor the brats. Bratwurst, not bratty children," she chuckled.

Johnny sat dumbfounded, a new pretzel not finding its way into his open mouth.

Diana skidded back to her pan, turned the heat off, and stepped back. "And you know this, how?"

"I'm a history and archeology major. In my senior year of high school, I took a cooking class on the side. At the end we had to write a short paper about any meat, so I picked a combination meat and, of course, I focused on its history. Someday, though, I want to go to Germany."

"And the beer brat spread like wildfire in the US," Peter said, untwisting a tie on a bag of rolls. "The Brooklyn Dodgers introduced it to New York sports stadiums and the rest is history."

Now everyone focused on Peter. "What's your excuse?" Diana said. "You're not a history major."

"No, but you forget I was a northeasterner for college and med school. You can't avoid ball parks and you can't avoid eating or hearing about brats when you spend your afternoon in the stands."

"I haven't added much to this conversation," Johnny said, "except for now. Where's the mustard?"

Peter spun around, took a yellow bottle from the pantry, and plopped it in the middle of them. "At least you know the proper condiment. Now open the fridge and grab the potato salad."

Diana divvied out a plate to each of them like dealing a deck of cards. She looked at each one of them and patted Tonya on the shoulder. "I think," she said, "we're all going to have a grand time."

"You know," Tonya said, solemnly. "I haven't had this much fun since my mom died."

Chapter 25

Peter and Johnny took turns driving Tonya's car to Winston-Salem. The Barns's car had stayed with Mel, especially to bus Jennifer back and forth to doctor's appointments after her discharge.

Johnny had never traveled to the Southeast. As I-40 dropped south past Knoxville and towards Asheville, they entered the Great Smoky Mountains National Park area. Johnny's eyes blinked only occasionally, not wanting to miss the winding curves, steep adjacent cliffs, and fall-away slopes down mountains. Hearty cold weather adventurers in their RVs dotted the non-passable double-lined road and trucks labored on the inclines and fought from following car bumpers too close on the descending hills.

Peter clasped the wheel with overt attention and then in the middle of a sharply curved area, he pulled over to a rest stop, much smaller and closer to the road than traditional stops. They stepped out of the copper Civic sedan and left their jackets on the back seat.

"That's pretty scary," Johnny said, looking up the mountain across the road. Heavy netting draped a section of gray rock and boulders right off the warty mountain face. At the bottom, a gully ran between the road and mountain, but its width made Johnny shudder. Stray rocks were peppered in its depth.

Peter surveyed the surroundings as well. "From here on in for quite a ways, it's not uncommon to pass rock slides. Sometimes they're so bad, I-40 closes for months for road crews to clean it up. When that happens, any detour around this section of the interstate can add hours to a trip." They walked leisurely towards the restrooms inside the center.

Johnny breathed in the crisp air. His head felt incredibly clear. "Not only are we lucky the road is clear," Johnny said, "but I think these mountains agree with me."

"Fortunate for you since you'll be having anesthesia in the morning and your upper airway will be less reactive."

When they came out of the warm brick building, Peter ambled to the vending machine area and stood before the coffee selection.

"We don't do many long drives but this stuff is creamy and flavorful." He put in three quarters and pressed 'large cappuccino.' The cup spit out, as well as the steamy liquid, and he took a sip. "Besides dinner later on," Peter said, "you better enjoy whatever else along the way. Nothing to eat or drink after midnight."

Johnny grinned. "If you say so, Doc."

Peter was about to reprimand him for calling him 'Doc,' but realized Johnny was egging him on and laughed. "Here." Peter dropped a few more quarters into the machine.

"Whenever my mom would take us places in Indiana or Kentucky when I was a kid," Johnny said, "I'd check the vending machine change dispensers and the ground around them. Usually what I would find would pay for half our snacks." Holding the hot chocolate, Johnny thanked him and they headed back to the car.

"Enterprising. You know, I did the same thing."

"They had vending machines when you were growing up?"

"Ouch," Peter said.

———

Diana approached her targeted cruising altitude after a perfect and uneventful take off. She banked the Cessna a little more and aligned it for the southern straight-shot flight. Few clouds dotted the sky and avoiding them was easy. She pointed downwards for Tonya's benefit, showing her the Ohio River's path and the tall industry plants on the west side of Louisville.

"This is amazing," Tonya said, "and so different than being in a commercial jet." Below them, brackish water churned and smoke billowed from factories. "Do you mind if I ask you why you become a pilot?"

Diana kept a close eye on the monitors and positioned herself more comfortable in the blue seat. "I don't mind at all," she said with zest. "It must have been in my blood. You know, whether girls play with dolls or boys play with miniature cars, they usually play make-believe on the floor. Well, no matter what I played with, I did it aerodynamically. My stuffed animals, my plastic dolls, even my books, I would zoom them around in my hands like a crazy kid. My mother pointed it out one day to my Father and they ended up

196

encouraging my exhilarating hobby. Next time they bought me a toy, it was a model airplane kit. By the time I was ten, I had my own radio-controlled model airplane. For a long time, I was the only female at Louisville's Tom Sawyer Park where guys met to fly their planes. One summer I spearheaded the flying club."

The density of the city started to dissipate as Tonya saw more farmland popping up further south. "It must've been nice to have your career path laid out so obviously. From a hobby, too."

"Not many people work at something they love to do. But I did set my mind up to make it happen. What about your history and archeology?"

"I'll probably attend grad school because I want to teach and be out in the field."

"For excavations and research?"

Tonya beamed. "I hope."

"Do more than hope."

Tonya quieted and frowned. "But see what happened to my mom? You can't always do something just because you want to."

"Tonya, life can deal you some lemons, but squeeze them out and make lemonade. Most of the time when something unforeseen gets in your way, it's temporary. You need to look at the bigger picture. Like now. Once your family home and the situation in Florida are under control, get right back on track with school. In the whole scheme of things, one semester, or one year won't put a dent in your entire life. People who don't get ahead often use an interruption as an excuse. They don't spring back on their feet."

Tonya looked over towards Diana and further out the pilot's window where a wispy contrail faded in the distance. She squeezed her brown eyes shut as if to imprint the moment and the advice to memory. When she opened them, Diana glanced her way with a warm smile.

"Thanks, Diana."

"Not to mention it. Peter and I don't have kids but I have a philosophy about giving advice to younger people."

"Which is?"

"I know you can't tell people what to do because they're usually going to do whatever it is themselves anyway. However, when I've looked back on the mistakes I've made, I wished my parents had been a bit more forceful in sharing their opinions or trying to make me understand the consequences of my actions. So rather than keep quiet as an adult mentor to younger people, I express my thoughts."

"You're easy to believe. I can see teens listening to your advice and taking it to heart."

"Maybe. For me, I see more philanthropy in my future. Working with some kind of big sister or big brother's program." Diana chuckled. "As if I won't have enough on my plate to help my Doctor Jonas Salk-like-husband render aid to Gulf Coast residents and two kids tackle unbeknownst property damage done by a killer storm. Young adults who by the way, have quite a bit of chemistry going on between them."

Tonya pulled at her hair and her cheeks reddened. When she saw Diana glance at her, she couldn't help but nod in agreement.

———

The next morning at Wake Forest Baptist Medical Center, Johnny tried to settle comfortably on the preop stretcher, the soles of his feet extending over the ends of the cushion.

"I don't understand one thing," Johnny said. "If I'm malignant hyperthermia susceptible, how can they give me anesthesia to find out?"

Peter put his Styrofoam cup on the side table inside the surgical waiting area. "Good question. I was wondering if you'd ask me that. Your anesthesiologist, who will talk to you soon, will explain. They won't use the anesthetic agents that are responsible for triggering MH. They'll use other acceptable drugs which will anesthetize you just as well."

Johnny narrowed his eyes with skepticism. "But I won't remember anything, will I?"

"Not to worry. Here comes someone with a syringe. In a minute or two you probably won't remember anything until you come out from your biopsy."

———

As Johnny opened his eyes, he heard Peter's voice. The curtain parted and a tall woman with green scrubs and a thick waist walked in. "There he is. Your numbers are looking good and as soon as you're up to it, I brought you some ice chips."

Johnny motioned for the cup as Peter trailed in behind her.

"What time is it?" Johnny asked.

"Before noon," Peter said. "You weren't back there very long."

Johnny slid his sheet to the side and edged the flimsy gown over to peek at his leg. A white dressing covered much of his thigh. "I thought they were going to make a small incision."

"It's only four inches," said the nurse. "They must apply a bandage which exceeds the surgical site. Any pain?"

Johnny grinned. "I guess not."

"Good," she said, "'cuz I'm short on sympathy today and pain meds." She smiled and patted his shoulder.

"We're going to know your results before we leave," Peter said.

An hour later, with little assistance, Johnny dressed back into black sweatpants and a maroon overhead shirt. Peter took the discharge papers and a prescription. With Johnny in a wheelchair, they went to a sunny lounge in the corner of the hallway. Johnny thumbed through magazines, finding information about deer hunting interesting, a science unto itself. He read a full article about the population dents in deer throughout the 20th century from hemorrhagic disease caused by a virus. He hated to read the symptoms - difficulty breathing, high temperature, and swelling – but admired the researchers who spent their time investigating and trying to cure white-tailed deer. Peter made headway through two chapters of a legal thriller, grinning at the sinister corporation running the behind-the-scenes campaign for a corrupt political candidate.

One round trip to a coffee stand and two hours later, a long-coated anesthesiologist with bifocals came in. "I'm Dr. Hanes. Since no one else is in here, you two must be Johnny Barns and Dr. Devlin." He pushed his bifocals up the scanty bridge of his nose.

"We are," Peter said, and they shook the man's hand.

"This is as comfortable as anywhere, so please sit back down. How's your leg?"

Johnny patted through the cotton. "Doing well." He fiddled with his hands, anxious to hear the test results. If he was positive, it would change his medical history in a flash.

"You're lucky to have your own anesthesiologist with you," Dr. Hanes said with a smile.

"Dr. Devlin took care of my mom during her liver transplant surgery," Johnny said. "That's how we met each other."

"I see your history," Doctor Hanes said. "Yes. Then it probably won't be too much of a surprise to learn that you tested positive for MH. In other words, you are Malignant Hyperthermia susceptible." Dr. Hanes let Johnny absorb that for a few seconds.

"In the future," the doctor said, "the most important recommendation you must live with is to share this information with anesthesiologists and surgeons prior to any surgeries. We'll talk at length but this folder houses a vast amount of information and the most frequently asked questions. You'll also be registered with the MH Association of the United States and be sure to familiarize yourself with their website."

After a lengthy talk and time for personal discussion, the two physicians and Johnny said the appropriate good-byes. With less favoritism of his left leg, Johnny encouraged Peter to walk his normal pace to the car, keeping up admirably.

"I wonder how the girls are doing," Peter said as he unlocked the car.

"I bet Tonya liked the plane ride."

"Let's call when we get back to the hotel. We'll give you one evening and night of rest and I'm the driver again tomorrow. No exerting undue motion or pressure on that leg."

Johnny agreed and then joked, "I haven't known Tonya that long but unfortunately, I must tell her I have defective DNA."

––––––––

Diana and Tonya neared the density of Pensacola from a bird's point of view, their eyes surveying from right to left in unison, peering once at each other with gaping mouths. The further south they went to the bay, Gulf Breeze, and the island, the overabundance of blue-tarped roofs stared up at them. As they swung out a little to the east bay, before their direct approach to the reopened airport, Diana swooped lower. It wasn't every day she saw a major interstate cracked in half, concrete dangling into the water below, and the water like an open mouthed fish with an appetite.

"I had no idea it would still be this bad," Tonya finally mumbled.

Diana gave her a concerned look. The discrepancy between the beauty of the sky and water with man-made structures was stark, even after the elapsed time since Ivan had swept over them.

"A remarkable view," Diana ventured, shaking her head. She kept a steady course, soared straight over Scenic Highway, landed down on the airfield, and taxied over to the fixed-base operator where she rolled to a stop.

Outside, warmer air than up north blew by on a thin breeze and brushed Diana's face as she stepped on the concrete. Not just any breeze, but one in which paradise came to mind, with the lovely overture of salt water churning nearby so the salty air hit her nostrils like rose petals. Tonya felt it, too, but she had the added relief and warmth of being home, the place where she and her parents and Putt-Putt had been a family.

Across the street from the airport, after shuttling over with the car rental company, they rented a dark SUV. With Tonya at the wheel, they proceeded down 12th Avenue and underneath the railroad trestle colorfully decorated with graffiti. When they stopped for a red light, the choppy bay lay in front, and they turned left to begin crossing the three-mile bridge to Gulf Breeze.

"I could do this," Diana said. "Live near all this water."

"Then you'll be mesmerized by the aqua gulf across from where we live. She charms you and doesn't let go."

The speed limit was twenty-five miles per hour across the expansive bridge, plenty of time for Diana to glance at cars and the parallel concrete structure off to the left and think about the damage she'd already seen in Pensacola.

"That's the old fishing bridge," Tonya said, "a favorite spot for locals and tourists. I doesn't meet in the middle but it looks like there was heavy damage. There are whole chunks gone."

A couple in a green sedan cut close in front of them and accelerated. "Wow, everyone seems to be in a hurry," Diana said. "I can see it; a hurricane must help the economy. Most of these pick-up trucks and cars have company slogans on them and they're piled high with ladders, generators, and building supplies."

When they pulled onto Gulf Breeze, the traffic snarled through the main core before they reached the base of the Pensacola Beach Bridge. The bulk of palm trees dotting the roads and shopping areas were slanted in one direction after previously standing upright.

They slowed behind a group of cars where some drivers were presenting papers to police officers. Tonya foraged through her bag on the floor and pulled out her resident's pass. She turned to Diana and waved the paper. "They're issued each year. Now, only residents and business owners can go over to Pensacola Beach or workers with permission."

Tonya crept the vehicle closer and stretched her neck. "It looks as if only this side of the bridge is open. The other side is closed for repairs."

Tonya stared hard over the median. The end of the northbound bridge concrete was damaged, construction equipment was parked nearby, and men with hard hats walked back and forth.

"Oh my God," Tonya said with a quivering voice. "On the other side, my mom had her accident. I guess after the wreck, Ivan slammed through, hurling his wrath right where my mom was hurt and Putt-Putt went missing."

Chapter 26

As Jim turned over, he spied his old faithful bedside clock, the red numbers glaring quarter-to-four. He failed to extend his legs any further because of the lump at the bottom of the bed. He peeked below at Sandy, curled up, wiggling a bit, and raising his head to check on his owner. Jim finally tucked his feet under the dog's warmth and wondered; the dog never slept in their bed until Janet's death and yet he always left her side of the bed unoccupied. Perhaps the dog was down there to monitor his well-being or in anticipation of Janet coming back to sleep on her side. But no, he decided, dogs can't think like that.

Sandy stretched his head towards his master and didn't put it back down on the homemade quilt until Jim breathed noisily in his sleep. At 6 a.m. he jumped off the bed and stroked Jim's cheek with his tongue.

Jim pulled his hand out from the covers and raked Sandy's neck. Were it not for the dog, he doubted he'd be so quick to rise every day. He felt an overwhelming desire to sleep. Each day was painful because his mind replayed memories of Janet and their daily routine and his heart ached.

He elbowed himself into a sitting position, arched himself forward, and got up. "Good morning," he used to hear by now, sometimes followed by, "you get your clothes on because I ain't dressing ya, and you and that dog take a walk if you both want food in your stomachs." He couldn't believe it. All the people he knew who had lost their mates were females. The guys always died first, so what was he doing here?

Sandy pranced back and forth in front of him and joyfully egged him on. Disheartened, Jim made it to the bathroom, brushed his teeth, and splattered water on his face. When he looked in the mirror he saw an old man with two days of hair growth.

"Okay," Jim said, "I better look as groomed as you." He picked up a razor and went about his business.

———

At the door, Jim leashed Sandy and they left the house. A minor breeze stirred and the freshness of the day was palpable. It occurred to Jim, as he appreciated the swinging tail and determined trot of his buddy, that the day was more tolerable than the day before, and the day before that.

Down the block, an arthritic woman came ambling down her driveway to her parked vehicle. She carried a purse and a stack of mail and opened her car door to place them on the front seat. "Good morning," she said as Jim approached. "What's his name? I see you walk him in the mornings."

"Meet Sandy," Jim said proudly.

"You're a good dog, aren't you, Sandy?" She petted his head while he sniffed her paisley skirt. "Nice to meet you, neighbor," she said, looking at Jim with crowded crow's feet. "I bet he takes care of you as much as you look after him. You two enjoy the day." She turned and placed a painful hand on the driver's door.

"You too Ma'am," Jim called after they continued their walk. By the time he arrived back to the house, Sandy's presence had caused Jim to encounter three people. He eyed the perky dog that momentarily shot him a glance, melting him with his soulful eyes. If it weren't for you, he thought, I'd still be holed up in the house, feeling sorry for myself and letting memories cloud the fact that I still love Janet even though she's gone. Because of you, I can still get on with life and live with purpose.

———

When Diana and Tonya made it across the bridge to the unmanned toll booth, they were surprised to find most of it intact. But driving deeper into the core, their mouths opened with disbelief. A monstrous sailboat, having seen its last water legs, lay sideways, flat out across the median, and a thirty-foot palm tree flanked the ground next to the giant water towers with painted dolphins. On the left, the only remains of a prominent seafood restaurant were its empty posts jutting upward from the bay, and the front stucco was ripped off the first high-rise hotel at the corner like someone had torn a page out of a magazine. They made a right and followed Fort Pickens Road a short way to the National Guard officers stationed there, their armored truck serving as their hub.

Tonya again pointed out her resident pass for 2005. She knew the men were a source of information but her mouth froze as she realized the disheveled piles of sand everywhere. The adequately cleared road had been clearly breached by storm surge and stripped of the dunes previously occupying both sides.

"What are your plans, ladies?" asked a young man with a heavy southern accent. He stood proud doing his job in a camouflage uniform.

"We're going to my house," Tonya responded almost in a fog. "I have not seen it yet."

Worried concern crossed the young man's face and he scratched the side of his military crew cut near the rim of his hat.

"If we can, we'll be staying," Diana added.

"I'm sure you know," he said, "there's no electricity or water yet. And on this side of the island there are only a handful of residents staying like that. You ladies are going to tough it out?"

"Yes," Diana said firmly. "How safe is it, sir?"

"We check everyone coming in. We're a barrier to looters and gawkers, so I don't think you have to worry about people. But be careful in any case. The island is dangerous. And FEMA is still working on the sand. That'll be going on for quite some time. You'll have to park on the side of the road; you can't gain access by car deeper into the residential areas. You'll see your property marked. Don't stay if there is big black lettering labelling it structurally unfit."

Diana nodded and thanked him and Tonya slowly accelerated west, passing the long fishing pier into the Gulf and cruising the narrow curves. She couldn't tell if the longest pier in Florida was damaged or not but, from her viewpoint, the pillars seemed to be intact.

All structures on the south side of the island were in total shambles. Whole condo units exposed their interiors to the road, or what was left of them, and blown out structures on the ground floor were strewn across sand. A mattress dangled from an open, previous bedroom while wires and pipe guts ensnarled each other in ghoulish twists in open living areas. An upstairs bathtub and toilet stood eerily open to the public while the bathroom walls had vanished. A navy sedan roof peeked out from the sand and a half intact beach gazebo mockingly waited for someone to sit and gaze at the remnants of the natural disaster around it.

A shudder ran up Diana's back. No wonder they talk about absurd monetary values placed on hurricane damage. She thought she arrived with an idea of what to expect but this went far beyond her imagination.

Around the last bend before the road straightened out, Diana and Tonya's silence became more penetrable, a bulky sand dune came into view. High atop the dune where sea oats sprouted, stood the memorial barrier island cross, a ten-foot cast concrete cross commemorating the first Christian mass held in the United States. The mass had been performed by the Spaniards in 1559 with 1500 settlers and soldiers present to celebrate Don Tristan de Luna y Arrelano's beach landing, which in essence established America's first European settlement.

"Almost all the gulf-front dunes are flattened for several miles east and west, as far as I can tell," Diana said, "except this one. How long has the cross been here?"

"Forty-five years," Tonya said. "I've heard it said that throughout all the hurricanes, the cross and that dune gets spared every time."

Diana took a deep sigh and another shudder raced up her back. It was as if God signified the last word by leaving His symbol intact after Ivan pranced north wreaking insults on a materialistic culture. Tonya also wondered and thoughtfully questioned her few religious beliefs. For the time being, she was willing to grasp faith in a supreme being due to the mysterious spectacle on the side of the road.

————

Down another mile, Tonya's heart knocked against her chest cautioning her to what she might find. She nestled the car on the side of the road, careful not to sink too deep an area of sand, and the two women got out. Tonya peered over the car roof. At least the house still stood; she settled for a big breath to calm her nerves.

First, they surmised the entire south side of the house. Many shingles had blown off the roof and a gaping black hole made Tonya realize the top floor must already be a mess with water damage. All the aluminum shutters on the second and third floor doors and windows had held fast but the third deck outside ceiling had only a few panels left in place. Tonya's eyes settled on the ground floor. The structural pillars stood firm but the bottom walls were ripped apart like old discarded tax returns.

Tonya and Diana walked to the house. Sand washed high into the right side where a storage closet was pitched against the cellar staircase, mashed items within the mess. The handle bars of a stationary exercise bike poked out of the thick water-laden sand as well as unrecognizable stored household items. On the left, landscaping tools, a bench, and pieces of Styrofoam body boards were poking up from the sand and little remained of the side wall. The garage doors were twisted, gnarled pieces of aluminum and the main staircase on the side of the house was missing half the bottom steps. Even more ominous, the foundation of the house there was precarious with a gap between the concrete and washed-out sand below.

Diana sighed with relief and gestured for Tonya to take a look. The stucco pillar on the north-east corner of the house was marked; the home approved for structural soundness and safe enough for entering. Tonya patted her chest with her hand. "Phew! At least we have a floor to sleep on tonight."

"That's the spirit," Diana said. "But get a load of that."

Little stucco remained on the ground floor of the pink house next door and only a trace of their garage doors stood. To their amazement, jutting out from the driveway of sand was the driveway itself – a concrete monolith sprouting forty-five degrees into the air. "Seeing is believing," Diana said, shaking her head.

"Truly,' Tonya agreed. She peeled her eyes away and looked across the would-be street to another neighbor's, where an impaled motorboat pierced through part of the ground floor, or what was left of it. "It's their boat which they stored in their garage," Tonya said, signaling from the next door neighbor's property to across the street.

"Those people across the street," Diana said, "aren't going to be very happy with their neighbor's boat -method. But we better try to go inside. We have a lot to do before nightfall."

———

No carpet covered the first eight steps going up the center staircase from inside the garage and a thick dirty water line remained against the staircase wall. They rounded the first landing and went up the next six steps with little light. Tonya pulled from her pocket the most important item she had carried. With the pinch light, she wiggled her key into the door and pushed with some effort, the humidity and moisture having made an invisible paste along the door frame.

"Priorities," Diana said, looking at Tonya, who waved her blue light straight to the covered generator in the passageway. Tonya pulled off the cover. "And here's the gas can to get us started. And there's the ladder." Tonya pointed to the great room which had sufficed as storage space.

"The shutters need to come down," Tonya said. "Not only to open up and get some light, but we have to run the generator out on the deck."

"Your mother and father explained things well to you. Peter says people don't detect the buildup of carbon monoxide from enclosed space generators. He says the carbon monoxide replaces oxygen in blood and people are dead before they suspect a thing."

"Dad pounded in our heads not to use the generator in an enclosed space." Tonya stared at the bulky machinery and turned to Diana. "I have to go back downstairs and bring the bag I left, especially for my mother's ashes. I need to put her on the fireplace mantle until I spread her to rest in the Gulf."

When Tonya came back, she tried to keep a tear from falling. She put the urn on the mantle and shook her head. "My mother's death was the worst but then Mother Nature's storm surge wreaked havoc on the ground and the hurricane's wind took care of everything above it. All of this is an example of bad things happening in three's."

Diana chose not to remind her of her missing dog.

Johnny didn't stand a chance fighting the residual effects of the biopsy and anesthesia, and never made phone calls. The next thing he knew when he plopped on the bed and closed his eyes, was that he found himself in a dream playing basketball in a hockey arena with Peter and Tonya as spectators. Peter didn't fare much better. His eyes shut after reclining on the hotel sofa with the complimentary copy of *USA Today*.

Johnny called home the next day while they weaved into Alabama, windows cracked, and their plastic garbage bag full of banana peels, granola bar wrappers, and empty Styrofoam cups.

"I was about to call you," Mel said. "After all Mom's been through, she's worried about you." Mel glanced at Jennifer, who smiled when she realized it was Johnny.

"I'm sorry, Mel. I fell asleep when we got back to the hotel yesterday."

"Well, Mom's sitting right here and except for being skinnier than a Twizzler, her complexion looks much better and she's smiling again."

"And no problems so far with her being home?"

"No. Except that it's not the same without you. Nobody is telling me what to do. And my friends haven't come over, probably because you're not here."

"They're just being thoughtful and letting Mom rest."

"When are you going to break down and let your head swell a little because they all like you? Anyway, does your leg hurt and what did they tell you?"

"I'm susceptible for the same diagnosis as Mom. They said you just need a blood test later. Dr. Devlin will help us out with that."

"So I'm off the hook as far as surgery?"

"You are. Guess I'll talk to you tomorrow. Can you put Mom on?"

Mel handed the phone to Jennifer who leaned again into the throw pillows wedged near the armrest.

"Johnny?" Jennifer said with renewed vigor.

"Hey, Mom. How are you feeling and how'd your discharge go?"

"A day at a time. Mel will take me at the end of the week to see Doctor Liu and Doctor Bhagat. But I want to hear about you. Do you have a long incision and what were the test results?"

"I'm positive, Mom. But compared to you, the biopsy was minor. There won't even be a scar."

Johnny glanced at Peter who drove down the ramp to a rest area..

"I'm sorry I brought on all these problems for anesthesia," Jennifer said.

"Don't worry. It could have been far worse. We could have inherited some unspeakable genes from our father."

Jennifer didn't comment, but said, "Please tell Doctor Devlin that I can't thank him enough for taking you under his wing. And also tell him Doctor Bhagat said I'm doing so well, being that I could've died after his surgery."

"I'll tell him. We'll talk tomorrow."

"Bye then. Love you."

Chapter 27

Tonya smoothed her sleeping bag down on the deck and fluffed two pillows at the top end. She sat cross-legged facing the Gulf. A three-quarter moon shone brilliantly, casting light over the water and island like a fairy's wand in a Disney movie. Bright stars twinkled and she picked out the Big Dipper. Never before had she seen it so demarcated, as if the sky above was a laminated poster for an astronomy lecture. And the barrier island lay quiet except for the peaceful surf lapping at the shoreline across the way.

The serenity broke with the ringing of her cell phone. "Hello?"

"Hey, it's Johnny."

"Johnny, I have so much to tell you. Where are you?'

"We just had to stop. Peter was too tired to keep driving and he won't let me drive due to my leg." Johnny sat in the unoccupied business center of their hotel, the flat screen TV muted, and a glass of water nearby.

"So how did it go?" she asked tentatively.

"A snap."

"And?"

"I have the same genetic problem as my mom."

"So no accidents or emergency health issues for you," she said lightheartedly. "You'll have to avoid those anesthesiologists as much as possible."

"I think I'll order a medic-alert necklace so no one gives me the triggering agents."

"Good idea."

"So what's it like down there?"

"Right now is the highlight since Diana and I arrived. I'm sprawled on a sleeping bag on our second floor deck. No human noise and the most beautiful night sky. It's warm and stuffy inside without air conditioning, and we've shut off the generator. Diana decided to sleep in a bed. But we're lucky. We found and paid two men after their work day today moving sand with a tractor. They removed all the shutters for us."

"I'm glad you didn't wait for us."

"But the destruction ...," she paused, "is horrible. I can't fathom how Pensacola residents are going to put it all back together again. This island has withstood centuries of pounding storms, but I don't think it can recuperate. There is now a breach across the island between here and the west end. Water is flowing from the Gulf to the Bay. Maybe we can go down there when you're walking better. I want to see for myself the nasty areas highlighted in the aerial shots."

Johnny smiled to himself, happy she thought about him in the plan. "I'm looking forward to being there, especially to see you."

When they hung up, Tonya made a mental note of the perfect gift for him. A medic-alert tag.

———

Peter and Johnny easily followed Tonya's directions, counting down the mile markers as they hit the last stretch from Montgomery, Alabama. They became painfully aware of the increasing number of battered signs off the interstate and exit ramps. They split a long hero sandwich before veering off I-65 and slowed their speed on the smaller roads of the northern Florida panhandle, especially after reading one of the sunshine state's welcome signs: *speed checked by air surveillance.*

Two hours later, they presented the beach resident information that Tonya had given them - Rick's copies - to the police officers monitoring the entrance to the bridge and the National Guard officers stationed on Fort Pickens Road.

They made their way down the sand strewn road keeping most of their comments to themselves. "Newspaper pictures don't capture this," Johnny finally said.

Peter pulled into the first parking lot on the Gulf side, almost two miles down, where Tonya had suggested they park. "I guess this is it," Peter said as they opened their doors, "or what's left of it." He pulled a light fleece jacket from the backseat for sun and wind protection and Johnny put on his sweatshirt. A boardwalk from the asphalt to the beach looked like the contents of a thrown box of pick-up sticks.

Johnny inhaled deeply and twitched his nose. Although he sneezed, his nasal passages were wide open.

"I can appreciate that this is normally a beautiful place," Peter said as they began walking.

"We can aim over to the black posts of the subdivision entrance," Johnny said, "but the house is the second one to the left of the entrance. Don't see why we can't walk straight through. This must be it." He pointed at the beige-colored three stories with the torn-up roof and ground floor.

Peter nodded and stepped into a large chunk of red brickwork. He paused and looked closer. "Tonya told us to go through the subdivision entrance because she probably had no idea that the previous retaining wall would be gone. Whatever wall, or drop to their yard, or landscaping that existed, is buried or washed away."

"This must be the house because the door on the second floor is open."

"And that's a generator outside. We'd hear it if they were using it."

Johnny narrowed his eyes and ran his hand along the back of his head. He slowed his trudge over the sand.

Peter turned around. "It'll be fine. I bet she can't wait to see you."

———

Cross-legged, Tonya scrubbed a squirt of bleach spray into the back synthetic board of her father's dresser. She made circular movements with a cloth to remove as much of the black furry growth as she could, but the last remnant would not budge. "Pig-headed fungus," she whispered and got up, stepping over peeled-up carpet. Wet carpet had caused the furniture to mop up the moisture from the bottom end and the rug had gotten wet from the dripping ceiling from the breached roof. She looked from the dresser to the exposed floor boards to the ceiling and shook her head.

Tonya stepped through the open door for the fourth time in an hour and quickly forgot her unpleasant chore. The timeliness of her break made her smile because down below, Johnny and Peter had arrived and wore puzzled expressions ... trying to make sense of the

213

former retaining wall. Her heart pounded faster than the speed with which she spun around and bounded down the two flights of stairs to the ground. There she halted to unclench her dirty rag and drape it on the banister. She tugged at her hair extra hard and took a deep breath while stepping into the higher sand on the garage floor.

"Johnny, Doctor Devlin!"

Johnny's eyes swept over towards her pearl-white smile and elated steps.

"Help has arrived as well as your car," Johnny said.

"Thanks for coming, Dr. Devlin. Diana is in the front of the house. She was just talking to a neighbor who came in with an insurance adjuster. More people are here today to assess damage, start cleaning up, or bring in an adjuster. Our FEMA flood insurance person came today, too"

"And how did that turn out?" Peter asked.

"Nothing on the ground floor is covered, which we knew, except major structural damage and electric or plumbing damage. Which, in essence, affects the whole house."

"You mean all the busted-out walls and garage doors aren't included?"

"No, not here. Mom and Dad took a chance on this property. And they believed other insurance owners shouldn't have to pay higher premiums because folks like them bought a house on what amounts to a sand bar." She grinned.

"Please show us around, and stop calling me Dr. Devlin."

"Yes, sir." Tonya laughed to make him smile and walked them under a warped front garage door.

Peter spotted Diana walking away from the departing neighbor. "There's my one and only," he said. "It didn't take long to acquire the beach bum look, did it?" He wrapped his arms around her and they lingered with a kiss.

"The baseball cap is an extra from Tonya's closet," she said, "if that's what you mean."

"But your body belongs on the beach: shapely legs, a killer curve under that non-plummeting top you're wearing, and a thin waist."

Diana punched his arm. "What's gotten into you, you redneck?!"

"I don't know. I guess I possess another buried personality beyond the OR. Actually, I missed you."

———

"I think we have enough water to float a boat," Tonya said to Johnny as they made two trips to the car to unpack supplies. She carried a grocery box filled with snacks, canned chicken, and tuna fish while Johnny carried the bottles.

They went up the stairs and placed their things on the counter as Diana ruffled through her luggage. "I think I have everything. Are you sure you two will be all right?"

"Yes," Tonya said. "We have your cell phone numbers and you won't be that far away, especially compared to my dad. What you both are going to do at that clinic sounds great."

Peter handed them a piece of paper. "This is Fred and Ginger's house number where we'll be staying. Don't work too hard, both of you, and be careful of all the debris around here."

"And careful using the generator," Diana added and laughed. "I'm sorry, we must sound like parents." She tugged on Peter's arm and picked up her bag. "We're out of here with the rental car. See you in a few days or sooner."

Peter shook Johnny's hand with a solid grip; each couple now had their own itinerary. As he followed his wife, Peter felt remorse for leaving them at all. He took Diana's hand when they were downstairs and she frowned to leave them as well.

———

"I've never seen two kayaks in a living room before," Johnny said as they rearranged clutter.

"We've been so busy," Tonya said, "we haven't tackled this room yet. There is a couch under here somewhere."

Tonya folded the throw blanket lying over the ottoman while Johnny put one of the Puno's paintings back above the fireplace.

"How is your mom and Mel?" Tonya asked.

"They are getting accustomed to being back home. Mom believes it's a miracle that she's there." Johnny widened his eyes and shuddered at what her condition would be if not for the transplant. "You know, Mel's really surprised me. I sense she's grown up even more because of our mother's illness and surgery. Two years ago, she balked at helping out at home if it interfered with her own agenda. I don't hear her complain like that anymore."

"You're lucky there are two of you to help out." Tonya stepped to the counter and stripped open a Twix package and took a bite. "Want one?"

Johnny put his hand out and thanked her.

"How about moving the buffet back towards the wall with me?" she said when they finished eating. They each lifted an end and moved the heavy Stickley piece over by a foot.

"You're lucky these walls stayed dry," Johnny said.

"Just a few more items and we'll call it quits."

"Good plan, especially since there's no water for a shower."

She tilted her head. "We could always go swimming later."

———

Like Tonya, Johnny decided to sleep under the stars. He spread another of the Puno's sleeping bags and two pillows on the other side of the second floor deck. After turning off the lamp and generator, the teens each carried a flashlight and positioned themselves on two plastic chairs outside the door.

Tonya's thoughts cluttered with things to talk about but, over the next minute, those thoughts faded to the background as the island's spell captivated her like it usually did. Even with all the destruction and the hassles of the day and the lack of comforts, she felt enamored with the open sky, water, and beach, and the teenager who had befriended her.

"What do you think?" Tonya said softly, wondering if Johnny was also contemplating the sky.

"I'm certainly not in Indiana."

"Neither of us! And can you believe we go to school in the same state?"

"The flat state with the bad reputation? Wander Indiana. Where you can spot the bad drivers all over the place. Wandering like they need a map, going twenty miles under the speed limit, clueless."

"You're not complimentary of the drivers where you live."

"You're being nice because you're not a real resident."

"They're not that bad. Have you ever driven in New Jersey?"

"I've never even been to New Jersey."

"You can rack up more expletives at the wheel than cruising in Indiana. When a driver there is in the far left lane and all of a sudden wants to get off at the exit a couple of lanes over, he or she just slides over. Drivers call it the Jersey slide, but it happens in New York, too. You can end up dead on the Long Island Expressway because of a slider."

"I don't think I could handle that. That sounds worse than the college students who leave a party after too many beers and slide behind the wheel."

"At least there are ways to handle that. Like getting a tipsy tow."

"A tipsy tow?"

"That's what they call it in California. You know, calling triple A to get their vehicle towed home, and then getting a ride home from someone."

"I have a friend," Johnny said, "who called his father after drinking too much. He thought his dad was coming to fetch him but, his father arrived, took his car keys away, and left him to sleep in the car all night."

Tonya laughed. "Mean."

"Better than getting a DUI."

Tonya uncrossed her legs and placed her bare feet on the railing alongside Johnny's.

"What do you call a tailgater," Johnny asked, glancing at her.

"A tailgater, because I won't tell you what I'd really say alone in my car. What do you call them?"

"Bumpersuckers."

Tonya laughed. "I like that. What about old people who sit at a red light with their right turn signal on and don't move until it's green or they go straight through a stop sign?"

"Old goats. But you know you can't fault bad drivers. They have a genetic problem like mine. Thirty percent of bad drivers possess a bad driver gene. They can't help it." He eyed Tonya seriously, his feet up on the railing, the chair balanced on its back legs.

Tonya's big brown eyes narrowed in the radiance of the moon. Slowly a smile crept across her face. "Get out. I almost believed you for a minute." When she poked his arm, his feet dropped off the rail, and the chair landed.

They sat in silence as a streak of light shot across the night sky, a distant meteor trespassing into the earth's atmosphere.

"Bet you don't see that very often," Tonya said.

Johnny sighed. "You're right. The southern Indiana city lights drown out the darkness. This is something else." His eyes wandered back down and he admired her slender legs all the way to her ankles.

"Tomorrow afternoon," Tonya said, "let's find some real food in Pensacola and visit the Escambia County animal shelter. I must start looking for Putt-Putt."

Johnny reached across, cupped Tonya's soft upturned hand, and gave it a squeeze.

"I miss that happy-go-lucky dog," she said. "I hope he's all right ... wherever he is."

Chapter 28

Johnny and Tonya wore sneakers to protect their feet from unseen objects as they stepped through the sandy subdivision towards the bay. It was midnight as Tonya carried a flashlight and Johnny held two towels. They walked straight back into the cul-de-sac and onto the boardwalk where Tonya used to sit on a bench at the end with a book. She also used to go there to drop her bait trap for crabs or gather her crustacean catch.

"I should've figured," Tonya said, taking a few gingerly steps and seeing the abrupt end of a shattered walkway further ahead where most of the boards were scattered, twisted like pretzels. They jumped into the sand and approached the water while despising the potential for getting injured.

"I'm sorry," Tonya said, "that I didn't know about this sooner."

"It would be too dangerous to go in" Johnny said, "especially without good light."

Tonya stooped down and made ripples in the water with her hand. "This doesn't have to stop us. Tomorrow we should go down the beach past the condos and parking lot to the Gulf Islands National Seashore where we can go swimming. There shouldn't be the man-made debris in the water like here." She saw a bump in the water out further and strained her neck. "That looks like our black glider out there. My mom couldn't carry it herself into the garage. It used to be on the small concrete south patio." She smiled and patted Johnny's arm. "Guess I can't swing on it anymore."

Johnny glanced down the beach and noticed a tossed sailboat, and another small personal pier ruined. "That's odd," he said. "There's a beached motorboat over there which doesn't look damaged."

"Let's check it out tomorrow if we get down there." Tonya brushed her hair away from her cheek and faced him to go. But with feet planted firmly and no inclination to move, they gazed into each other's eyes. Johnny slipped his hand behind her neck while Tonya's fingers landed on his biceps. The distance between them closed and their lips met. The bliss deepened as Johnny's arms embraced her shoulders and she held him along his lower back. The curves of their bodies compressed and when Johnny came up for air, he smiled at the smell of gardenias from her shampoo.

———

Their midnight swim plan aborted, Johnny and Tonya walked west and cut through between two houses to the buried street which curled around more houses to the Puno's. They went straight through a blown-out garage, where a wave runner lay jammed in sand and a central-vacuum canister dangled from a beam. A quick thud-like sound caused them both to stop short and exchange looks.

"Sounds like something fell," Johnny said softly.

Tonya nodded and they listened for another moment. They stepped ahead, emerging before the next house with a north facing side staircase, partially intact. Tonya happened to glance up at an open door, an open invitation if the island were inhabited. "What the … " she muttered.

A dark duffel bag flew from the doorway and landed several feet in front of them followed by a masculine figure taking several steps down and leaping off the staircase. He landed and reached for the bag but stopped cold at the sight of Johnny and Tonya silhouetted like art.

Above, a skirmish broke more silence as bagged objects were thrown towards the doorway. "That's enough," a tentative voice scolded. "I told you I'm pulling the plug. We've been here way too long and it's my boat."

"Gary," a deeper voice growled from upstairs, "I've got two words for you. Shut the fuck up."

Johnny and Tonya held their breath as the stealthy shadow in front of them stood, startled, but poised like a cat. After the freeze, all three of them moved ahead, Johnny and Tonya intent on minding their own business and getting home. The dark figure lurched his entire body forward, pitching all his weight into Johnny's side, ramming him to the ground. The man quickly wheeled a right punch while gaining better footing, hitting Johnny's shoulder prematurely instead of settling it into his face.

Still in the same spot, Tonya belted out a scream to scare the stranger off and hoped the sound would travel far. More loaded bags fell around her and the two men from above landed nearby. A pair of hands slammed into her chest before her eyes could settle on either of them. The wind sucked out from her lungs like a deflating balloon and she stumbled backwards, doubling over. The man who had smashed his hands into her stooped and grabbed the last sack. "Quiet, bitch," he said. He turned and fled. His partners grabbed their goods and sped off behind him.

———

On the edge of the bed, Jennifer Barns slipped into her fuzzy slippers. She got up and stabilized her balance, turned and straightened her sheets, and glanced at her alarm clock. The house was quiet. Mel had left two hours ago for school.

She stopped in the hallway bathroom and sat on the toilet with relief to have a normal colored urine and volume. She hoped to never again stay in the hospital with a tube running out from her bladder. It was practically too good to be true, to feel halfway normal. Every day her gratefulness bubbled over for her good medical fortune. Sometimes she thought about her family's low income but now, more than ever, she realized that economic poverty did not translate into a poverty of spirit. She was more happy to be alive than ever before. The day before she'd also made arrangements with the school principal. Next autumn the school and her doctors would allow her to sub if she continued to gain more daily endurance.

In the kitchen, Jennifer poured two cups of water into the coffee machine. Her taste for a strong cup had diminished as well as her desire to pour seconds; when it finished brewing she poured in a generous amount of vanilla creamer. She peeled a banana and carried her coffee and fruit to the table. She heard a truck rumble past outside and sat thinking before opening the previous day's newspaper. Half the time, Mel picked one up for her on the way home from school and also bought the necessary groceries.

Jennifer finished the banana, savoring the perfectly ripened flavor, and sipped from her mug. There was something different, however. Johnny didn't come in and out as he had routinely done in elementary school and high school. It was the longest absence from her son she could ever remember. She missed him so much; those thoughts took precedence over her concern about a possible liver rejection, worrying about side effects from anti-rejection drugs, and pondering about the next doctor's appointment. At least she had Amelia, who had grown as capable as her brother. The two of them were her biggest blessings and her reason for living, getting a new liver, and recovering well. In the last two years she had given up on ever seeing grandchildren, but now that possibility existed and she fostered it as a secret hope. A major shift in thinking, she contemplated.

The phone rang and she welcomed the interruption. She picked up the hard line in the kitchen corner and moved it, wire and all, to the table as she announced her "hello."

Exuberant to hear Johnny on the line, she settled back down. "I bet you're busy down there. How are you and how is Tonya, the doctor and his wife?"

"First, how are you feeling, Mom?"

"You don't need to ask me that regularly anymore. We've turned a huge corner, remember? I'm doing well." She stopped herself from telling him how much she missed him.

"Glad to hear it. Peter and Diana left to start helping at that clinic and to stay with their friends." He paused, uncomfortable. "But Tonya and I had a little trouble last night."

"Trouble?" Jennifer twisted the phone cord.

"Don't worry though. I'm all right. We stumbled on a theft in the middle of the night. The looters weren't too happy about that and pushed us around."

She gulped hard, as if the banana lay stuck in her throat. "Did either of you get hurt?"

"We're sore, but nothing's broken. We called the island police and they took a full report. Now we're waiting on a cop from Gulf Breeze. It's a different county and they're both going to be involved."

"But I thought no one was there."

"It's basically Tonya and I. But these people came over from Gulf Breeze or Pensacola by boat in the middle of the night and broke into a house or maybe more than one."

222

"Oh my God. I don't think you two should be sleeping over on that deserted island."

Johnny grinned at Tonya as she watched him, her elbows on the counter and her face nestled in her hands.

"But there's so much work to do. We'll be careful."

When they finished talking, Jennifer held the phone a little longer. She replayed the conversation in her mind and reluctantly put the phone down. He couldn't be any more grown up. Finally he'd ventured out of his hometown, was travelling with other adults and a nice girl, and had engaged himself in a helpful cause for the very family who gave her so much. How grounded he acted about it all, even after having an altercation with thieves. She smiled. How about that? She acknowledged to herself that she could take some credit for her fine son and his actions. But, she faced an adjustment - he wouldn't be around like before, and she was missing him like hell.

———

Kent Milton's life would never be the same again, for that he was sure. On arising every morning, his brain incessantly reminded him of pulling out in his cruiser and crossing the base of the bridge. Crossing, that is, until he plowed into Karen Puno's Honda dismantling her and her dog's future forever.

Since getting back on regular duty the week before, Kent promised himself to be a more cautious police officer. To get the job done, it was also an officer's duty to do no harm. Maybe that should be more emphasized in police training, he thought. How could he have been so rash about hurrying to the southbound bridge lane? He bet his police captain father and his FBI twin brother wouldn't have made that mistake. They had no record of spinning a woman into a comatose state and death due to their unprofessional actions.

Kent's knee and arm discomfort also reminded him daily of the accident. Before, he never gave credence to theories about payback or retribution for mistaken or purposefully bad human behavior. But now, he'd never be convinced otherwise. In the police station, he tapped out an ibuprofen from a pill bottle and slid it down with a gulp of warm coffee. Hopefully, his boney aches would lessen in a little while.

"Tyrone," he said, "I'll go work the call we received about the Pensacola Beach incident last night."

Tyrone eyed him from his desk as he crushed a paper bag from a late morning bagel. "It really is my turn, Kent."

"No. If you don't mind ..." He put on his cap, adjusting it for comfort on his sculpted head. "I'm so excited to be out on the beat again, I want to do it." He started for the door.

"You don't look excited," Tyrone said, tossing the bag into the basket.

––––––

For a short time on his drive, Kent thought about another dilemma. Several months ago, proposing to his girlfriend of three years had been imminent. He took a deep sigh. For a marriage to be successful, he had to feel responsibility for a wife. Not just to love her, but to be a full man, capable of providing in any which way - emotionally, physically, and financially. For now, thinking about that was a burden, his mind was already cluttered with enough grief and responsibility. It wouldn't be fair to his girlfriend. Not only was a proposal on the back burner, but he considered backing out from the relationship all together.

At least the sun basked down on the little battered island as he made a right turn onto Fort Pickens Road. He stuck a pen from the console into his uniform pocket so he wouldn't forget. The clipboard next to him had the preliminary data reported to their office from the island police. He noted the tiny police station as he passed, strategically located near the core and the long fishing pier where most of the island's drinking occurred.

Unlike some working relationships between counties and law enforcement, Kent knew, Santa Rosa County and Escambia county police forces got along just fine and politely shared information and tasks. They had to. The cooperation of both counties was essential for the huge Blue Angels' summer air show on the beach which could only be pulled off due to their mutual cooperation. A huge chunk of money came into both departments indirectly from those tourist dollars and that translated into money for police salaries. Kent thought of his medical bills which still streamed in and was grateful he was even able to return to work.

———

Having a sore upper left arm didn't make shoveling sand from the garage any easier for Johnny, but they had at least paved a narrow walkway area clear to the foundation. He stopped to take a swig from his water bottle and evaluated the growing bruise.

Tonya perched her broom against the wall and grimaced at Johnny's shoulder. She wasn't any better. Her upper chest was tender to touch and she was lucky her ribs were intact and that the perpetrator had not slammed into her breasts. Johnny passed her the bottle and she took a hearty drink.

"Sounds like more help's arrived," Tonya said. Outside, slowly making its way, a bulldozer worked on sand removal, hoisting it into the main field every time it had a load. As it backed up, the silence was permeated by noisy alarms. "They work for FEMA, but the subdivision is paying this man after his regular hours to finish clearing our streets. Otherwise, we would still be waiting." The full yellow scooper hoisted its claws and ambled backwards as a Gulf Breeze policeman walked across their neighbor's property, glancing up at the house address, and continued across the adjacent empty lot.

"Are you two the witnesses to last night's crime?" he asked, approaching closer.

"Unfortunately. I'm Johnny and this is Tonya."

"I'm Officer Milton. Can we go somewhere so I can take your statement?"

"Upstairs," Tonya said. They went in single file through their path, up the center staircase. "It's not too bad in the kitchen. The generator is on as well as a portable room air conditioner." She guided Kent to a kitchen stool.

"That's quite a punch you took there," Kent said eyeing Johnny's arm. "That from last night?" Kent placed his clipboard down and pulled out his pen.

"Yes, sir. But Tonya was hurt, too. In her chest."

"You two are lucky you're not worse. You could have been shot. All right, I'll start from the beginning. Are you John Barns and you're Tonya Puno?"

They both nodded as Kent looked again at the typed form. Somehow Tonya's last name was familiar. Then again, in the recent past, he had been the paper king expert at work, so names were floating around in his head like carp circling a meal.

Kent wrote down the pertinent basics. "So there were three men; you heard each of them speak. Can either of you describe them or your attacker?"

"The guy who came after me," Tonya said, "seemed to be in charge because he told the other one off upstairs. I had a flashlight beam on for a short time. He was medium height and lanky and wore a T-shirt with a fish picture on the back. The guy with him was only about five-five and stocky. Meaning muscular stocky. And one guy called the other guy Gary."

"How old would you say they were?"

Johnny and Tonya looked thoughtfully at each other. "Early twenties," Johnny said. "And the guy that came after me acted more polished and quicker. His hair was short and light brown and he definitely had on some kind of long-sleeved water shirt. You know, the kind that's tight fitting." He rubbed his nose as Kent scribbled notes.

"You didn't go to the hospital?"

They looked at each other sheepishly. "It scared the life out of us," Tonya said, "but we didn't need stitches or anything, so we just called the police. Plus, life has been way too complicated lately."

"Don't worry, officer," Johnny added. "We're going to see a doctor we know. We were waiting for you first."

"What were you two doing outside late at night?" Kent asked, turning to another page. "Is this your house?"

"I'm a college student," Tonya offered. "Well, we're both college students, but not right now. This is my family's home, but my dad's in South America on work and my mother died in a car crash. She was evacuating the island because of Ivan."

Kent eyes never left the page as he listened to Tonya's soft voice. As each word parted from her lips, he sensed an oncoming

226

dread like suffocating under a heavy pillow. By the time she finished, his bronze complexion had faded from his face and his wrists and hands felt pulseless. Nausea crept up from his belly.

Chapter 29

Officer Milton's attention to his report stopped and Tonya wondered why his movements slowed, his face turned pale, and he dropped the clipboard. Johnny reached across the counter to give him a bottled water.

Kent shook 'no' to Johnny's offer. Now the name 'Puno' registered, he thought. His forehead crinkled up with wrinkle lines like he was in pain and his eyes welled-up with moisture. He looked imploringly at the daughter of Karen Puno not knowing how to explain what he did to her mother. He finally sighed after holding his breath far too long.

"I was ... working the bridge closure that morning." Kent's gaze slowly filtered upwards. He searched Tonya's eyes. It was now or never.

Tonya gasped. Her chest began to ache a lot more than from the incident the night before and her shoulders slumped like a rag doll.

"I was parked, but a car sped down the Gulf Breeze ramp - it was going back onto the bridge and we were closing the island. I shouldn't have tried to get over. I should've left it for the officer on that side. I didn't see your mother coming with the chaotic wind and sand and the decreased visibility but I didn't look conscientiously enough at what was coming over the bridge."

Tonya's emotions were in limbo while the generator on the deck rattled its mechanical sound and the air conditioner ran steady and blew air out the rubber hose vented out the window. Every few seconds the bulldozer's triple alarm sounded outside. From where she sat, she didn't know if she wanted to strangle him or console him. Ever since that day she had avoided forming a mental picture of the cop who had killed her mother.

"I'm sorry." Kent's breath escaped in a sob. "I'm so sorry."

———

After a further discussion about that horrific day and after Ken finished his written report, Tony and Johnny accompanied Kent downstairs. Although the sun shone brightly, it was no longer sunny at all.

"I'm walking over to evaluate the house which was broken into," Kent said. "It may happen again. The thieves chose a clever way to bypass security back by the core by coming across by boat. Looters may come again, but we'll do everything we can to investigate this. You both be careful."

"We will," Johnny reassured him.

"If there is something else I can do to help …" His eyes lingered on Tonya. "Please, I hope you can forgive me."

"It happened," Tonya said. Bereavement had been difficult enough, but forgiveness takes time, too, she thought. She searched for the right words. "It was an accident. We can't take it back."

"I know,' he said disheartened. He slipped the clipboard under his arm and gave Tonya his card. "If there's anything else you both remember about those men, please call me. And have those bruises looked at." He took a step to leave.

"Officer Milton," Tonya said, "there is something else. Do you have any idea what happened to our dog? He was in the car that day with my mom."

Kent couldn't believe his misfortune. He was like the bearer of grim news. "He escaped and made it out of there," he said. "During my own recovery, I wanted to find him."

Tonya anticipated his information and glanced at Johnny with optimism. Johnny rubbed her shoulder.

"I can tell you good news and bad news," Kent said. "A dog that fit his description was taken care of by The Gulf Coast Animal Clinic. They patched up his back leg. But after the hurricane, the Humane Society picked up all the new strays from vets and the shelters and took them north. The Panhandle was swamped with lost dogs so they had a better chance of being adopted in northern states or found by owners through internet search sites."

Tonya looked at Johnny despondently.

"I'm sorry, again," Kent said, wishing now that he had tried harder to locate her dog.

"No. Thank you," Tonya said, "for looking for him. At least I know he escaped the wreck. Maybe he's safe somewhere." But the little optimism Tonya previously had was shot. She suspected Putt-Putt had ended up a number in a mass of hundreds of dogs.

"We can still look for him," Johnny said and Kent nodded.

Kent put his paperwork in his left hand, leaned forward, and lightly squeezed her shoulder with his other hand. She closed her eyes during his embrace. "Bye," he said, holding back tears. He walked away and couldn't look back.

———

The shelves lining the room contained prescription and over-the-counter medications donated by pharmaceutical representatives and local physicians' offices. A drug store chain had lowered the price on certain stock generic drugs for the clinic's patients, and a retired male nurse labeled and alphabetically stocked the shelves based on categories: heart, blood pressure, GI, allergies, antibiotics and more. Volunteer women manned the front reception area or screened patients for need based on income. Fred and Ginger used their initial financial backing to cheaply rent the office building and they had secured publicity for the grand opening.

Diane, and particularly Peter, thought the project was amazing. Most helpers had their own post hurricane problems and yet, for a few hours here and there, they made the clinic a reality born from the dreams of the older couple dedicated to a spiritual calling. The couple's project had blossomed because of their hard work, perseverance, and dedication. Once other people met the couple, they were motivated by their zest, charity, and concern for anyone who needed help.

Diana straightened the kitchen area and then packed packages of crackers, pretzels, and nuts into a basket. She measured ground coffee and started a fresh pot for the half-dozen people staffing the place while Peter walked in between patients.

"Would you mind doing this?" he asked. "Calling over to the hospital's radiology department and telling them I'm sending this patient over? Tell them he's a clinic patient, and ask if they could cover him under their free care for us?" He handed her the chart.

230

"Consider it done." Diana could not perform the nursing tasks, but she fit in perfectly doing the odds and ends. "Stop a minute for some fresh coffee. This is the first time we're working alongside each other like this."

"I hope you don't leave me because of it."

"Quite the opposite. And the patients seem to like you. After seeing you inside those examining rooms, they walk out to the front desk quite satisfied. Bedside manners after all?"

"Perhaps. But I still prefer the challenges when patients are asleep."

"You're so modest." She poured a half cup of coffee into a mug and handed it to him as Fred rounded the corner with a spry step and a wide smile.

"Here's one for you, too," Diana said, pouring again without asking.

"Peter," Fred said, "Ginger is bringing back a young couple. Special walk-ins for you to see." Fred extended his long fingers and clasped Diana's offer while Peter poured in a sugar packet, stirred, and sipped.

"There are only two other patients to see besides them," Fred said, "so we're almost finished. And Thursday I have another doctor recruited. A family practitioner who can commit to once a week. We're growing," Fred beamed.

A silver-haired woman wearing a pink blouse entered from the other doorway. "I think you know these two," she said, as Johnny and Tonya trailed behind her.

"Looks like you've all met," Diana said. "Came to see us so soon? Fred and Ginger will recruit you both if you don't watch out."

Peter surveyed the both of them. "You two appear to be tuckered out. What happened?" Peter pointed to Johnny's arm. "I can examine that."

"And Tonya, too," Johnny said. "She was pushed in the chest."

"Come on, you two," Ginger said. "Sit down here."

Ginger and Fred pulled chairs out from the square table. "Hon, you don't look so well," Diana said to Tonya.

Tonya stared down at her hands and verbally spewed forth with her upsetting news. "We were assaulted in the middle of the night, I had a face-to-face with the policeman responsible for my mom's wreck, and my dog was relocated out of Florida." Tears slinked down her cheeks and fell into her lap.

Diana crouched down in front of her and took her hand. She pressed it into hers and let Tonya cry. Johnny sat perched on the end of his chair right beside her and stayed silent.

"This is a lot to handle all at once," Diana said. After a long pause, Tonya slowed down the sobbing and wiped her face with a tissue.

"You know," Tonya said, "I'm relieved I met the policeman. And relieved that he met me. He's mourning as much as I am."

Diana squeezed her hand again and stood. She signaled for them all to leave the room and give Tonya some quiet time with Johnny.

———

Peter ordered a tetanus shot for the last patient who cut his hand while jamming it into a debris pile. Then he took a look at Tonya and Johnny's injuries. "I think you're both going to live," he said.

"You're serious about delivering good news, Doc," Johnny said.

Peter frowned. "That's going to turn shades of purple before it goes away, however." He pushed his thumb into the teen's upper arm and Johnny flinched. "And Tonya, you're lucky you haven't broken any ribs or your clavicle. In case either of you have more discomfort tonight or tomorrow, we'll give you some ibuprofen."

Peter stopped in the pharmacy room, grabbed a bottle, and tossed it to Johnny. "Now, let's say goodbye to Fred and Ginger for the day and, as Diana would say, 'Let's go get something to eat'."

———

The two couples sat in a booth as the waitress placed a large pepperoni pizza in the middle of the table. "Enjoy," she said, and walked away.

They slid a slice on each paper plate and passed paper napkins. Tonya folded hers, held it carefully to keep the oil on top, and took a bite. She swallowed and beamed. "Papa's is the best."

"I think I agree," Johnny added.

"College students are probably the best judges of pizza," Diana said. She bit the end, agreed, and Peter followed.

"New York Italian pizza in Florida," Tonya said. "The owner's from Brooklyn, it doesn't get any better."

"I think I've gone to heaven," Diana said.

"I could eat Italian food every day if I had a choice," Johnny said.

"But pizza goes back before the Italians," Tonya said. "Ancient people in the Mediterranean area used to make bread with olive oil and seasonings. Later, some Italian baker named Raffaele made flat bread with tomatoes, mozzarella cheese, and basil for some visiting royalty. He conjured it up to be red, white, and green to represent the colors of the Italian flag. And voila, pizza was born!"

Johnny swallowed and stared at her. "Do you learn the history of food in your history and archeology classes?"

She caught some dripping oil off her chin with a napkin and giggled. "A little. And some of it comes from my dad. He possesses a worldly view of things so we often discuss the origins of food at the dinner table. I remember him once telling Mom all about the ancient Inca's diet."

Diana slid a second slice on her plate and glanced at Peter. "We're gaining on you. If you snooze, you lose."

"I'll claim it then," he said, and lined up his next slice. "So tell us about your dog, Tonya."

"Johnny and I were going to check around to find him, but the policemen said he was relocated by the Humane Society. The only chance I have of finding him is looking on line or calling places in northern surrounding states." She grabbed the shredded cheese shaker. "Now the chance of finding him is pretty slim. There'll never be another dog like him. I'd give my right arm to find him."

———

Sandy wagged his tail and raced to the door as Jim put on a baseball cap and followed. Outside, the morning's sultry humidity hung in the air. "This is the kind of day that Janet found it hard to even breathe" Jim said. "God rest her soul." Sandy looked up and furrowed his forehead.

Jim had been in the doldrums. Today he was going to use the pass his neighbor had given him. The next-door couple owned a rental condo on Pensacola Beach in need of repair, but to raise Jim's spirits they urged him to use it for access to the beach over the coming week.

"Take that dog of yours and go stroll on the beach or go in the water before the beach opens back up and there are crowds," the man had said. Not that that would happen anytime soon, Jim thought, but he knew they were concerned about him due to the loss of his wife. Changing his mind, Jim put off a beach visit for another day and went straight down the block for his usual walk. Sandy ventured little from Jim's side, didn't tug on his leash, and followed Jim's every step on reentering the house.

———

On the beach house's deck, Johnny leaned over from the plastic chair and put his cell phone on the sleeping bag. "Mom says to say hello."

"How is she?" Tonya asked.

"Optimistic. She's starting to sound relieved as she's realizing life is going to be more normal now."

Tonya smiled. "Your mom deserves it."

The waves churned more vigorously than the previous night and the cresting, rolling foam glistened in the moonlight. Their afternoon had been productive. They threw unsalvageable bedroom furniture over the top deck railing and hauled it to the front to wait for a future pick-up of big items. The water company also came through the west end of the island and turned the water back on since all repairs had been made.

Tonya wiggled her toes against the railing and sighed. "This is an extraordinary night. A real shower!"

"What a luxury." Johnny leaned over and took Tonya's hand. He rubbed her palm and massaged her fingers. She watched and wrapped her fingers around his. He stood, inching her up with him. As their eyes rolled over each other's face, they drew closer. Tonya

234

put her hand around his neck and Johnny leaned in, planting his lips on her moist lips. Their embrace grew tighter and Johnny slid his hand in between them, feeling her breasts through her sweat shirt.

"What are we going to do?" Tonya asked. "You can't help me here forever."

"Maybe we can attend some college together. We can figure it out."

"Would you consider going to Butler with me? As long as your mom stays well?"

Johnny's eyes grew wide. "But I can't afford a school like that."

"I'll ask my dad. I think he'd be happy to cover some of your tuition. I mean it. I'll ask him."

"Tonya, I couldn't ..."

"I'll call him tomorrow."

With that, Tonya placed her fingers over his lips to silence him as they slid down to her sleeping bag. Johnny rolled on top of her and lingered over her hair, her eyes, and her lips and then covered her mouth with his own.

Chapter 30

Sandy darted across the room and leaped onto Jim's blue jeans and back to the kitchen floor where dirty shoe and paw prints were accumulating. He spun around a full circle while Jim swiped the car keys off the counter. Jim arched his eyebrows and grabbed Sandy's leash. "It hasn't been that long since I gave you a car ride but come on then, let's go."

The dog bolted as soon as Jim opened the screen door and waited next to the sedan. His morning walk had already been full of fresh smells from birds, trash, and a strange cat, but now the day was going to turn out even better. He gave a mighty jump when Jim opened the door and scrambled to the passenger side when Jim nudged him off his seat and got in.

"It's bad enough you're spoiled to ride with me half the time, but you're not qualified to drive, too."

Sandy poked his head close and swiped his wet tongue on Jim's face. Jim studied the dog for a second before starting the ignition. His face softened and he cleared his throat.

"Yeah, well, you're going to love this." Jim dug his hand into his pocket and placed the borrowed beach resident's pass on the dashboard.

As the vehicle went down the road, Jim rolled the window halfway down and Sandy craned his neck to sniff the incoming whiffs of air. A strange calico cat sat beside a neighbor's garbage can. Sandy voiced his displeasure and woofed several times. But even an intruder couldn't hamper his delight while riding next to Jim, even if later he had to wait in the car a few minutes at their final destination. Sometimes Jim left to do a chore and it made Sandy that much more happy to see him reenter the maroon sedan and get the ride going again.

A mile down, they didn't make the usual left turn but made a right and drove the exit off of Route 98 for the entrance to the Pensacola Beach Bridge. He planted his rump down and voiced a little whimper. They made the bridge incline with few other vehicles.

After the feeling of dread had left, Sandy stood again as five pelicans flew in formation parallel to the bridge and, with heightened awareness, he sniffed the saltier air.

At the core area, Jim stared transfixed at what damage still remained on the little island. The contrast with the rest of Pensacola was significant. He made a right and a left into the pier's parking lot. There were few cars but the cab doors opened up from a pickup truck which had just parked. Two spry men jumped out and picked through the bed, pulling fishing poles and boxes and coolers as they went. Jim stopped and idled for a while, watching.

"I think we'll go further down, boy. There's probably enough junk in the sand to cut your paws but, if we stay near the pier, you may encounter fishing hooks, too."

Slightly further, back on the road, Jim showed the borrowed resident's pass again to the road block crew and slowly they made their way down Fort Pickens Road. Sandy stood fully at attention now. This was familiar territory and they were approaching his old home. His tail sped up and, with anticipation, he whined incessantly.

Jim glanced at his buddy as much as he watched the road. "What? You sure are wound up!"

Sandy stared straight out the front window as much as he focused outside the half-cracked window. As Jim pulled into the Gulf-side parking lot one mile down, Sandy pawed at the door and extended his nose outside the vehicle. He spun around and jumped at his owner as Jim shut the motor off.

Jim clasped the keys and picked up the leash from the dirty floor. "Jeez, I didn't know you were this crazy about visiting the beach. You must be a water dog." He flung open his side with the intent of going around to the passenger's side for his best friend, but Sandy peeled across his lap, spit out the door, and was gone.

After recovering from Sandy's surprise exit, Jim stepped out and realized with horror that Sandy wasn't headed toward the flattened dunes, aqua-green rolling surf, and the sandpipers fleeting up and down the shoreline. He was headed in the opposite direction.

———

Due to habit, Johnny pinched the bridge of his nose as Tonya pulled off her rubber work gloves. "We need to take a break from working with this bleach solution," she said.

"It sure would clear out my sinuses if we were in Indiana."

"Probably because it burns away all the hairy cilia lining nasal passages."

Johnny grinned at the bucket. "It probably causes cancer, too."

"Yes, we need to call this quits for the day." She beamed a flashlight into the back corners of the master bedroom's bathroom, the separate little toilet area, and nodded. "I think we removed all the furry mold growing back there."

Outside the toilet area, she placed the light on the sink because she didn't need it anymore and sat on the edge of the Jacuzzi tub. "It'll be so nice to see the contractor guys today. At least something's going to get started." She'd been told that construction of the ground floor walls would start after supplies were brought in the next two days. And when the foreman arrived in the afternoon with picture catalogs, she was going to select the garage doors.

"Come on," Johnny said, "let's go have something to eat."

"How about some fruit and one of those cappuccino muffins we bought yesterday?"

Johnny pulled her up with a hand grasp. Standing on the tub's step, she stood taller than him and she ran her fingers through his hair. He breathed into the curves of her top and then stepped back.

Tonya dumped the dirty water from the bucket into the tub and chased it with running water. She rinsed out the nearby sponge and sopped up water which had splashed along the back rim of the tub. When she finished she looked out the bathroom beach window. The usual bulldozer moved sand to the west and an apparent insurance agent carrying a clipboard stood with a man looking up at a house to the east.

Directly across the street two cars sat far apart in cleared areas. A thin man with a baseball cap looked across the street towards the house with a look of concern. She guessed him to be in his retirement years but, by wearing jeans, she figured he could be working on hurricane related beach repairs. The man stepped away from his car rather quickly and it was then she noticed a dog's leash in his hand as well as a dog racing over the sand.

Cute dog, she thought, and what vitality. She took a double take. Hell, if that wasn't Putt-Putt, then someone was cloning dogs. She dropped the sponge and bounded from the bathroom down the steps. When she got to the bottom by the kitchen, she yelled loudly, "Johnny, come quick. It's Putt-Putt. He's come home."

Tonya fled out of sight down the basement steps and Johnny quickly chased after her.

"But Tonya, how can that be?" he shouted.

———

Sandy zoomed along his old territory faster than a chipmunk, alongside his old house and the empty lot next to it. He took that route because there were less gnarly bushes and clutter. It was the old way anyway ... running to the front of the house through the vacant lot. He made a wide left and began to understand that the bottom floor had drastically changed. He could see through it from one side to the other.

His previous home made him so excited, he lifted his leg to a mound of sand circling a Sego Palm and tried to mark his familiar territory, but he couldn't squeeze a trickle, so he dropped his rear leg back down. He ran again, into the garage, looking for Karen.

A girl exited from the basement steps and he plummeted straight into her.

"Putt-Putt, it is you!"

It wasn't Karen but Tonya, and he pranced and danced and couldn't stand still as she tried to embrace his entire torso. His nose jiggled like on a hot scent, gathering up the new and old smells about her. Finally, he settled himself between her legs as she squatted down in a fixed position. He felt a heartfelt embrace and someone behind her said "So this must be him?"

While Putt-Putt's face was locked in Tonya's hands, Johnny leaned over to study his face and stroke the top of his head. Putt-Putt smelled his mellow lime fragrance, a new scent also discernable on Tonya. The quick rate of his heart started to relax and he lifted his front paw and dug it into her thigh.

Putt-Putt backed out from between Tonya's legs and looked up the staircase. He voiced a bark, a question to them, which he hoped Tonya would understand right away. Communication with people was not always as easy as he wanted. Sometimes they just didn't understand, no matter how hard he tried to tell them something.

"Oh," Tonya said, and her voice lowered. "She's dead, Putt-Putt. Karen didn't make it after the accident you both had."

Sandy's thick furry tail stopped churning. Dead. The way he'd found Jim's wife, Janet. Motionless, cold, and with no more voice. Hands that didn't reach out and pet him. A non-stirring person who no longer responded.

His deep dark eyes glassed over. He backed up once more and sat. He studied Tonya's face, and then Johnny's, and then glanced back at Tonya.

"I'm sorry boy," Tonya said.

Johnny rubbed his fingers into Tonya's right shoulder and gasped. "He knows what you're talking about."

Out of the corner of his eye, Johnny caught a figure coming towards the garage from the driveway. He turned his head as Jim stopped. "Can I help you?"

"My dog bolted over here. Oh no…" Jim's voice trailed off. He swallowed the lump in his throat. "It appears he knows you."

Tonya stood up and the teens walked over. Sandy trotted slightly ahead and acknowledged Jim.

"He's my family's dog," Tonya said, "but we lost him when Ivan was imminent. He escaped my mother's car accident, but we were told he was rescued by the Humane Society and taken to another state. We were still hoping to find him."

"He almost did get shipped out," Jim said. "But I found him cut up bad and took him to the vet before the center of the storm hit. Afterwards I found them loading him into a truck to take him away. I couldn't bear to see him go with dozens of other homeless dogs, so I grabbed him real quick, and brought him home. He spent a lot of time with my wife." He lowered his head. "But she died and now it's just him and me."

Jim dredged up a small smile, and longingly looked at Sandy. "I'm happy to have known him. You've got a sweet dog." He leaned forward and patted Sandy's head as he continued to lock his gaze into his best friend, his heart cringing at what he must do.

"Well, I better go," Jim said. For the time being, he could not display the emotion he felt. He would let the tears spill at home. He took several slow steps as Johnny leaned into Tonya's ear to whisper.

Putt-Putt watched Tonya and Johnny hold each other's hand. He glanced at Jim's drooping head and slow gait, then stepped towards Tonya and barked as tears formed in her eyes. Tonya reached for his muzzle, held it, and kissed his snout. When she let go, Putt-Putt lurched his mouth into her face, swiped his tongue once, and spun around. He trotted off to join Jim - for a walk on the beach and a ride back home. Jim needed him a lot more than Tonya did.

———

In the afternoon, after two rounds of building materials were unloaded from trucks and left underneath the house, Tonya and Johnny went to the core area. They ordered a gumbo soup and sandwich from The Market on the second floor over the marina, and brought their food outside to the deck.

"This place is like the Beach Cross," Tonya said. "It stands up to anything because it sits on massive stilts and is shielded by the bigger buildings over there. You won't find gumbo like this anywhere else."

"I thought that's what's good in New Orleans."

"Okay, Johnny Barns. It means you're taking me there one of these days. For beignets, too."

Tonya opened a pack of plastic utensils and slipped out the napkin. "Which reminds me. You may be able to afford beignets and gumbo, but your tuition comes first." She pressed her father's contact number on her cell phone.

"Dad. How's it going down there?"

Rick hadn't spoken to his daughter in three days and excused himself from an informal meeting. Tonya heard him rattle off some fluent Spanish.

"I'm making more contacts and signing up more contracts than I deserve."

"Then we're both making progress. Construction work has started on the house. You don't have to worry about anything here and right now I'm introducing Johnny to The Market's island gumbo."

"That's my girl. In any case, I'll be there in two weeks to shoulder some of the responsibility."

Tonya gestured to Johnny to take a spoonful of soup. "Dad, you won't believe this. Putt-Putt showed up today. He's been living with some man since the accident and has not been far away after all."

Rick squeezed his eyes closed. How Karen had loved that dog. "That's incredible. How is he?"

"He appeared to be well and happy. But Dad, he made a choice. I think he realized things are different now and Mom isn't here. He wanted to be with the old man. It broke my heart. He's still breaking my heart."

Rick looked down at his shoes, dusty from the morning walk at a new job site, and thought of the additional loss to the two of them. "I'm sorry, honey."

"Me, too. But it'll be okay. How many dogs are so loved that more than one family wants him? He's so special. I'll miss him, and I'm going to remember him forever, just like Mom."

"You're very mature. It will take time for me, too." Tonya smiled at his remark and also at Johnny who gave a thumbs up on the gumbo.

"I have a request," she said into the silence at the other end of the phone. "Do you think you could help Johnny out with tuition costs through the spring, maybe longer? Johnny may join me at Butler."

"May I talk to him?"

Tonya raised her eyebrows. "Sure." She handed Johnny the phone after he put down his spoon.

"Hi, Mr. Puno."

"What do you think of the island's best gumbo?"

"I'm converted."

"Good. I want to thank you again for helping us out. Tonya asked about your tuition. I'll be happy to help out but there'll be a condition."

"What's that?"

242

"That you chip in by working ten hours a week towards your expenses."

Johnny erupted with a big smile. "I can bartend on weekends or be a dorm monitor. I'll find something. Is that all?"

"That's all because I suspect you're already my daughter's best friend."

Chapter 31

The Good Samaritan Clinic, after a successful opening, accumulated a bucket of trouble. The clinic didn't take any money for visits so it had problems a paying clinic would dream of - more patients coming through their front door than the little building could handle. Island and Gulf Breeze subcontractors showed up with back pain, cuts, and lack of prescriptions, and the displaced people living in FEMA trailers came in because they ran out of meds and they had sprouted new medical problems. Those who lacked health care before the storm came in droves after the hurricane. They all found the staff compassionate and diligent and down to earth about providing a service because they wanted to, not because they had to. And where else could they get free care?

Fred and Ginger called Peter into the kitchen after he treated the last patient for a skin infection. A new volunteer ENT doctor, Diana, and the rest of the staff filtered in for a surprise cake in honor of the visiting couple who was about to depart.

"We're going to remember your philanthropy down here, Dr. Devlin," Fred said, "and your help, too, Diana. When you come back to visit the Emerald Coast, stay with us again, but expect to be put to work." Fred laughed. "Now come on, somebody cut that thing."

Ginger sliced the creamy sheet cake and slipped slices on paper plates as everyone huddled around the table and said their good-byes. Diana savored a piece as Peter gave Ginger a small hug.

"Don't let your husband work you too hard," Peter said. "The two of you should be slowing, not plowing ahead like you're planting a new crop every day."

"Hah," Ginger said, "a road block won't stop him."

Diana faced her husband, handing him his slice. "Here, honey, eat up. Your wife's taking you back north, my way."

———

Peter and Diana returned the rental car and a shuttle dropped them at the small aircraft terminal. Diana filled out paperwork while

Peter glanced at the *Pensacola News Journal.* With fast steps, she walked outside to her bright Cessna, lining herself in front of the nose, and mused over the plane's magnificence. She slipped her hand out of her pocket to block the sun and stepped around the entire plane to do her safety inspection.

After completing the preliminaries, she popped back into the office and dragged Peter from his newspaper. When they got airborne, Peter studied the sights below; the houses, the railroad tracks near the bay, the three mile bridge, and the narrow island with the infinite body of water to the south. He glanced at his wife. She maneuvered the plane for the scenic route and in the next few minutes he realized she swung it over the Puno's house and waved the wings of the airplane as a good bye.

"You're a modern Amelia Earhart," he said, "but even she may not have loved flying as much as you."

"That's a strong possibility." She soaked in the blue-green water one more time and spun around to head north.

———

Tonya heard the plane before she spotted it. She stepped out of the ground floor to throw a garbage bag into the dumpster and saw it heading away from the house. She threw her hands into the air and waved excitedly. "Johnny, Johnny," she yelled.

Johnny raced out of the second floor and leaned against the railing. "That's Diana and Peter," she belted out. "There they go."

Johnny shielded his eyes from the sun and scanned the sky to where Diana's Cessna made its way towards the bay. Along with Tonya, they both waved their arms.

"I doubt they can see us now," Tonya said.

"They didn't have to come this way," Johnny said, "but I suspect Diana wanted to say good-bye."

"Both of them. If I adopt a second pair of parents, it's going to be them."

"I'll second that."

Tonya continued looking up at Johnny. He smiled at her and he still wore the stylish hair cut she created for him. In a short sleeved T-shirt, his arms and shoulders were more developed and less Ohio-valley white than when they had arrived. She finally tore away from looking smitten at him and gazed across to the Gulf and made up her mind.

"I think today's the day," she said. "The conditions are perfect out there. Let's launch the kayaks and properly say good-bye to my mom."

———

They carried one kayak at a time across the street and over the sand. As Johnny placed the second bright-yellow kayak next to the edge of the water, black shadows glided as far as possible to the shore. They formed a V in the water just like the pelican formations above which he saw so often.

"Tonya, what are they?"

She smiled at his bewildered face. "Sting rays."

"Too awesome," he mumbled.

"Come on. You'll see. The visibility to the bottom is crystal clear until we are out deep and past the sandbars. You'll see sea turtles, sharks, fish, and dolphins out here if they're around. The dolphins will even play with us."

She took off a small backpack, placed it in the front of her kayak, and threw him a life jacket. They both zipped up. Tonya edged the kayak into the water where gentle rolling waves lapped the shore. "No trouble getting out today at all. This is perfect for what we're about to do."

Tonya straddled the two sides with her water shoes, sat, and took several easy strokes waiting for Johnny. He followed her method and they both grinned. Paddling was easy. Although the breeze was from the south, it was negligible and the small swells further out wetted Johnny's appetite for future excursions.

Out further, they both rested their paddles across their laps. "Listen," she said. "How quiet it is out here. Just us, the water, and the horizon as far as you can see." Tonya pointed. A streamlined cormorant dove, and after propelling himself underwater, bobbed up closer to their hulls. Johnny smiled.

Tonya picked up the long paddle again. "Just a little more, okay?"

"You're only doing this once. As far as you want is fine with me."

"Thanks. I'm going to remember this day and I'm going to tell my dad every detail. He said it is dependent on the cycle of life and if only one of us took care of her remains, it was more important that I do it." The kayaks bumped as they slowed and closed the gap between them. "You can't believe how religious my father is. He has a soulful way about him and cares deeply about family, God, and all of nature."

Tonya laid her paddle lengthwise along her left side. "This is far enough." She slid the backpack over and unzipped it. Carefully, she took out a brown ceramic container.

"Is there anything you would like me to do?" Johnny asked. "Why don't I hold us together? I'll grab the strap."

Tonya nodded as Johnny eased alongside her and wrapped his hand into the kayak's front end handle.

"The light breeze is blowing towards shore," she said. "I'm not going to spread my mom's ashes into the air. I'm going to place them in the beautiful water she loved."

Tonya screwed open the top. She looked all around. The blue sky, the rippled water, the young man next to her. She closed her eyes and listened to the miracle around her. She opened her eyes and slowly lowered the urn down. The shimmering water seeped in and mixed with the ashes. Tonya held it in front of her. "I love you, Mom. I'll have your memories tucked away forever. Today I'm letting you go – just what's left physically – into this beautiful big grave. And Dad loves you, too."

Tonya lowered the urn again into the water. She swiveled it and brought it back up again empty into the kayak. She placed the container into her backpack and wiped away the moisture in her eyes. Besides the Gulf, a part of her mom still lived on in Johnny's mother, Jennifer. When she composed herself and let the moment sink in, they picked up their paddles and headed to shore.

―――

The rare first day back to work gave Peter mixed emotions. On the one hand, he anticipated whatever challenges the day would bring him and he was itching to perform the various procedures he loved to do, but he also knew the calming effect of having had time off would quickly dissipate within the first half hour. That's the way it was - plunging back into the realities of his specialty in a complex medical center.

Several doctors nodded or stopped to talk to Peter in the lounge as he poured his first coffee after changing into scrubs. He turned to face Dr. Liu arriving off the Doctor's elevator.

"Good morning," Peter said. "Glad I ran into you. How is Jennifer Barns?"

"Glad to see you back," Dr. Liu said. "Mrs. Barns's daughter brings her in for her appointments. Her blood work is fine and she's a trooper. I think she'll have the maximum projected life expectancy with her new liver." He glanced over his spectacles as if he were solving a puzzle. "Sorry you aren't able to follow her progress."

"I rely on you to clue me in. Plus, I spent some time with her son."

"They're a nice family." He smiled and started walking to the locker room.

"Keep me in the loop," Peter said and walked into the OR hallway.

Joan rushed from the main OR desk. "Dr. Devlin, I'm up to my shoulders with scheduling problems this morning. The electives are overbooked, there's a stream of add-ons, a hand emergency on the table, and a bad case coming up from the ER."

Joan stopped to catch her breath and motioned to him all the while to follow her. "I've sent Cindy downstairs to get as much patient information as she can about the ER case. She's heading home after working all night. You hurry now; I need for you to do the case yourself. Cindy will drop the anesthesia preop with me and I'll bring it into you."

"Which ..."

"You're in OR 9. Big trauma. All I know is the guy got hit in the parking lot, has a belly full of blood, and is crashing. They'll be up with him within minutes."

At least OR 9 was always set up for emergencies, Peter thought. He would be able to do a quick but efficient check of equipment and drugs and run to get narcotics from the drug dispenser. He stopped in front of the double doors and Joan continued on her way.

"Oh, and Dr. Devlin," she said, "welcome back."

———

The Cuban cigar tasted exceptional. Sukhdev selected three from his humidor that morning and was trying out that brand for the first time. It had cost a few extra dollars compared to the normal expensive labels. As usual, he thought, it proves he gets what he pays for.

The doctor's parking garage only had a few stragglers coming in this early; the cars were filling in the parking spots between the doctors who had stayed for over-night call. But he didn't want any morning bull shit with anybody, like 'good mornings' and all of that, so he leaned against the front bumper of his Lexus facing the wall and puffed with sheer pleasure. He needed to make rounds a little earlier because he was scheduled for an elective case right off the bat and there was a deluge of patients to see. Lately, his work load had been a flood rather than a drought.

Sukhdev took a substantial pull on his fine brown vice and finished it off, highly satisfied with his early fling. He needed to still pull his brief case from the car, lock up, and get into the hospital. He took his right foot off the bumper, turned, and stepped aside from the front of his vehicle while studying the cigar wrapper, making a mental note. He was buying this one again. As he took his eyes from the lady stogie of his life, he faced a silver vehicle pulling into the parking space next to him. His eyes grew wide as the driver hit the accelerator instead of the brake and Sudhdev was pinned against the wall. The crush felt like the foot of an elephant boring through his belly straight out through his spine.

———

Sukhdev surmised they were doctors and ER personnel and onlookers as a storm of people were around him and a stretcher glided him into the hospital. Craziness erupted in the ER trauma room as cuffs and IV's and machines and people came at him from every direction. He smelled the rubbery scent of a mask and tasted the oxygen. A voice sounded familiar, like one of the trauma surgeons, and he heard someone shout "filling up with blood," as he shot through the CT machine. He was aware of doors closing and someone shouted "BP's dropping" as the elevator went one flight up.

Horror gripped him as he realized he went through double doors and he had entered the familiarity of the OR. Surgery was one thing, but his mind searched through significant data trying to pin point an even more important issue which made him tremble like a house cat confronted by a bobcat. What was it?

Yes, as important, he remembered, was the need for an anesthesiologist. Shit, he thought. What if it's Devlin? He hated Peter's guts but – and he would never admit this – he is the most proficient anesthesiologist he ever knew. If given the choice, he would hand pick Peter to take care of him. But did Devlin harbor thoughts of retribution like he did? Maybe he would see to it that he didn't 'wake up.'

Personnel wearing scrubs and masks lifted the sheets around him and placed him on the OR table. The bright surgical lights glared in his eyes. He felt like he was beginning to pass out. A face from the top of the table came directly into view above him as a new oxygen mask covered his mouth and he realized his life was now in Peter Devlin's hands.

- END -

From the Author

Barbara Ebel is an author and a physician. Since she practiced anesthesia, she sprinkles credible medicine into the background of her novels and her O.R. scenes shine. She currently lives with her husband and pets in a wildlife corridor in Tennessee but has lived up and down the East Coast.

The following books are also written by Barbara Ebel and are available as paperbacks and as eBooks:

The Outlander Physician Series:

Corruption in the O.R.: A Medical Thriller (The Outlander Physician Series Book 1)

Wretched Results: A Medical Thriller (The Outlander Physician Series: Book 2)

Stand-alone Medical Fiction (besides Outcome, A Novel)

Her Flawless Disguise

EBook Box Sets:

The Dr. Danny Tilson Novels Box Set:
Books 1-4 (The Dr. Danny Tilson Series)

The Dr. Annabel Tilson Novels Box Set:
Books 1-3 (The Dr. Annabel Tilson Series)

The Dr. Annabel Tilson Novels Box Set:
Books 4-6 (The Dr. Annabel Tilson Series)

The Dr. Danny Tilson Series: (Individual paperbacks and ebooks):

Operation Neurosurgeon: You never know… who's in the OR (A Dr. Danny Tilson Novel: Book 1).

Barbara Ebel

Silent Fear: a Medical Mystery (A Dr. Danny Tilson Novel: Book 2). Also an Audiobook.

Collateral Circulation: a Medical Mystery (A Dr. Danny Tilson Novel: Book 3). Also an Audiobook.

Secondary Impact (A Dr. Danny Tilson Novel: Book 4).

The Dr. Annabel Tilson Series: (Individual paperbacks and ebooks):

DEAD STILL: A Medical Thriller (Dr. Annabel Tilson Novels Book 1)

DEADLY DELUSIONS: A Medical Thriller (Dr. Annabel Tilson Novels Book 2)

DESPERATE TO DIE: A Medical Thriller (Dr. Annabel Tilson Novels Book 3)

DEATH GRIP: A Medical Thriller (Dr. Annabel Tilson Novels Book 4)

DOWNRIGHT DEAD: A Medical Thriller (Dr. Annabel Tilson Novels Book 5)

DANGEROUS DOCTOR: A Medical Thriller (Dr. Annabel Tilson Novels Book 6)

Author's website: http://barbaraebelmd.com

Also written and illustrated by Barbara Ebel (a children's book series about her loveable therapy dog):

Chester the Chesapeake Book One
Chester the Chesapeake Book Two: Summertime
Chester the Chesapeake Book Three: Wintertime
Chester the Chesapeake Book Four: My Brother Buck
Chester the Chesapeake Book Five: The Three Dogs of Christmas

The Chester the Chesapeake Trilogy (The Chester the Chesapeake Series); eBook only

Chester's website:
http://dogbooksforchildren.weebly.com

DEAD STILL

by Barbara Ebel, M.D.
A Dr. Annabel Tilson Novel Book One
(copyright 2016)

Chapter 1

She had started the surgery rotation the day before so Annabel Tilson barely knew her patients from the list of names that had been shoved into her hands. As a third-year medical student, the day had been hectic; therefore, a short introduction to them and a quick listen to their chests with her first shiny Littmann stethoscope had sufficed. But this morning as she squeezed in close to the bed and looked down at a dead corpse, she remembered the sixty-five-year-old woman, Mrs. Hardy, with clarity from visiting her in her room and watching her surgery in awe.

During the first surgery that Annabel had witnessed on her clinical rotation, the chief resident performed a minimally-invasive gallbladder removal - or laparoscopic cholecystectomy - causing the long mechanical instruments to protrude from her patient's belly like the squirming arms of a squid. No one indicated at the time or postoperatively that anything had been complicated about the case, so why was her patient dead? She admonished herself for missing the resuscitative attempt before she'd walked into the room; medical supplies, carts, and equipment were scattered about the bed and floor but personnel paid no attention as they began exiting through the doorway.

"Most likely a heart attack," Marlin Mack said, waving an EKG and signaling her to follow him out of the room. Excluding the chief resident, he was one of the two residents on the team, an unkempt-looking fellow with a ridiculous mustache for his age and a lab coat that needed ironing.

Annabel lagged, taking a last impressionable stare at the deceased woman: mucus smudged her cheeks, urine soaked the bed, and the smell of bowels having opened up was pervasive. A nurse moved the patient's stocky legs closer together and covered them with a sheet, hiding the unnatural way they seemed to lay. Someone else jammed a pillow under her head before housekeeping came in and started removing the black bags from the trash cans.

As she peeled her eyes away, Annabel tried to shake off her conflicting thoughts of sadness, unsettled nerves, and nausea before rushing out like a puppy after the resident. This was her second day out from the two first years of course work during medical school and the second day on clinical rotation in hospitals. She shuddered. Already this was emotionally difficult.

Outside, Dr. Mack waved her over to a desk in a small cubbyhole. "You're going to deal with life and death," he said. "It's not all a bed of roses. Do you know that blood pools at the bottom of a dead body, whatever area is most gravity dependent?"

Was that something she needed or wanted to know? She didn't see the relevance of him telling her that and she shook her head.

"Furthermore, since there's no more circulation and no more heat, the muscles harden, thrusting a corpse into rigor mortis which sets in after about four hours. Then you better do something with it because if it's left for a day it'll start to bloat and blacken. And I won't even mention the smell."

Annabel gulped. She was beginning to regret that she'd been assigned to surgery right off the bat. Were all the residents as blatant and cold as he was?

Marlin glanced her way. "Oh, sorry. My dad owns a funeral home. It's natural for me to know about cadavers. Anyway, now comes the second part. I have to go talk to the deceased's sister. The patient wasn't married, no kids, not much of anybody in her life it seems." He got up and brushed past her.

"What's the matter, Annabel? You look like you've seen a ghost." The other female medical student on her team, Ginny Young,

254

sat on the edge of the main desk's counter and gave Annabel a warm smile. She was thirty years old compared to Annabel's twenty-three and had sought admission to medical school after reconsideration of her first career in biological research.

Annabel leaned over. "Mrs. Hardy, one of my few patients passed away," she said in a low voice so no one overheard her. "She went from being a living, breathing person with whatever past and with whatever ties to family and friends, to not leaving the hospital. Dr. Mack makes it sound like she's a lifeless disposable sack of flesh."

"Sorry to hear about your patient," she agreed. "That's too soon after we just started. She frowned and, in a few minutes, settled her eyes on Marlin Mack as he walked towards them.

"Good morning, Dr. Young," he said. "Annabel's gone and lost her first patient before official rounds with our attending doctor. Anyway, the sibling of the deceased doesn't want to see her sister but wants to wait until she's beautified by the funeral home. She's pretty much in shock."

While Marlin grabbed the patient's chart, Annabel and Ginny stole a glance.

"Come on, don't just stand there," Marlin said. "Let's assemble the team in the office and be ready for Dr. Burk."

They filed out and, as they passed the dead patient's room, stopped so Marlin could talk to the transporters waiting in the hallway. A nurse in the room put a blouse on Mrs. Hardy, holding her forearms with a tennis-racquet grip; the body fell quickly back on the mattress when she let go.

Two male transporters filed into the room while Annabel dawdled in the hallway. They lifted the dead woman and her head, arms, and legs fell away as they put her in a big black bag. Annabel closed her eyes for a moment. In the last few years, her physician father had been a role model with his religious overtones. She thought of him and then gave a little blessing for her patient to rest in peace.

Barbara Ebel

Made in the USA
Middletown, DE
12 May 2025

75402547R00146